AND THE WILDNESS

Susan Maxwell

Bibliothèque des Refusés

First published in 2023
by Bibliothèque des Refusés
Reprinted 2025 with minor changes to text and layout

ISBN 978-1-7396037-1-7

No part of this work is the product of generative AI.
Image details and attribution are provided at the
end of the book.

www.biblioref.com

ALSO BY SUSAN MAXWELL

Hollowmen
Fluctuation in Disorder

'Hibernia Altera' Sequence
Good Red Herring (Muinbeo Chronicles 1)
A Wild Goose Hunt (Muinbeo Chronicles 2)

Quill and Thornapple
Death at Hallowtide

SUSAN MAXWELL is an independent author and scholar who writes literary/slipstream and fantasy fiction, and mystery fiction as R.S. Maxwell. She has published five novels and a collection of short stories, and her work has appeared in magazines and anthologies. She has worked as a profess-ional archivist in Ireland, the UK, and the Netherlands, holds a PhD for her research on archives and the margins, and writes non-fiction on themes related to archives and literature. Maxwell is a regular juror for the British Fantasy Awards and reviewer for the *BSFA Review* and *Inis*, the magazine of Children's Books Ireland. Literary influences come mostly from speculative and modernist fiction. When not writing, or painting, or being an archivist, the author can be found in the vegetable patch, listening to music, reading books, watching old detective series, or catching up on sleep.

Praise for *And the Wildness*

"Gorgeous and hilarious and profound." *Siobhán Parkinson*

"A universal adventure story that riffs off Irish mythology ... accomplished, intelligent, deeply witty and important ... it assumes a thoughtful and imaginative and intelligent reader." *anonymous editorial reader*

Praise for *Good Red Herring*

"Imagine a book like a Pogues concert! Chaotic, powerfully creative ... littered with classic and classical Irish references all united in a glorious cacophony of intense delight and beauty." *Nigel Robert Wilson*

"This is the kind of book I absolutely love – it creates a dense world for the reader to move through, makes few if any concessions in terms of explaining itself ... The nearest comparison I can think of is *Lud-in-the-Mist* by Hope Mirrlees meets *The Dalkey Archive* by Flann O'Brien."
Karina Clifford

"Maxwell is to be congratulated ... on her inventiveness [and] skill in keeping such a firm grip on the inter-weaving strands of her narrative, entertainingly employing in the process many of the tropes of the classic noir detective story." *Robert Dunbar*

"With a very precise social/political structure, the action weaves its way ... with expert rhythm and timing to create a story that is compelling and driven. I was captiv-ated by this world, complex and having an eery beauty." *Mary Esther Judy*

With sincere thanks to Siobhán Parkinson for being so generous with her time, her editorial nous, and her enthusiasm for And the Wildness.

What would the world be, once bereft
Of wet and wildness? Let them be left,
O let them be left, wildness and wet,
Long live the weeds and the wildness yet.

Gerard Manley Hopkins

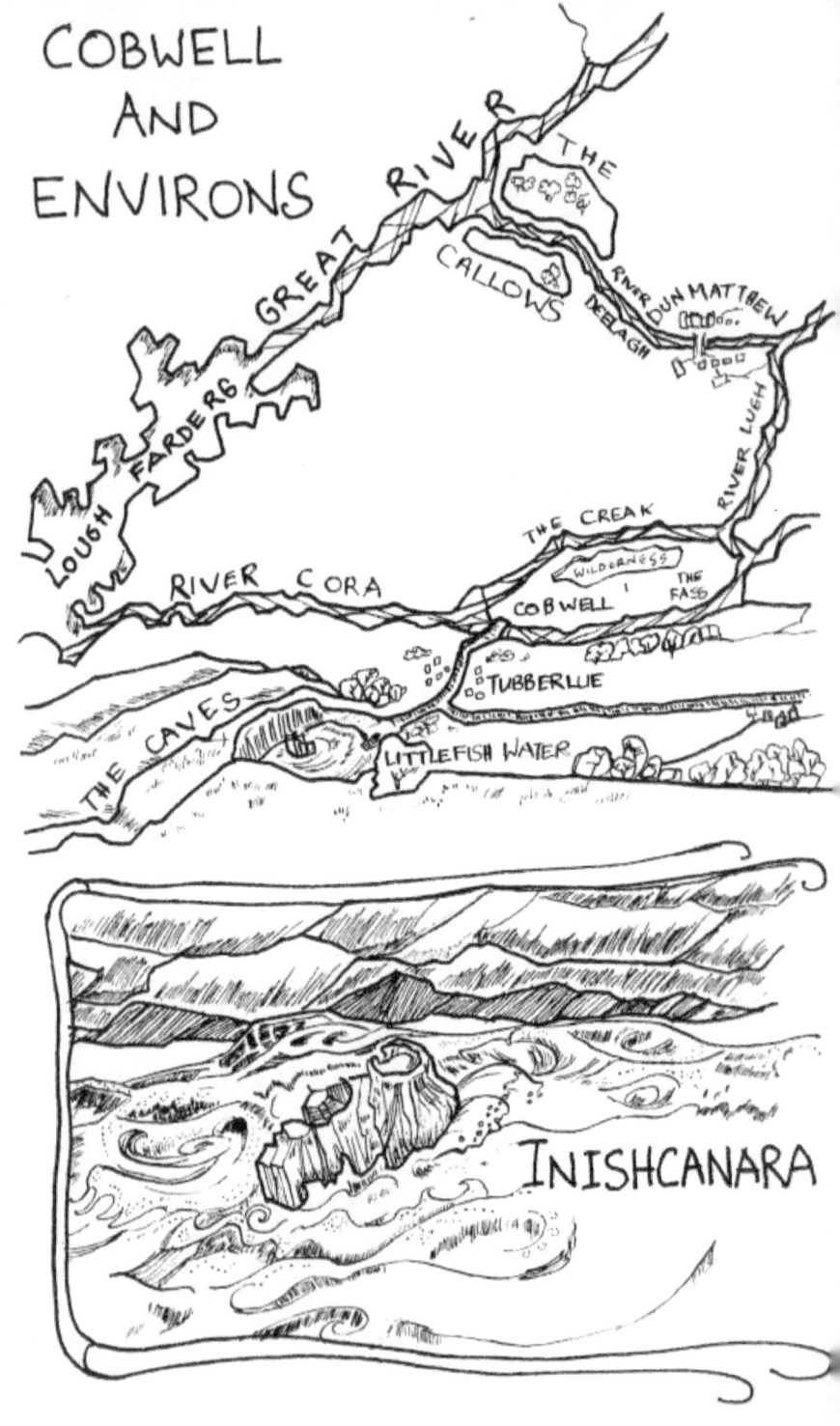

COBWELL
AND
ENVIRONS

GREAT RIVER

LOUGH FARDERG

THE CALLOWS

River DUN MATTHEW

River DEELAGH

RIVER LUGH

THE CREAK

WILDERNESS

COBWELL

THE FASS

RIVER CORA

THE CAVES

TUBBERLUE

LITTLEFISH WATER

INISHCANARA

Prologue

Naturally, being part of Cobwell Farm, The Wilderness was bigger on the inside than it appeared on the outside.

From the outside, The Wilderness revealed only the stingiest shaving off the reality of it: some rolling grassland, a few groves and spinneys of round-crowned trees, and the sun glinting on a pond, on a glasshouse, and on a sprightly little river. On the inside: when there was rain, it drenched the leaves and soaked the roots of a thousand different species. If there was sun, it glinted on miles of lake, on the glossy scales or hairy hides of thousands of browsing or basking animals, and on the windows and ornate metal of the acres-wide Glasshouse. When winter came, frosted berries and hidden seeds fed thousands of birds, and the trees, the grass, and the tangled, teeming soil were home to sleeping multitudes.

Anyone looking at The Wilderness, or Cobwell Farm, might wonder why they appeared so lush, and green, and vibrant, when the rest of Hibernia was being fried to a crisp in a drought. They would certainly wonder. They might even ask. They were always free to ask.

Inside in The Wilderness, in the middle of August, bears were doing what bears do—fishing in the crashing waterfall of the river, ambling along their own paths to hunt out beehives, and eating berries off the hooping brambles. While they hunted and basked, they heard but hardly noticed the sounds.

> *The Wilderness takes its cue from the belling of a stag. Trees are rumbling their roots, their faint roaring is embellished by the high tingling of rootlets vibrating, the tinkling of jangling nodes. The river thunders all the louder over the precipices, and in the immeasurable deep of the lake, the current rolls, roaring.*

One young bear, trying its paw at fishing, caught instead a new scent on a puff of wind as brief as a note of music. Across the river, a figure emerged from the trunk of a lightning-split tree. It was hardly visible at first, being as dappled in gold and green and brown as the bark. It was a human figure, apart from being covered in ivy and vines, and the bark-like appearance of the face, the knots of leaves and small fruit that bunched around its shoulders and waist like a fancy collar and belt, and the fine set of ten-point antlers. Apart from that, absolutely and entirely human. It dusted some dried leaves and dead insects from itself, and stood listening.

The Wilderness seems to be silent again, but it is more than that. It is the silence that happens when the orchestra is poised but the conductor's baton is still. Instruments are tuned, bows at the ready, reed to the lip, finger to the key, waiting for the sign. Into the alert silence, there comes the urgent, disproportionately loud, yell of a wren. The figure is off, bounding over the rocks that make a dangerous crossing above the gurgling waterfall, and onto the path that curves east before the wren's voice died away. The important thing is to be on a path, any path, before the rest of the music starts. Otherwise — well.

The figure trotted briskly, and was lost to the bearcub's short sight by the time the blackbirds' chirruping bloomed and the corvids started their gravelly calls. Leaves and small branches hissed like cymbals in the breeze. Mice agitated fallen leaves and crickets snapped their joints. The robin's clear whistle was blurred by the soft cooing of the doves. The Standing Stones, and to the north the Old Trees, gathered the sounds.

The figure did not so much as break a rotten branch, startle a wolf, or dislodge a ladybird as it ran. The air seemed to part for it, and trees to sway away. By the time the figure reached the grass-scalloped edge of The Wilderness, its hands were full of foraged things. It crossed

3

through the hip-high grass, where the forest had dwindled to saplings and bushes, and clambered carefully onto the stile that linked the edge of The Wilderness to the lane by Cobwell Farm.

The stile appeared to be very simple, though so old that the wood from which it was made was as hard as iron and as slippery as ice. It was a narrow two-bar fence, forcing open a tiny gap in the dense hedge that was the boundary of The Wilderness. A thick plank of wood had been threaded through the bars, and each end rested on an upright post, one on either side of the fence.

The figure stepped up onto the plank, folded one long leg up to its chest, and unfolded it again over the top of the stile to the plank on the other side. It could feel the air of The Wilderness clinging to its back, vibrating gently, and letting go only reluctantly, slowly, sliding away like whipped cream from a spoon. The horned figure stepped out onto the farther post, and waited for the dizziness to pass. Then it stepped down onto the dry, churned ground of the lane between The Wilderness and Cobwell Farm, retracting its horns, and replacing its ivy and vines, its ash keys and rowan berries, with clothes more suitable for the human side. To its right, towards the south, the path widened, and there was a patch of short grass sheltered by a tangled thicket of dog-roses and blackberries.

Bridie the Vet was sitting on the short grass, with a fox kit and a leveret sitting in her lap, and a sprig of hyssop protruding from the side of her mouth. Her sister Britta the Smith sat beside her, with her face turned up like a sunflower and her eyes closed. They wore overalls, and while Bridie was barefoot, Britta wore thick-soled sandals. Bridie was saying, to Britta,

"We *can't* ignore it. Something's brewing, and you know it. Something's going to give."

"Lookit— "

"Don't 'lookit' me. You weren't with me when I met the Cailleach back in February."

Britta opened her eyes reluctantly. She dragged her attention away from the chorus of birds, the blackbird and the wren in a struggling duet, and the wood-pigeons cooing mournfully. She saw the approaching figure, and waved.

By the time Tima reached Bridie and Britta, she was conventionally clothed and shod, with her hair twisted up and pinned on the back of her head. She had put the things she had foraged into a wide, shallow basket, and this she handed to Bridie.

"Good day to you both," Tima said. "Here's your pharmacopoeia—everything on your list."

"You're an angel," said Bridie, sitting up properly, and beginning to sort out the contents of the basket.

"Not exactly," Tima said, sitting down, "but I'll take the compliment. What's this about the Cailleach? Not trying to elbow in on your territory?"

"I met her back in February," Bridie said, "with a hundred ox-hides filled with firewood."

Tima raised her eyebrows.

"Is she planning to freeze the world? Did she say why she was collecting so much?"

5

"She didn't know why," Bridie replied, "she just collected it. And she's asleep now until October, so we can't ask her anything at all."

"Maybe she made a mistake?" Britta said, and Bridie rolled her eyes.

"She's the Cailleach. A winter immortal does not make mistakes any more than a summer one does. The Cailleach collects enough firewood before the start of every summer to get her through the next winter. When I saw her in February, she had enough fire-wood to last a thousand years. That's not a good sign. Something is wrong."

"If it came to it, Cobwell would prefer eternal winter over that broiling summer they're having out there," Britta said, jerking her chin towards the land beyond Cobwell's boundary. The far bank of the River Fass, away from Cobwell, shimmered in a heat-haze. Its covering of grass and herbs had burned to copper-yellow, with nothing moving except mayflies on the languid water, and cattle trying to find shade in shelterless fields.

"I know that," Bridie said, "and I know why. But you know and I know that that summer they are having out there is not natural, so maybe neither is the winter."

"It won't be very healthy for us," remarked Britta, "if we have to sleep for a thousand years."

"We're immortals, but," Tima said, uneasily.

Bridie and Britta looked at each other, and Britta said at last,

"That might not make the difference you expect."

She sighed, flattening to the ground the feathery grasses in front of her. She got up.

"I'd better get back to work," she said, holding out her hand to haul her sister to her feet, and Bridie said, sympathetically,

"It's a hot ol' day for blacksmithing."

"It is," Britta said, "but even on Cobwell, gates and scabbards don't make themselves."

"I'll walk with you," said Tima, "I have to get to Dunmathew. A meeting with… oh it's too dull even to describe. All this nonsense about the St. Maur Kers' Rain-Maker. Unbelievably tedious."

"Oh, you poor thing," said Britta, "that's the downside of your responsibilities, on this side. It must be exhausting."

"I always thought it would be rather exciting to be a spy," said Bridie, picking up the basket, but Tima shook her head.

"It isn't all dry martinis and fast cars, I can assure you. Mostly it is keeping awake during very dull meetings. At least this meeting is up at the castle, so it might be boring but we won't be fried by the sun. I think that's why the High King wanted me to host it. Better air-conditioning."

They parted ways, Britta on her short journey to her smithy by the Great River, Tima on her longer journey to her home in Dunmathew Castle, and Bridie to return to the farmhouse on Cobwell. The kit and the leveret, dislodged, scampered off to their separate destinies.

Bridie walked up the lane that divided The Wilderness from the garden behind Cobwell Farmhouse. Muddy in wet weather and churned by the hooves of cattle, the lane had been baked in the blistering sun during the drought. It joined onto a smooth, gravel path, blindingly white under the sun, leading through the yard to the back door of the house. Bridie skirted the house, and started to cross the yard to her infirmary, but when she heard a hollow clattering of metal on stone, she changed direction at once. There was no mistaking the sound.

Out of the yard, past the ancient oak, and a scrubby bit of ground cluttered with machinery, the field rose in a low ridge. In the middle of the ridge, a neat cylinder projected out of the ground like a chimney. The mouth of it was wide enough to fit a small tractor, and it was encircled by a low wall, a foot and a half of biscuit-yellow brick. This was known, for no reason that anyone was particularly willing to explain, as The Pot. A long metal spike was rising from the centre of it; the spike, like the dorsal fin of a shark, was a signal that something was approaching the surface.

Bridie took longer strides, and had just reached the lip of The Pot when a bathysphere, rising through the dark water, bobbed up to the surface as abruptly as a duckling. The hatch of the bathysphere made a loud whine as it was unscrewed, and the pilot clambered out, dragging a chain. She dropped the ring on the end of the chain over the huge hook that was embedded in the wall.

"'Sup, Murph?" asked Bridie. "Find any wilder than usual life?"

"Nothing doing the day," said Murph, hauling herself over the ledge, and perching there to catch her breath while she took off her gloves, "for which I suppose we must be grateful. I might go for another spin under Littlefish Water later, see if there's anything new there."

"I thought something old would get your nostrils flaring. No sign of the Littlefish Monster, then?"

"Well you may mock," Murph said. "There must have been *something* that made people think that a monster sleeps under Eightfoot Island."

"If it's there," Bridie said, basking, "you're the púca to find it."

Glad to be out of the stuffy bathysphere, Murph refreshed herself with deep breaths and then rested, idly slapping her gloves into her palm. The water in The Pot gurgled and plashed gently. No-one knew quite how deep it was, but it was a blessing on a hot day, full of clear, fresh water that was quite un-enchanted. A body could swim in it, even, and come out the same as they had gone in. Deep it certainly was, and though it opened out, after a few hundred feet, into caves on either side, no-one had ever been to the bottom of The Pot, not even Murph. The light afternoon breeze stirred her green mane, and she twitched her ears to stop the thick hair tickling. After a few seconds, she slid her red eye sidelong at Bridie, and said,

"Do you think we need to worry about this? This heat, I mean, this drought. It's burning up on the human side. The hens are laying the eggs hard-boiled."

"Not on Cobwell," said Bridie, "even the St. Maur Kers can't banjax Cobwell, whatever about burning down their own house to make a few bob. Come up to the house and eat with us. You'll never guess what Peg has done."

"It was a bad day when the Habsburg Emperor opened the doors to that family," Murph said, shaking her head and jumping down from the low wall. "They've a taste for power and wealth now. One empire won't be enough for them, you mark my words. They will have their finger in every pie going, if they can."

"Not Cobwell," said Bridie confidently, "I've never found anyone's fingers in Cobwell's pies. And before you start worrying about our magic little fishie, the waters the Salmon swims in can't be touched by the humans, not even the St. Maur Kers, whatever lies they might tell about their origins."

They walked down from the rocky ridge of The Pot, through long grass and the weedy patch of machine-strewn scrub that separated The Pot from the yard. Once in the yard, they both stopped to dust pollen and cleaver-seeds from their clothes. Murph, being a púca, only wore clothes out of politeness and currently looked like she had raided a ballet-dancer's dressing room, so a bit of pollen or a few seed-heads hardly mattered. She followed Bridie to the infirmary, through the passage between the various beds, ponds, byres, artificial crags, dens, horse-boxes, and insect hotels for the patients, to the pharmacy, where Bridie stored her medicine.

"Are St. Maur Ker still banging on about being descended from the inhabitants of Atlantis?" asked Murph, leaning on the door-jamb, watching while Bridie packed away what Tima had foraged from The Wilderness. "What are they like?"

"It has done them no harm," Bridie said. "Look how

cosy they are getting with the Pharaoh's Court. I knew a Queen of Atlantis," she added, sweeping bits of leaves and berries off the big wooden table, "back in the day. She wouldn't have given Cosimo St. Maur Ker the algae off her flipper. The Emperor in Prague has lower standards."

"The Emperor has expensive tastes, that's what he has, and the St. Maur Kers have a lot of money. Come on, I'm famished."

Cobwell's kitchen was full when they went in, and noisy with it. The long table was heaped with food, and the queue of farmworkers shuffled along briskly, then peeled away to find a cool spot to eat in. The huge fireplace fitted three or four eaters easily, several took their loaded plates into the little scullery, between the kitchen and the long, dark, pantry behind it. Others risked the flies outside, and sat either on the fence between the yard and Home Farm, or in a half-finished shed attached to the stables.

Bridie and Murph helped themselves to food, and stood aside near the back door, Bridie watching to see when Peg was free, and Murph looking out into the workshop, filled with musical instruments in various stages of completion or repair. Now and then she caught a glimpse of shirt, or a hand, signs that Peg's husband was hard at work. Every time Peg took a step closer to the table, someone stopped her with a question, or a dog or a chicken had to be dug out of trouble, but finally she got to load up a plate, find a seat, and get her snout into the trough. Bridie waited till Peg finally pushed away her plate, and was handed a cup of tea by a passing swineherd.

Then Bridie sat down beside her.

"So, Peg, my old segotia, I hear you are foisting four mortals on us. Children, no less."

"It's a favour for a friend of mine."

Murph joined them, and said,

"What kind of sprogs are they, exactly?"

Peg shrugged.

"The older twin prefers books to people, so she should be no trouble, but I don't know how much work we'll get out of her. Her brother, though. His ambition in life is to work for St. Maur Ker."

"Ah, here," said Murph, "we don't want any of that."

"You may as well know the worst," Peg said regretfully. "His father is a liaison lawyer for the St. Maur Kers. Any negotiation between them and a king or a caliph or a countess, he's the man to call."

There were cries of alarm, and protest, and Peg raised her voice.

"You think that's bad? His mother works with Dorian Decker. Works as a botanist up in that Academy they're after setting up. What do they call it? Better Food Academy?"

"Ah, here," said Murph, "this is desperate altogether. You may as well invite Cosimo St. Maur Ker to set up shop in the yard outside!"

"Put your dampers down," retorted Peg.

"Are they human children, is what I wanted to know."

"Hardly," Bridie answered Murph, and then said to Peg. "Aren't they were related to Gale McCabe? Her that married the O'Malley chap?"

"They are," said Peg, "Gale is their grandmother. Thelonius O'Malley is her husband. Their daughter Gráinne is the mother. So they're *mostly* human."

"A grandchild of Gale McCabe wants to join St. Maur Ker?" Murph cackled. "Love a bit of irony, me. Is there just the two kids coming?"

"No," Peg dragged out the word reluctantly, "there's another two. Another girl, who sounds like a hooligan. And a seven-year-old boy."

"How long are they here for?" Bridie asked. "It doesn't do to have even partly-human strangers around too long on Cobwell. Especially not children. Inquisitive. They get everywhere. You couldn't swap them, could you? We could do with a few more cattle."

"Bridie, quit complaining," Peg said, but she was clearly uncomfortable. "I've told Lou—that didn't go down well. Humans are not Lou's favourite thing right now."

"You can see why," Bridie retorted.

"I owed their granda a favour," said Peg defensively. "Anyway, they're just kids. What could go wrong?"

A resounding silence, bristling with all the things everyone knew perfectly well could go wrong, followed. Then Peg sighed.

"I'd better go and break the news to Mick," she said, "he'll have to get the boundaries all fixed and secure. He's going to love me for this."

"I suppose you want me to pick up the rug-rats?" Bridie asked, without enthusiasm, and Peg nodded.

"If you would. Mr. Gabriel will explain that there is no

13

other way of getting to Cobwell, but I doubt the parents will listen."

Bridie snapped her fingers several times in quick succession, and all the cutlery and crockery used in the meal were instantly clean and returned to the shelves and presses where they belonged.

"Look on the bright side," she said, "there's always a ton of work to be done round the farm. That should keep them out of mischief."

One

North from Cobwell and the River Fass, the sun beat down vigorously. The sky was bright and bald as a shield, too shining to look at, and glimmering with brilliant swifts. Another river, the Creak, flowing west to join the Fass, watered the town of Dunmathew, that had grown up around the castle and fort of the O'Connell Beares.

It was a small, lovely, lively town and today was livelier than ever, because the High King was on his way to the castle to talk to St. Maur Ker about their Rain-Maker. He could have insisted that they came to him—he was, after all, a High King. But the O'Connell Beare family had been nearly as rich for nearly as long as the St. Maur Kers, and their history equally riddled with technomancers, engineers and scientists. The result was that, among other things, the O'Connell Beare castle was far more comfortable in a months-long heatwave than the High King's official residence in Dublinia.

The High King hated using portals to move from place to place, but he had heard tales of the castle's cool stone rooms, and the technomantic marvel that was their air-conditioning. So he endured the nauseating plunging and jerking of the portal and the disorienting vibrations and colour-bursts. Finally horsed out in an undignified heap at the other end, the High King was set on his feet and smoothed down by two enormous bodyguards. He looked enviously at the citizens of Dunmathew, dangling their feet into the brisk river and eating ice-cream, while he was being led between towering royal guards, down narrow stone-paved passageways to the Castle.

Some people waved at him, shouted "How're'ye, king? How's she cutting?" He waved back, thinking stickily that it was alright for them. They got to splash about in the river, and play with their dogs. He had a four-hour meeting to sit through, during which he had to be on the alert all the time. It never did to let this branch of the St. Maur Ker family catch you napping. They would be running the country before you had had your morning tea. Their swift wile was how they were rising, bit by sneaky bit, in the Empires and the Pharaoh's Court. They would, his wife said, live in your ear and rent out the other one.

The High King tugged determinedly at his long robe, and briskly straightened his crown. He wasn't accustomed to the weight of it, but everyone had insisted. The St. Maur Kers' request had been debated long and hard among Hibernia's local rulers, most of whom welcomed any way to end the drought, but wouldn't trust a St. Maur Ker out of their sight. Everyone felt that the High King wearing the crown would show determination, that he was not to be trifled with. Hibernia had agreed to one thing, and one thing only. The High King had to make sure the St. Maur Kers got nothing else.

The room in which they were to meet was gloriously cool. The High King strode to the table, and all the politics started.

"This is our gift to the world," said the St. Maur Ker Chief Diplomat, rising to his feet and bowing all about him. "It is our solution to this unprecedented heatwave. It is, we hope, the start of our solutions to Mother Nature's capriciousness—this year, a crippling drought, last year, rains of frogs and crickets. We want Hibernia to be the first to benefit from our visionary plans to make Nature play fair with us."

"What you want," said the High King, "is to use the model made in this castle to help you finish your Rain-Maker. Let's stick to the immediate point."

"Hibernia would be extremely suitable for our whole research programme," said the Diplomat encouragingly, "you do get such a lot of... *weather*... here. Forty-nine types of rain. Thirty-two words for 'field'—imagine what our phytotekts could create in—"

"Back to the point," said the High King, crisply. "We're not talking about wealds or feathers. I mean, fields or weather. We're not talking about the kinds of new plants your phytotekts can make, or any other promises you might have made to the Habsburg Emperor. We're talking about Sylvestra St. Maur Ker wanting to use the model, built in this castle centuries ago by the O'Connell Beares' engineers, to help them finish their modern Rain-Maker. That's the question."

"As your Excellency says," said the Diplomat smoothly.

"He's a king," said one of the royal guards curtly, "or did you not notice the big lump of a crown on his head? He's a Highness, not an Excellency."

"The St. Maur Kers have their research team ready," another man butted in hastily, before any tempers frayed. He stood up, smoothing back already smooth hair, and made a few bows. "Terence Grace, your Highness, the family's liasion lawyer. Our gracious host, the O'Connell Beare, is showing the antique model Rain-Maker to our chief Magi, Boitumelo and Fleming, as we speak, but if you have any questions, the St. Maur Kers' lead Engineer is present. Dr. Breck."

Two hours later, the agreement was made. Despite the Diplomat's, and Terence Grace's, best efforts, the High King stuck firmly to his guns. Sylvestra St. Maur Ker had permission to send the tiniest possibly handful of researchers to Hibernia for the shortest amount of time, so that they could study the model Rain-Maker made by a distant ancestor of the O'Connell Beare. Based on the intricate and complex mechanism devised in those past centuries, Breck and the other engineers could finish their modern Rain-Maker. They could bring their machine to a place called the Callows, on the edge of the Great River, to test it out. If it worked, the High King thought to himself as he followed his host out of the Great

Hall, Hibernia would be the first to say goodbye to the drought. Then the St. Maur Kers could take their machine, and their researchers, and they could take their double-dealing and scheming, and they could go the hell home to their Emperor in Prague.

Once the High King and the St. Maur Ker diplomat had left with their entourages, everything relaxed very slightly. The O'Connell Beare returned with St. Maur Ker's two Chief Magi, and invited everyone to go into the Blue Room for refreshments. The room was gloriously cool, and the French windows at the south end had been left open, with the bright curtains pulled right back, just in case a breeze might start. The walls were hung with tapestries, the blue limestone floor laid with thick rugs. There were two tables decked out with linen tablecloths embroidered with thistles and buttercups, and laden with dishes of food, and a huge bowl of fruit punch.

Terence Grace came in last, bringing with him two of his children. One, the one with green hair and grubby, tattered, clothes, he told sternly to go and sit on the chair near the window. The other, impeccably turned out, he guided towards the main party, who were waiting for it to be polite to start eating.

"Dr. Breck," he said, beaming at the engineer, "I'd like to introduce my son, Bram."

As they shook hands, Magus Fleming collared Terence to quiz him about the exact terms the High King had set. Bram's attention was mostly on the table of food, but he noticed that Dr. Breck was wearing a short, dark velvet jacket with slim, knee-length red suede trousers, and black stockings. This outfit was so unsuitable for the weather that he suspected it was part of the Pharaonic Court's new ideas about clothing regulations. Bram followed news of the Courtiers very closely indeed.

"I understand that you will be going to Prague for the summer," she said, "that will be—oh. I see you are not."

His face had darkened glumly.

"We were *supposed* to be going to Prague," he said. "My mother is taking over the St. Maur Ker botany summer school this year, and we were all supposed to go with her, me and my siblings. But my visa—all us children's visas were cancelled."

"How very—unfortunate."

Bram darted a resentful glare at his little sister, who was ignoring Terence's instruction not to move on pain of being turned into a frog. She was moving, the little horror, making a bee-line for the food. Breck raised her eyebrows at the sight of the unevenly spiked green hair, the grubby shirt and the well-worn shorts, and the general appearance of having been dipped in glue and rolled through a hardware shop.

"Ooh," Breck said very sympathetically, smoothing a loose curl back from her forehead, "I see. Relations are so difficult, aren't they? I had a cousin like that…"

Immediately cheered, and wanting to impress her with his polished social skills, Bram turned the conversation to Breck's own work. He was rewarded by finding that she was not only an engineer but the lead model-maker, too. He was so engrossed in the finer details of how to build a Rain-Maker that he did not notice when the O'Connell Beare detached herself from Terence's group.

"Why are you lurking in the corner?" the O'Connell Beare said to Bram's little sister. "Do you not like people?"

"Not much, as it happens," replied Villa Grace, "but I'm lurking because I am in big trouble with my parents, and I was told to sit here till Poppa is ready to go home. So I got some food, and here I'm sitting."

"Why the trouble?"

Villa turned her attention away from her sausage-roll and looked up—and up and up, it seemed—at the O'Connell Beare. The lights were low in the room, to try to keep it cool, so the long-legged figure seemed dim and shadowy. All Villa could see was hair piled up in a neat chignon, a long, broad nose, and the fact that one eye had a blade of gold through the brown iris.

"Well," Villa said, "I got expelled from school. It was the Gladdish Academy, and I got chucked out. So, the Imperial Offices refused to let us have visas to go to Prague. My parents can go, but the rest of us can't. Poppa had to pick me up from school today and bring me home."

"Why did you get expelled?"

Villa hesitated. Her father had warned her not to tell anyone "the sordid details." Remembering what he said made her outraged again.

"It was a matter of principle," she said with dignity.

The O'Connell Beare raised her eyebrows. Then she said, "That's an... interesting shade of green you have in your hair."

21

"Thanks," said Villa suspiciously, "that's another thing I'm in trouble about. Once I was expelled, I decided I didn't have to follow their rules any more. So I put on proper clothes instead of a uniform, and cut off my hair. I thought green spikes would be better than brown plaits. But I only had sugar-water and food-dye, so the hair is a bit... clumpy. And not very green."

They both turned their heads as Magus Fleming waved to get the O'Connell Beare's attention. Wiping her fingers on a napkin, the host said,

"A word of advice, Miss Grace. You have, I think, an inability to do what other people expect you should do. You fail to cooperate, or to be *nice*. This will cause you a world of trouble."

An automaton glided up to take their plates.

"Cling to that inability, and to that failure, as to a life-raft. Other people's expectations are their problem, not your responsibility."

The O'Connell Beare wafted her hand over Villa's head, and glided away.

Two

Oaklake, where the Graces lived, was not exactly owned by the St. Maur Kers. Their architects and technomancers, working at one of the family's homes on the western edge of the Habsburg Empire, had designed Oaklake as a perfect model village. They had bought land between the River Olla and Lough Uaill, built luxurious, semi-sentient houses surrounded with beautiful gardens. They provided the automata that looked after everything, and everyone who lived in Oaklake worked for St. Maur Ker, ate food produced by them, wore clothes imported by them, read newspapers published by them. So, they didn't exactly own Oaklake, but they threw a very long shadow over it.

At the start of the drought, Cosimo St. Maur Ker had a technomancer and a bevy of automata build an artificial lake to keep local residents comfortable despite the baking heat and the shrinking of the lakes and reservoirs. Now, months later, Flann Grace sat in the shade of some mulberry trees, listening to the noise of shouting and splashing, and writing a letter to a deceased philosopher.

Dear Mr. Wittgenstein,

I hardly know how to find the words but I will give it a try.

–<u>Angry</u>: feeling or expressing annoyance, animosity, resentment. (*Animosity*: powerful dislike, hatred.)

–<u>Devastated</u>: made desolate, ravaged, overwhelmed with shock or grief.

–<u>Outraged</u>: profoundly indignant, angry or hurt, as a result of a wantonly cruel act, or a gross violation of decency.

It is such a shock to me that I hardly know what I am to do next.

When I heard that Villa had been expelled I was unsurprised—blasé, unconcerned—because it was unavoidable, inevitable. She is unrelentingly weird. Most words to do with Villa begin with "un"— unpredictable, unmanageable, unruly, untidy and now, unforgivable.

This trip to Prague was the key to everything—the Klementinum has centuries and *centuries* of books in there. I read a newspaper article last year about how the monks have started a campaign to get a copy of every book ever published in any country in the Habsburg Empire. Actually, that seemed to annoy the Court, I'm not sure why. But the point is, they must have a gazillion books in there. It is imperative that I go there. The only thing in the world worth doing is thinking—about what words mean and about what is right to do, I have so much to read before I'm any good at it, before I can say "now I understand."

Anyway, Mr. Wittgenstein, here is the point I want to

make: I spent weeks planning how the library in Prague was going to change my life. I would be a whole new person. Practically. I'm always 'Dr. Grace's daughter' or, even more annoyingly, 'Bram's twin', or 'Mr. Grace's oldest child' or something. But a couple of months in that library would have changed everything. Everything. I would have caught up with Mama and Poppa, maybe even Granda. I'd be cleverer. I'd be quicker. I'd probably even be taller.

Villa ruined everything. As usual, I get the blame. I should have kept an eye on her, according to Mama. She said 'Bram and you', but she doesn't really expect Bram to do anything he doesn't want to do. All he gets is an eye-roll and 'honestly, Bram'. I get 'if you can't be trusted' or 'you should spend less time reading rubbish.' Keep an eye on Villa, indeed. It's a padlock we should have on her.

How am I ever going to catch up with Granda? And Mama and Poppa? If I am to be foiled in the attempt by my wretched little sister?

Yours sincerely,

F.G.

P.S. I have written letters to you since I was twelve, so two and a bit years. Perhaps I should point out that I am aware that you are, in fact, dead, having lived some centuries ago and that, even if you were alive, you are unlikely to want to correspond with a teenaged randomer, even if she is quite clever, and her maternal Granda is Thelonius O'Malley who teaches at the university about your books. So, in writing these letters to you I am not expecting you to reply. Though of course if you were able to reply, that would be most interesting, even if a little strange and spooky. But I need someone I can talk to, and ~~your~~ you're it.

F.G.

P.P.S.: Please don't think that Mama calls philosophy 'rubbish'. But a couple of years ago, she found me reading an author she disapproves of, and she has a particular tone of voice when she says 'your other reading choices' that other people might use to say 'your habit of eating snot'. I haven't read any since, but I don't think she believes me. I was mortified when—

Hearing her name being called startled Flann, and she immediately folded up her sheets of paper. But it was her Granda who was striding up the grassy path to where she sat near the Civic Pool, his high-heeled shoes stabbing the grass, and a ball-gown flapping around him. The minute she saw him she knew he would somehow wangle her into not being angry. Granda sat down in a whoosh-ing cloud of organza and muslin, and Flann said quickly,

"I know you always say I will learn more from un-pleasant situations than I will from pleasant ones, but I'm not finished with furious yet."

The first thing he said, sympathetically, was, "I see you have been letting Mr. Wittgenstein know the news."

Flann was folding up her letter, though she had no need to hide it from Granda. Flann's parents did not forbid much, but she had a bad feeling about what her mother Gráinne would say if she discovered that Flann wrote letters to a dead person.

"I'm sorry this—" Granda started, and Flann burst out,

"How could she do it! What was she thinking! And now everything's ruined. I could have—even if it would take more than three months to read all the books in the Klementinum—I mean it was my best chance!"

People turned at the sound of Flann's angry voice, but it was at Granda they stared instead. Thelonius O'Malley was the size of a well-built stables, with a face like a well-climbed mountain, and had a travel-diary of tattoos about his person. He was wearing a tangerine organza evening dress with glittering peach-coloured shoes the size of canoes, with heels on them like tent-pegs. He was wrestling these off his feet as Flann spoke, and now he held them in one hand, wriggling his freed toes in the heat. Flann was struggling not to sound either churlish or sulky. She said,

"I abhor—"

"*Abhor* is a great word, isn't it?" Granda said with enthusiasm. "It gives objection such a stately air."

"Poppa works for the St. Maur Kers!" she blurted out. "They could decide to send us to one of their summer camps! They all sound *grisly*! It'd be worse than school!"

She missed the dart of Granda's probing glance. He said,

"You will be glad to know, then, that you are not going to the summer camp in Galicia."

Flann was not given to displays of enthusiasm, but after the shock wore off she let a whoop out of her that Villa would have been proud of, and—overcoming her dislike of hugging people—seized her grandfather about the silky waist.

"I should have known that you would think of something!"

"It was really Gale," he said. "Your grandmother knows some… people. And don't cheer till you see the alternative. But neither Gale nor I could stand the thought that you would be subjected to a St. Maur Ker summer camp, which is by definition a propaganda machine run by nincompoops."

(*Nincompoop*, Flann wrote down later, idiot, foolish person, but much more satisfying to say).

"Now, I can tell you no more, because it is fair that you and your siblings all hear at the same time. I'll walk you back to the house, but I'll have to leave you there. Your Grandmother and I are heading away tonight, so I won't see you till the autumn."

As he spoke, Granda started wedging his feet back into the shoes.

"God, these are terrible yokes," he said, peering balefully at them, "bad cess to whoever invented them. Do you think anyone will notice if I go barefoot?"

"No, Granda," Flann said with confidence, "I think it's the last thing anyone will notice."

He stood up, but sat down quickly, and started putting on the shoes again.

"The ground's too hot," he said. "Better squashed toes than blistered soles. Damn this drought, too. Come on, we'll go home."

"Granda," said Flann as they set off down the path to the gate, "I meant to ask you. Why are you wearing an evening dress? And in the afternoon? The St. Maur Kers are getting strict about clothes. They like the Court's ideas about clothing regulations."

Granda looked down at his embellished silk and organza, with its thick lace and gold embroidery. He stuck out his sparkling shoes, one after the other. They were enormously wide in order to fit Granda's tattooed feet, and as a result, their pointed tip was extremely long, like the sting of some exotic and monstrous wasp.

"The Court is always trying to see how far it can go telling countries what to do," he said, "but the St. Maur Kers are not the boss of me. Why do you think I won't live in Oaklake? Anyway, as it happens, I'm writing a book, about what 'allowed' and 'supposed to' mean."

"That's brilliant!" Flann exclaimed. "Mama will hate it! Sorry—did I say that out loud?"

"To be fair," Granda said, "your mother is just anxious that I will get up to what she calls my 'old tricks'."

Flann pounced.

"What tricks were they, Granda?"

"Oh, I was a lively young fella, as you know," Granda said evasively. Before she could stop herself, Flann blurted out,

"*Were* you in the Resistance?"

"Don't tell me you believe that there are actual, organised,

29

protestors?" he said, as if in disbelief. "Are they not just a few disaffected troublemakers, as your father calls them?"

Granda was a harsh critic of all emperors, especially Ferdinand who, since acquiring the Habsburg title, had given the St. Maur Kers more and more authority to act on his behalf, in exchange for the benefits that the family's money and magic could bring. Nowadays, Granda was a professor of philosophy, but Flann suspected that, in his youth, his contempt for those in power, from the Pharaoh and his Courtiers down, had a more practical expression.

"You can't be the only one who thinks that the Pharaoh's Court is no longer protecting anyone," she ventured.

"Five hundred years ago," Granda said, as they reached the gate and turned for home, "the Pharaoh, the Court, and the Empires, were set up for mutual protection against the aliens invading us. Five hundred years is a long time, and the aliens are long gone. What job do the Court and the empires have now? The only thing they protect is themselves and their gravy-train."

"We have an alright life, though, with our Emperor," Flann observed, a little timidly. When Granda got well away about politics—or anything, really—he could be like a river in spate, submerging her in a deluge of pronouncements and opinions that she never felt equipped to answer.

"We do, yes," Granda agreed, "but at what price? You said yourself that the St. Maur Kers are becoming strict about clothes. What next? We're lucky enough in Hibernia, the Emperor of Thule does not stand much nonsense from the Court. But how long will the Courtiers let that go on? Come on, keep up, and stop fishing for scandal."

Flann scurried in his wake.

On his return from the O'Connell Beare's castle, Bram had spent much of the afternoon visiting friends around Oaklake, so as to tell them of the Great Villa Outrage, and of the fabulous morning he'd had amongst High Kings and diplomats. Blinded by the sun on the pavements, cooked on both sides by the relentless heat, and thickly peppered with the dust of drought-shrivelled gardens, Bram took refuge now in his room. He drew the curtains so that not the slightest gap remained. The daylight, thus filtered through heavy white cloth, was opaque and shady, and the room not quite so searingly hot.

Like his siblings, Bram had a large room, plainly furnished with whatever they needed most. While Flann's room was lined with books, Bram's shelves displayed his model machines. His early efforts had been made from kits, but the later ones were his own inventions, and his parents had had his drawings and blueprints framed. Bram had hung the best ones on his wall. He had a deep, wing-backed chair that the father of a friend had given to him, and it was in this green-leathered monstrosity that he now lounged, his EyeGram nestled on his face like an affectionate, if leggy, arthropod.

EyeGram was a new invention, the work of one of the Court's research corporations, and it was not yet on sale. But Terence Grace always 'knew a chap' or 'had a word' with 'a friend of a friend', and the EyeGram was Bram's last birthday present. The EyeGram harvested the wearer's biochemistry to create holograms, and wired itself to the electromagnetic impulses in the wearer's brain so that they could hear and see as the hologram did. These holograms could be received—once the right code or wavelength was known—by those who had a radio or a telephone.

The downside was that the design of the EyeGram was not finished. The result was that the visible circuit boards, the minuscule plugs, and adjusting camera-eye made Bram look a bit like an automaton whose facial panelling had taken a battering. The first time Bram wore it, his little brother Raftery had gotten such a fright that he had run away and hidden under the kitchen sink, whence he had to be coaxed with jellybeans and promises of something new for his Cabinet of Marine Curiosities. Bram did not like the look of the half-mask, but he loved what it could do.

> BRAM: ... so the actual reason I was calling you is because—get this—I am not going to Prague this summer at all. Surprise! Thanks, Villa. Just ruin my life for me.

SUNNY: *Your whole life? All of it?*

BRAM: Oh, here, look, don't get all 'it's only a holiday,' this was far, far more than that. Trust me, you've no idea how important this was. Mama and Poppa had been arranging for me to meet all sorts of people of importance. Maybe even— well, guess who with? Go on, guess.

SUNNY: *Just tell me, will you?*

BRAM: Guess.

SUNNY: *Honestly, I don't know. Someone from your father's law office?*

BRAM: (snorting): Honestly, Sunny— no! That's not a big deal, at this stage —I've met them scores of times. No, one of the St. Maur Kers. One of the actual St. Maur Kers themselves. They are going to meet with Sylvestra St. Maur Ker—

SUNNY: *No!*

BRAM: And now we can't go. And a family that Mama knows from her job with the Better World Academy offered to bring us on the Orient Express Train, too, you know, from Vienna to Byzantium. There have been technomancers working for a year or more on this stupendous bridge to get the train across the Danube. And Mama said she and Poppa had a whole raft of people I could meet. You'll never guess who they'd invited for our first night there?

SUNNY: *I don't* know—*God?*

BRAM: Though I suppose it hardly matters now, since Villa's only gone and ruined it for us all. No trips, no ships, no trains, no Sylvestra, no Cosimo. What on earth am I going to do now? How am I going to have a career if my nutso sister is going to keep throwing hammers into the works?

SUNNY: *You throw spanners, not hammers.*

BRAM: That will make all the difference, thanks, Sunny. It's a good job it is only spanners I have wrecking my life.

SUNNY: *Where are you going to be for summer?*

BRAM: Goodness knows what my alternative is. I can't believe Villa!

SUNNY: *When will you know your fate?*

BRAM: The axe is about to fall. I had hoped we'd go to the St. Maur Ker summer camp in Galicia, but Granda wouldn't hear of it. Grandmother Gale, of all people, has worked something out, and we are waiting for a visitor to come and give us the details. I hear a step upon the stairs—I had better go. Wish me luck.

SUNNY: *You don't need luck—your father works for Cosimo St. Maur Ker, you'll fall on your feet!*

Three

The visitor for whom Flann had been fetched home had declined a seat, so everyone was standing rather awkwardly in the kitchen. Gráinne and Terence Grace looked very shifty and uncomfortable as Granda strode in, ballgown rustling and shoe-soles pealing on the tiles. Grandmother Gale, on the other hand, was quite accustomed to Granda after so many years, so paid his appearance no attention at all.

Flann joined Bram beside the fridge, the coldest place in the house which simmered, despite the automata waving huge fans, the abundance of marble and polished stone, and the white furnishings. Peridot cufflinks twinkled at Bram's wrists as he ate olives from the bowl he was supposed to be putting on the table. Raftery was at a low table, negotiating with No. 6 Automaton who was trying to get Raftery to eat while Raftery wanted to rearrange his scrapbook of marine pictures. His bright yellow hair was sticking out at all angles, a sure sign he was busy.

Outside in the bright garden, Villa was peering into

the interior of a bicycle's dynamo. Bram frowned when he glimpsed her, partly because he was still annoyed and partly because he was trying to work out why her hair looked different. It was still green, and still in spikes. But the spikes were smooth, pointed and shiny, and in a more regular pattern around her head; the green was very lush and deep. She looked, Bram thought angrily, like a drawing of a virus. Villa wore cut-off dungarees and t-shirt, both liberally streaked with grease. She was crouched over the partially dismantled bicycle with a fuel-line in one hand and an oil-rag in the other.

In the middle of the kitchen there stood a short stocky red-head with a red shovel-shaped beard and large, tranquil, brown eyes. He wore a shabby, age-rusted black suit.

"It is so good of you to come all this way, Mr., Mr., Mr., hmmm, Gabriel," said Gráinne Grace, and then said brightly to Granda,

"I didn't know you knew anyone in that part of the country? Down, way way down in the countryside? Around Littlefish Water? How unexpected!"

She laughed very tensely but Granda said breezily,

"Oh, we know Peg well. Your mother knew her long ago—Peg's been the farmer on Cobwell since old god's time. Interestingly enough, I met Peg's husband entirely separately—Jolyon and myself go back a long way."

"Yes, well, that may be true," Terence said hurriedly, "there's no need to drag up your past."

Bram and Flann glanced and each other and Flann winked. Fond as he was of his father-in-law, Terence was ambitious and successful, and was not convinced that Granda's rackety background was entirely suitable for other people to know about. It was one thing for Granda to be known as a devout contrarian, loudly despising what he called *money-grubbing parasites on a corrupt system*. It would not do for Terence, trying to keep his career on track.

"You can hardly ask for a better solution, dear," said Grandmother Gale to her daughter. "The children will be as safe as houses."

"Peg thought you should know," Mr. Gabriel said to Grandmother Gale, "that Mr. Decker will be working in Hightide House for the whole summer."

Granda looked momentarily startled.

"I thought Decker was in Prague? Or Vienna?"

"No, Father," Gráinne said, very tight-lipped, "that's the whole bloody point of our trip! Sylvestra St. Maur Ker promised the Emperor that they can re-create the Atlantis Codfish, and that's what Decker is doing right now. Working in his laboratories, on Eightfoot Island, where he makes all his marvellous animals for the Better World Academy."

"With the Emperor and little Sylvestra hoping that the supposed capacity of the legendary Atlantis Codfish to regenerate itself will make the world rely on them for a never-ending supply of cheap food?" Granda butted in sharply, but Gráinne ignored him, and continued,

"With Decker away on Littlefish Water, Cosimo St. Maur Ker asked me—*me*—to organise Decker's *Clockwork Oranges Are Not The Only Fruit* conference. This means working *directly* with Cosimo St. Maur Ker! This is the making of my career. This is my chance to move from botany into phytotecture, from understanding plants to making them."

"Do you not think plants can do that already, without your help?" said her mother tersely. "They've been doing it a while, like."

Gráinne ignored her, too.

"This is months of work," she said, "and a summer school, *with the St. Maur Kers*. This is life-changing! Which is why it is so vitally important that this works out properly. That everything goes right and smoothly and doesn't get sabotaged and overturned and trampled into the mud at the first hurdle by my youngest daughter's accursed inability to not get herself slung out of the best school in the freaking country!"

Dr. Grace's voice had been getting louder and louder and Bram's eye darted to the French windows through which he saw Villa look up, and then determinedly look back down again, pretending not to have heard.

"If Decker lives on Eightfoot Island," Terence said quickly to Mr. Gabriel, before Gráinne started up again, "you must have met him?"

Mr. Gabriel said thoughtfully, "Mr. Decker is not what you would call a frequent visitor."

"No?" said Terence, "Too busy, I expect."

"Not invited, if I know Peg," said Granda.

Mr. Gabriel said, "Mr. Decker does not leave the island often, and always remains in his carriage when he comes ashore."

"Father, let us keep to the point," Gráinne said glancing swiftly at the children. "The point is—well, Cobwell—saving your presence, Mr. Gabriel, and I am sure we are extremely grateful to you and to, to, to, Farmer Peg but can we have your assurance that Cobwell is… respectable?"

"Respectable?" said Granda, shocked, and Mr. Gabriel shook the windows with a great and rumbling peal of laughter. "Respectable? Are we even related, Gráinne?"

"Respectability does not concern us," Mr. Gabriel said, when he had finished laughing, "but you must know your children will be perfectly safe at Cobwell. They may even be happy. We will do our utmost to take good care of them."

Gráinne was looking flustered, Flann noticed with astonishment. Rather pink, Gráinne said shiftily,

"I heard, I think, a rumour perhaps about, you know, Cobwell being…"

Even Terence looked at her without understanding.

"Being a bit close to…? You know? Oh for goodness' sake, a bit close to the border with the sídhe! Dangerous?"

"You're always close to the aos sídhe," Gale said, and Gráinne rolled her eyes.

"We don't want visits from— our aos sídhe brethren!"

"Maybe we should ask those technomancers that you so admire," Granda said slyly to Terence. "We have all heard the rumours that St. Maur Ker turns a blind eye to technomancers using elf-parts in their machines."

"Father!"

"Really, Thelonius!"

Unexpectedly, Mr. Gabriel snorted.

"I would not worry too much about Cobwell and the sídhe, or with portals to other worlds," he said.

"It's not so close as they say, then?" said Terence, and Mr. Gabriel looked out of the window with an air of unconcern. He cleared his throat.

"Let's go with that," he said, finally.

"Well, that's the best I can offer, Gráinne," Grandmother Gale said briskly. "The ankle-biters go to Cobwell, you go to Prague, and we go to your Great-Aunt Honey's. Unless you prefer to stay here scowling at each other while Gráinne's career goes down the toilet."

Terence and Gráinne looked at each other. There was an uncomfortable silence. Gráinne and Terence looked at the twins, and Raftery, at each other again and then looked at Mr. Gabriel.

"Silence means assent," said Grandmother Gale, and Terence said to the automaton,

"No. 6, could you follow the trail of bicycle grease out there and bring Villa in?"

Mr. Gabriel's way of travelling through the aether was quite unique: he simply crumpled it up, as a human might crumple a sheet of paper or cloth, and pushed it aside. He did not move through it, he moved it around himself. A very few minutes after he had left the Grace household, he was on the edge of Cobwell Farm.

Even towards evening there was a haze, and the bright corals, fresh yellows and crisp, limey greens in the fields shimmered under the searing sun. The lime-washed walls of Cobwell House, and the few little houses scattered between the fields, were dazzling. From where he hovered, Mr. Gabriel could see the routes of two rivers twisting down from Wolftrap Mountains, wrinkling the landscape, one shining gold in the dying sun, the other shining pink, the boundaries of the fifty or so acres of farm-land.

The Wilderness sprawled over the north half of the farm, and the evening light gleamed on the roof of its Glasshouse, which stood between the Wilderness lake and the stretch of meadow, and on the crown of the dense forest beyond. A third river cut The Wilderness in two, but this river flowed only through The Wilderness and it had no name.

Just on the Cobwell side of the Fass stood the jagged promontory of rock known as the Pike of Phoenix, and strewn along one edge of the farm, and hugging a curve of The Wilderness, were more rocks: standing stones, and lumps of granite that, though unhewn and the size of bulls, were nonetheless peculiarly smooth and polished. From Cobwell House there was a long road through the farm to its boundary at Fass Bridge, and the road led on then to the village, Tubberlue.

Seen from above in a hazy late-summer evening, with the sun burnishing the lakes and rivers and glasshouses, everything looked peaceful and unchangeable. Mr. Gabriel hardly wanted to land. He hovered a moment or two longer before beginning to diminish in size and descend.

He glided through the big iron gates by the bridge over the Fass, and oozed up the avenue to the house, leaving a smear of emerald-green behind him.

When Mr. Gabriel arrived, Peg was sitting at the table peering into the minute insides of a mechanical teapot. Her husband Jolyon sat near stone steps up to the back door, where there was a great deal of sunlight. He and his wife could not have looked less alike. Jolyon had a great deal of very dark hair tied back in a pony-tail. He was tall and willowy with large round eyes and a long smooth oval of face, and wore a lot of silver necklaces and bead bracelets. Peg was short, with bobbed grey hair, almond-shaped eyes in a round face and no adornment at all. Jolyon was wearing glasses that magnified his eyes till they looked bigger than his head, and he was using a chisel the size of a rat's tooth to carve a detail onto a wooden flute he was making.

"Are we sorted?" Peg said, as soon as Mr. Gabriel came into the kitchen, scattering green light behind him. "So—what do you think, now that you've met them?"

Mr. Gabriel shrugged.

"They seem like decent people, but we have to be careful. The parents are devotees of the St. Maur Kers; Sylvestra and Cosimo's branch, unfortunately."

"Lou? What do you think? Are you worried?"

Lou, who had just that moment appeared beside the wide mouth of the fire-place, wore a long and very shabby coat and a wide-brimmed battered hat with slumped crown, and was eating an apple.

"Worried," said Lou, "Why worry?"

An apple-butt cartwheeled through the air and landed in the empty grate. It hissed then burst into flames, scattering the seeds. The seeds turned to pearls and showered, bouncing, over the stone floor while the apple-butt dried into flakes of gold that settled down among the ashes. Jolyon sighed and took a broom.

"Stop messing, Lou," he said mildly, "you'll only annoy Mr. Gabriel."

The rafters rang with Lou's laughter. Peg said,

"Lou, this is serious! I had to take them in, but we don't know—well, we don't know whether they pose a threat to us."

"At the very least, Lou," Jolyon said, "you have to make sure that they don't see anything that could get back to—anyone."

"Oh don't sweat the petty things," Lou said cheerfully. "Even I can't stop them seeing."

"But you can stop them remembering," said Mr. Gabriel quickly. "We want nothing of Cobwell to reach the ears of the St. Maur Kers, or anyone like them. The Pharaoh's Court is starting to tighten its grip on the Empires, starting to see how much control the Courtiers can start grabbing. We don't want them getting any ideas. We already have Dorian Decker nearby, and now the Academy has research permission for two weeks in the castle in Dunmathew. Cobwell is surrounded."

The back door opened, and there was a lot of grunting and shuffling as someone struggled out of their boots.

"I heard," said Lou, "that they plan to re-build the Rain-Maker."

"And we know how they are planning to make that work, don't we?" said the new arrival, blocking out the light briefly as he padded across the kitchen in his bare feet. "Elf-parts."

"Mick, we don't *know* that they use sídhe-parts. Okay, there are very strong *hints*. If there was proof, then Tima could have refused permission. As it was, she had no option."

Mick scattered sapphire-blue specks of light as he moved around, putting on the kettle and taking out mugs for tea. He was a big bruiser of a man with red-blond hair and a bright red beard.

"Besides," said Peg, "the Rain-Maker is not their invention. They are just sprucing up the model that was made by the O'Connell Beares back in the Middle Ages. That isn't built to have elf-parts. The O'Connell Beares wouldn't have stood for that."

"Only humans could think drought is a good thing," Mick muttered, and Mr. Gabriel gave him a dig in the ribs and jerked his head vigorously towards Jolyon. Mick blushed the same red as his hair and his beard.

"Sorry," he said, "Jolyon. And the rest of you. I meant … other humans. St. Maur Ker. Their supporters."

"The most important thing is," said Peg, "that no-one knows more about Cobwell at the end of this visit than they did at the beginning. Not the Graces, not the Court."

"There's no harm in the children seeing the way the farm works," Mr. Gabriel said with decision, "once we keep them out of The Wilderness, and especially out of the Glasshouse."

"The Wilderness itself will take care of that," Lou remarked, and Mr. Gabriel continued,

"But the last thing we need is that any connection of the St. Maur Kers gets wind of—our duties here."

This seemed to decide the matter, but then Lou said,

"You have to worry about the right thing. Go big, or go home. These sprogs aren't a worry because they have a connection to St. Maur Ker. They're a worry because they're human. Humans think the St. Maur Kers, and people like them, are the best of the species. Their hubris knows no bounds now."

Mr. Gabriel said, suddenly uneasy,

"Lou?"

"The St. Maur Kers, their diplomats, their academies, their private army," Lou said, "the Courtiers, these corporations they have started up. That whole, rotten layer of wealth, of greed. Pfff. They're nothing. They never had real magic. They depend on people believing them, and they depended on stealing magic from the bones of the sídhe."

Everyone stopped moving, and no-one spoke.

"But I think they are going one step further, now," said Lou, getting up, "the St. Maur Kers. They're trying to get ahead of their competition, trying to make their emperor more powerful than anyone else's. So, they're stealing something very big. This drought is no accident. Neither is it the end."

The silence became, though it hardly seemed possible, even more profound. Bridie broke it.

"You have always said that everything has its season,

though. That which rises falls, be it star or empire, you said."

"They will fall," Lou replied, "St. Maur Ker, the empire, all the empires, everything they have seized."

"Cobwell—" Mick said, and stopped. "Cobwell… is Cobwell, remember."

"If they go too far, if they fall too late," Lou said, "then the St. Maur Kers and their sort can break Cobwell as badly as they are breaking the Other Side, before they go. And the humans let them have control of everything, because the St. Maur Kers, and the Courtiers, and the emperors and empresses give them cakes and ale, bread and circuses, promises of happiness. The St. Maur Ker in particular have been thinking the unthinkable. The humans have stopped taking care of things for themselves. They are starting to worry me."

Lou stretched, and the house bulged.

"Actually," said Lou, "they're starting to piss me off."

Four

Night, when it finally fell, was a clear one, hot and humid, and very quiet. Lou went out the back door of the farmhouse, and in a single step reached the polished rocks and standing stones on the north side of The Wilderness. It was like standing in an auditorium, where every distant sound was amplified. Lou's hearing was as sharp as a basilisk's.

Miles to the north of Hibernia, beyond the source of the Great River, beyond the rock-toothed sea near Malin Head, and the heaving greens and blues that eventually came to crash or swash against the edges of Scotia's western islands, there was a right barney going on. Lou listened with every ear—of which there were more than standard issue, for someone wearing human form—and was grimly certain that such a terrific rannygazoo at sea could be created only by Storm Kelpies. Storm Kelpies, who lived in the wild water between Hibernia and Scotia. Who ought to be keeping an eye on the sleeping Cailleach. Who should make their appearance only when the Cailleach emerged in October, and ruled for winter.

Every evening for what the humans called 'a week', Lou had gone into The Wilderness, and had listened. The storms had started under the unsailable Corryvrecken Whirlpool, and spread south in slow, wide spirals. Lou could hear them rising from the black, cold currents of the deep seas up to the sunlit world. Very soon, they would be visible even to the humans. So too would the Storm Kelpies. Storm Kelpies who were up and about, giving the leather lungs of banshees a run for their money in the lethal-shrieking stakes. Who, Lou wondered, had spat in their ambrosia, if not the St. Maur Kers?

The sounds of The Wilderness were a balm, and Lou turned to them in relief. It was a quiet evening, but Lou's hearing was as acute as a hound's sense of smell. Everything made a noise: a hawker dragonfly hit a leaf, a gadfly stepped over the surface of the watering-pool where wolves were lapping, rooks chivvying as they rounded up their roosting-mates. Ladybirds tapped out onto leaves to avoid the scampering paws of pine martens, and the crepuscular and nocturnal hunters began to set out for a night's work. Grazing animals dozed, and Lou heard the soil beneath the cattle and horses humming and crackling, teeming with far more lives, from bacteria to worms, than lived on the surface.

The drought had not touched The Wilderness. The sizzling of water and the cracking of soil and rocks that Lou could hear were from the banks of the River Fass, or from under Littlefish Water, the lake a few miles south of Cobwell. Miles to the west the Great River, broad and majestic, flowed on between the worlds, between Hibernia and the sídhe, and off into the dark between the stars. But to the north, the Kelpies were rioting, and the storms were rising higher, and getting wilder.

The moment Mr. Gabriel left, Dr. and Mr. Grace took action. They weren't happy about the children going to Cobwell, but were less happy at the thought of contacting the St. Maur Kers and saying *sorry, 'cos—Villa.* The biplane was leaving before dawn the next day, and the children would leave for Cobwell after lunch, so there was not much time to prepare. Everyone's suitcases had been packed for Prague which meant they had to re-pack for a holiday spent on a remote farm. Automaton No. 6 was still out, making arrangements to get the children, with the maximum amount of luxury, to Cobwell. Gráinne was scribbling notes for minding the house plants in the family's absence, and Terence was preparing food for an early breakfast. Without thinking, he said,

"Pity we can't just use a bit of magic."

Gráinne said nothing, and Terence turned to look at her. She was clearly tempted. But then she shook her head.

"No," she said regretfully, "they said they didn't want any magic or technomancy in Oaklake."

"I wasn't thinking of using any," Terence said hastily. "Anyway, I hear the Pharaoh is less keen these days, too. Some of the Courtiers have been extremely critical."

"Seems a bit ironic, considering the history."

She bit the end of her pencil, and then scribbled some notes about checking leaves for red spider-mites.

"Anyway," she added, her mind elsewhere, "it's been so long, I'm not sure I'd be able..."

Her voice trailed away, and she finished writing. She held out two lists and a pencil, and said to Terence,

"Here—get this lot packed. Check if there's anything else they want to bring. Get Raftery to bed, and make sure Flann isn't sitting up writing letters to Mr. Dead Philosopher. You've got one hour."

Dr. Grace's packing list for Flann
– *The Secret Diary of Ludwig Wittgenstein, Aged 14 ½*
– *The Reflective Child's Guide to Ethical Eating*
– Paper and pens
– 6 sets of identical trousers, skirts, and tunics, three pale, three dark. [That's it? That's the lot, Terence? It seems... Spartan.] [Have you met Flann lately, Gráinne? Of course it's Spartan!]

Mr. Grace's packing List for Raftery
– Wellington Boots
– Sun-Hats [Note: Plural? He has one head.] [he keeps losing them!]
– Waterproof Everything

- Shrimping net, sea-binoculars, other marine-related items
- Four scrapbooks [note: he doesn't need four!] [I know but he couldn't decide between them]
- *Maps of Impossible Places*
- Tin whistle

Dr. Grace's packing list for Bram

- *Getting Ahead while Keeping your Head: The Ambitious Child's Guide to Life in the Imperial Courts*
- *From Atlantis to Tyre: The History of the St. Maur Ker Family*

[How many jackets and pairs of co-ordinated trousers can he need? He's packed fourteen shirts, seven ties with matching socks, unspeakable amounts of gels and potions for hair and skin, handkerchiefs, cufflinks, comb, brushes, and a hair-dryer that asks you if you have any holidays planned. Is this normal?] [It's how the St. Maur Kers do things, so, yes.]

- *The Hungry Child's Guide to Eating*
- His Eye-Gram [in my young day, a smart-phone was good enough.] [In your young day, old-timer, you didn't plug a circuit-board into your face so a hologram can chat to your friends. Don't forget the vitamin pills —using that Eye-Gram is tiring.]

Mr. Grace's list for Villa

– Telescope
– Ship's Logbook
– 9 Ordnance Survey maps
– Pen, nibs and different coloured inks
– That camera she got from Great-Uncle Barnabas, that looks like a tool-box
– *The Explorations of Miss Gertrude Bel. Illustrated by her Budgie.*
– *To Hy-Brasil in a Wave-Sweeper: Legendary Voyages to Legendary Places*

[Note: Some clothes, maybe?] [She's agreed to a tooth-brush. Otherwise it's the clothes she stands up in, apparently.] [Terence! Pack some clothes!]

Villa was sitting at her desk, writing in a blank ship's log-book that she had found in an antique shop. The only time she was careful about her handwriting was when she filled in the orderly, narrow columns, and especially, the unlined spaces for comments. Granda had bought the book when she found it, and made a ninth-birthday present of it, but it had been months before she had dared write in it. Not until she had carefully copied a drawing of a clipper ship—with Bram's help, back in the lost days where he still spoke to her like a person and not a nasty infection—did she feel like she really owned the log-book. Now she wrote in it every day.

CALL SIGN: Oh–Villa!

HOUR: 22:00. Am supposed to be in bed asleep. Ha!

WIND SPEED/DIRECTION: None. Not a breath of air.

TEMPERATURE: 30°C/86°F outside. In interior of Grace Family Home: sub-zero. Arctic conditions prevailing (twins and both parents angry).

PREVIOUS COMPASS COURSE: To Prague, first. But trip arranged on the Orient Express, a train that stops in Byzantium. A city which is on two seas, and where the St. Maur Kers have a fleet, Sylvestra St. Maur Ker has a two-masted schooner, as well as their navy-ships that they gave to Empress Justinia. So plan was to go to Byzantium, but to slip off the train just as it started the return journey.

CURRENT COMPASS COURSE: West of the Middle of No-where in Hibernia. Land-locked.

SPEED OF TRAVEL: New plan has immediate effect–we're being sent to Cobwell Farm tomorrow.

FATHOMS: Unfathomable.

COMMENTS: Scuppered Plans: (1) Learning to sail properly, not just dodging about on the fishing boats.

(2) Escaping family and start new life by stowing away on a clipper-ship headed for Cathay and when it was too late to send me back, oblige captain to let me work to earn my passage when I was already aboard (that is, sail before the mast). Contingency Plan (for if they threw me out in Alexandria): there are tons of ports there, I would've found someone stuck for a cabin-boy to take me on. If Granda could do it, so can I. Stayed at sea. Learned to be an explorer, for when I

get my own ship. Photograph the high seas, and the icefields of the Arctic.

Not feeling a bit sorry for Flann. All she was going to do in Prague was moulder away in a library—you can do that anywhere. Well, except possibly Cobwell, I don't think farms have libraries. Bram would have spent the entire time with Poppa, learning how to be a smiley-face. But I feel a bit sorry for him, he blooms like a lily with other people and an isolated farmhouse will give him horrors. Raftery would have been shown things, and people would tell themselves that it would be a wonderful experience for him even though he is seven and will have forgotten all about it in two minutes and all he really cares about are his marine scrapbooks and his curiosities.

Villa put down her pen and bit her thumb angrily. The world was unfair, and adults took delight in frustrating the plans of future explorers. She heard Flann and Bram chattering on their way to their bedrooms. She closed the log-book and returned it to its proper place, between a model of a currach and a ship's lantern that she had been given by Grandmother Gale. Then she climbed into bed, shut her eyes, and picked up her adventure where she had left it. *The fog shrouded them so visibility was only a few yards. There was no sign of another vessel in the ice-packed sea. With the fog so dense, it was impossible to guess from what direction the howls came, but they were getting closer. The battered crew armed themselves as best they could, but whatever was approaching was big. The Chief Mate strode up.*

"Orders, Captain?"

"Send up a distress flare."

The Captain went below, and wound up the radio: Mayday! Mayday! This is clipper-ship Wave-Sweeper...

As the clocks around the Grace house struck midnight, Dr. and Mr. Grace finally crawled to bed, exhausted. Just as they were drifting towards sleep, Dr. Grace said,

"I'm not entirely happy about this, Terence."

Her husband's voice was muffled by the pillow.

"Neither am I, but the children will be perfectly safe. They might even enjoy it."

"Terence."

"Okay, maybe not enjoy. We'll find a way of making it up to Flann and Bram."

"I don't think Mr. Gabriel is right about Cobwell not being close to the borders with— well, Over Beyond," said Gráinne.

Terence struggled to open his eyes.

"Your mother wouldn't have let them go anywhere they were likely to fall through a portal into—her home country, shall we say?"

"No, but there was this war, wasn't there, about two hundred years ago, the sídhe tried to invade? There was some, I don't know, weak spot in the boundaries, and they broke through? Wasn't that somewhere... you know... near Cobwell?"

Terence said, "I'm not sure if that was really true. Anyway, if there was any trouble from the sídhe, St. Maur Ker would have put paid to it by now."

They fell asleep.

By midnight, Bram was already asleep, and Flann— though she had determined to stay awake being angry —was not long behind. Raftery slept the sleep of the just, and dreamed of myrmidons. By the striking of the one o'clock chimes, only Villa was awake, wondering about places where on a map it says *hic dragones, here be dragons*.

Five

CALL SIGN: Who Knew?

HOUR: Dawn.

WIND SPEED/DIRECTION: None. Not a breath of air.

TEMPERATURE: 25°C/81°F outside. Cobwell is not boiling like everywhere else is, even outside, and inside the house is very cool. Captain's bedroom perfect: desk and chair, bed, wardrobe, chest-of-drawers, white walls. No fuss. Skylight.

PREVIOUS COMPASS COURSE: Prague, and then Byzantium and the sea now impossible.

CURRENT COMPASS COURSE: Cobwell might not be without interest.

SPEED OF TRAVEL: This was hilarious. Parents arranged all sorts of luxury for us, to keep Bram and Flann happy, even though Granda kept saying *there's no point, Gráinne, Cobwell's not like other places*. A car came to collect us and the luggage, but it broke down a mile out of Kilcam. Driver got a lift for us, but not the luggage, but the second driver got lost, and after two hours still couldn't find the right road; the engine finally shouted *stop bloody asking me, I'm not a navigator!*, the paper map had a huge rip right across the middle, and the road-signs were blank.

Finally found a different route to the marina on the lake, but the luxury river-boat, said to be unsinkable, had a mysteriously shattered bow, and was on its way to the shipyard for repair. It looked to me like it had been wrung out, twisted tight. Got an automaton to drive us to the Rathivshe train-station, because we'd be just in time to catch the sleeper from Aircal to Rothe Hall, but we'd barely got the far side of the town when the train fell apart. It slowed down for no reason, and we were all sticking our heads out of the windows to see what was going on, and the engine just fell out. All in bits, it sort of unravelled, engine innards everywhere.

Flann came along, looking really grim, and said, "Get your bags, this is not going to end well." We only had our small bags, because the rest of the luggage was still up at Kilcam. By then, the train boiler was neatly standing by the tracks, and the smoke-stack—made of opal? Odd—had rolled away. Axles and cogs and all sorts of gears, all shining and polished and studded with pearls. There were mechanics and stokers and ticket-collectors all standing about, scratching their heads as though to scare up some ideas of what to do.

Bits of train started to fall off, carriages collapsed onto the line, someone started singing *Are you right there Michael are you right?* And the trainmen didn't look a bit impressed but it was kind of fun, everyone knew the words. *Do you think that we'll get home before it's light? It's all depending whether the old engine holds together, and it might now, Michael, so it might.* Lots of verses, lots of gusto, not much grip on the tune.

Finally, the train-driver told us all to get off what was left of the train. A flat-bed truck had arrived, and they were piling up bits of train to take it back to the goods-yard to be put back together. The driver and the stoker picked up a sheet of metal and there, neatly stacked up underneath, were our suitcases. None of us looked at each other.

"Someone doesn't want us to get there," Raftery said, while we were trudging down the road to a bridge across the River Bearu, where a bus, apparently, would bring us somewhere. What actually turned up was a jeep, and the driver leaned out of the window and said, "Are youse the four childer for Cobwell?" Raftery said, "Wese is", and the driver said, "Well, I've been sent to collect youse. Bridie's my name. Get in. Mind the animals." Flann said suspiciously, "How did you know the transport broke down?" Bridie said, "Only what comes from Cobwell can find Cobwell." We got in, and I got belched at by something that seemed far too large to be in the car, and then I had a hare on my lap. I wondered if we were being kidnapped.

It was rare excitement.

FATHOMS: Unfathomable.

Dear Mr. Wittgenstein,

The less said about the journey here, the better. Even poor Raftery, who never complains, looked on the verge of tears when he saw the bockety vehicle that finally brought us here. And it was full of animals that the driver —Bridie, her name is, she's a wildlife vet—was bringing home. She gave Raftery a frog to look after, so that cheered him up. Villa had an unfortunately windy hare on her lap. I was sick as a parrot the whole way and I— well, we will draw a veil over the whole Vomiting on Arrival incident. Raftery asked Bram if I was turning inside out.

I have been interred in a mean little upper room, practically in the attic, bare apart from the bed, a desk and chair, and—this at least is something—some book shelves. There's a tiny press to keep clothes in. My suit-case is still on the floor, unpacked.

There is a skylight through which I could see Orion's Belt, and a window through which I saw the moon rise, and the rustling crowns of trees. If you can see Orion's Belt, you can find the Pole Star, and from there, you can find your way anywhere.

I have been lying awake for a long time, and I have made a decision. I decided that I will not stay here. I don't care that I have been told to, it isn't fair, I don't want to stay, and I am going to leave. Granda was made to work on a farm when he was my age and he hated it, but he did something about it. He didn't just put up with it. He ran away to sea. I don't care if Mama thinks this makes me a contrarian, I don't even care if I'm expelled. Granda was fifteen when he ran away and if he could make his way to Manchuria, I can make mine to Prague.

Flann woke up. She turned her head to look up at the skylight, and yelped aloud in pain from a stabbing crick in her neck. She had fallen asleep halfway through her letter, and slept twisted onto one side, with her head hanging at an angle. She had also dropped her fountain pen, and there was a large blue ink-stain on the sheet. Flann went cold, staring at it in horror. She was abruptly very angry. She jumped out of bed, but then didn't know what to do. The ink-stain reproached her. She was angry, and she was obscurely sick of being reproached. Bad enough people interfering with your life, she thought, the material world has to join in.

She yanked the bedclothes up. If she had her way, she would be a ghost, a surge of energy, and not be constantly bothered by this corporeal existence, by having limbs and insides, by all this hair-brushing and nail-clipping. She stopped yanking, and fished her pen out from the fold of sheet in which it had become entangled. She wrote 'not be constantly bothered by this corporeal existence' on the back of her letter to Wittgenstein. She often made a note of thoughts she was pleased with, that she was sure she had not read somewhere else. Then she jerked the bedclothes into a semblance of order, put away her writing things, and looked out of the window.

She could just see the River Fass glittering in the light. The sound of feet clumping down the hall outside told her that Villa was up and about. Even in an empty room, Flann grimaced.

A small hallway separated the workroom from the kitchen, and off the hallway was a utility room, where a battered wooden bench was used for fixing things, and where the surrounding shelves were tidily packed with boxes of tools and equipment. Bram was there, hunched over the workbench on which he had dismantled his EyeGram. He was using a set of pliers so infinitely fine they were occasionally invisible, and he was detaching filaments from one surface, and with evident difficulty, he was re-attaching them elsewhere. The filaments looked larger than the pliers. They were mostly gold and sapphire, and they gave off fiery sparks as they struggled and thrashed. Villa hurried on before he noticed her and started whingeing about Prague.

Raftery was in full flow in the kitchen. Villa recognised Mick, who had carried the grumpy, tearful Raftery up the yard to the house on arrival yesterday, and amused him with card tricks. Villa looked about her. The bright sunshine caught the pots and pans hanging from the ceiling, and the polished stone surfaces. One side of the room was taken up with the vast fireplace, with a curved black oak beam above it and space on either side of the grate where a person could sit, or a loaf of bread could rise. The back wall, when Villa peered at it, was black with soot and so cavernous and dark that light rarely fell on the tiny silver cauldron dangling from the hook.

Opposite, across the black and white floor-tiles, there were two big wooden dressers, and between them was a very large green oven with plenty of doors, drawers, wheels, levers and winches. From the belly of this behemoth, Mick was taking potato cakes and beans, while Raftery's spate of questions went gloriously unchecked. For every question that was answered, he had two more. Mick had told him that not only did Cobwell have a river, but also a duck-pond, an unmeasurably deep cave full of water, called The Pot, and a small lake on the top of the Pike of Phoenix. Raftery wanted to visit them all, preferably at the same time.

"I was looking at the map on the way down," Villa said, "before the train fell apart on us, and isn't there another lake—Littlefish Water? Where do I get breakfast?"

"Here, in the oven," said Mick, answering her second question first. "Littlefish Water isn't on Cobwell Farm. Raftery would have to get permission to go there, or onto Eightfoot Island."

"There's nothing in the oven," Villa said indignantly, when she had opened the oven door, and Mick closed it again, and said,

"What do you want for breakfast?"

"Why's it called Eightfoot Island?" Raftery demanded.

"Eggs and sausages and pancakes."

"Open the door again," Mick said to Villa, and as Villa exclaimed in delight at a plateful of food, Mick answered Raftery. "Who knows why it's called that. But sure there is plenty of water for you to explore here. Maybe we'll take you up some day to the Great River, or the Callows."

"I'd like to explore the farm," said Villa, shovelling eggs and sausage into her mouth. Flann, suddenly appearing behind her, said sharply,

"For goodness sake, Villa, don't talk with your mouth full. And don't eat like a pig."

Villa slapped her knife and fork on the table, and Mick said,

"You can't go exploring by yourself on a farm, Villa, you might come to harm. I'll get Lou to show you around. Flann, stop snarking at your sister, and eat some breakfast."

"I—"

"I said stop snarking at your sister. You should have better things to do with all your brains than bother them about how Villa eats."

Flann was so surprised that she went silently to the oven, and took out a plate of mushrooms on toast.

"Raftery," said Mick, "myself and a couple others are going down to the duckpond to lay a hedge. Do you want to help out?"

"Where's this Lou person?" Villa demanded, not wanting to be left alone with Flann, and the threat of Bram. "Where can I find her? Him? Him or her?"

"I never thought to ask," said Mick, "but finish your breakfast and by then you can find Lou with the pigs, in Home Farm Field."

"That'll do me," said Villa.

Mick and Raftery went out, and Bridie came in with a very tiny, sad-looking, lamb wrapped in her jacket. She opened a different compartment in the oven, and put the lamb inside it. Mr. Gabriel came in, yawning and scratching his beard. He put the kettle on to boil, and stooped to pet the lamb.

"Bridie," said Flann innocently, "I wonder, you know the River Fass? Which way does it flow?"

Bridie looked at her, and Flann looked back, keeping her expression open, and blank. After a couple of seconds, she had the uneasy feeling that Bridie knew what was in her mind.

"It flows," said Bridie, "from its source to the sea, which is the way of rivers."

There was a short moment of deep silence. Mr. Gabriel was looking intently at Bridie. Villa, her spoon halfway to her mouth, was looking at Flann.

"C'mere to me, though," said Bridie, and everyone relaxed, "I believe you're a great woman for the books."

"You're a vet," said Flann, "you must have read a few books in your time."

"My sister is moving house," Bridie went on. "She was living in that wee cottage near Home Farm, but she decided she needed a change. And she could do with a hand unpacking her library. If you were to help out, I'm sure she'd lend you a book or two to tide you over."

It was not so easy to obscure the library at Prague, but Flann's bibliophile sense tingled.

"She's just down in Tubberlue," Bridie said, "I'll gi'e you a lift down, and you can walk back, easy enough, it's only a mile. Or two."

"Well—thanks," said Flann. "What's your sister's name?"

"Bridget," said Bridie.

"Bridget? Your sister's name is Bridget?" Flann said, managing only just in time not to laugh. "And you're Bridie? Is Bridie not short for Bri… Oh, okay. Fine. Never mind."

Bridie finished eyeing Flann beadily, and said,

"Finish up your breakfast, and be at the car in ten minutes, or you'll walk there, too."

Six

The hallway between the kitchen and the back door was square, tiled in white and red, and full of dogs. The youngest ones dashed at Villa, and skidded about on the tiles as she stopped to greet them, while adults sat upright and alert, looking for signs of food or a walk. Three dogs with grey muzzles thumped their tails at her in a kindly manner, but remained where they were, propped up against each other, dozing. Villa waded through the dogs, greeting them to left and right, and reached the door of heavy wood and battered brass, and through it a lean-to filled with bicycles, bits of machinery and old engines, broken armchairs where cats had kittens and chickens laid eggs, and rough wooden boxes filled with the kind of thing that can never be found when it is needed, like string or scissors or thumbtacks or boot-laces. Outside, Villa stopped to squint around, shielding her eyes with her hand.

The yard was cobbled, the stones worn shiny in the busy places, and the walls of the stables and sheds that closed the yard in on two sides were brick. Even in the morning, the sunlight leached away colours, so the normal dark orange of the walls was faded, and the random clumps of wild violets and speedwell looked bleached. The farmhouse and the few sheds around it threw navy shadows, and in these sat various cats and dogs, and a small goat was nosing about, its back end as bright as daisies through a half-open door. Beyond, a big dark stand of trees sheltered everything from the coldest winds, from the north and the east. Directly in front of the house grew a stout oak tree, its crown blazing green, and the wide circle of grass under it was cool in the shadow.

Everywhere was very quiet—or at least, Villa thought with surprise, it was not at all quiet, but there were no human voices. There was distant barking and birdsong, and horses' hooves striking a hard surface, and chickens chattering and occasionally a rooster crowing. She could not identify the smell, either, but it was strong, and musty. It was not unpleasant. She thought suddenly of being by the lake near her home, where she sneaked from Oaklake as often as she could, and of the smell there, that was tiny amounts of all sorts of things—dried water-weeds, new rope, the wet wooden posts in the ma-rina, dead fish, even—all pressed together. She wondered what tiny separate things made this distinctive Cobwell smell. Oaklake never smelled of anything. *This could be interesting.*

Near the oak, uneven tracks of dried mud and gravel met, and swung away. Villa skirted the oak tree, and stood in the middle of the knot of paths, looking around her again. The pale-brick cylinder, like a chimney, but sticking up from the ground, she guessed now must be The Pot that Mick mentioned. The stretch of scrubby ground that ran up to the ridge from the path was cluttered with bits of machinery of such intriguing natures that she was very tempted to investigate. She decided it would be better to find out who was the mechanic, and persuade them to let her help. All around her, all she could see were trees, and glimpses of fields and an occasional cow in between them.

Just as she takes her first step onto the grassy centre of the lane to Home Farm, Villa stops, startled, and listens. A chorus of birds seem to have just died away, and into the silence that followed, comes the sound of a very distant note. It sounds by itself, and then around it cluster more muffled sounds, fitting around each other like a mosaic, rather than joining together in a single line. Over them, a loud sweet whistling trails, and more sounds cluster and heap together, the whistling speeds up, and seeming to rock forth and back: louder on one side, then the other.

The moment Villa stepped fully onto the path, the peculiar impression she had of the music vanished, and she heard only the more familiar scolding of robins and alarm-calls of blackbirds. Everywhere was busy. In one field, someone was using an ancient little tractor to cut the long grass, in another, someone was pruning trees, in a third, someone was cleaning donkeys' hooves, and having their hat eaten by a foal, from another—Villa began to walk faster—came the grunting of pigs.

The first thing that Villa saw was several full-grown pigs, and uncountable piglets, near a sheltering grove of trees and bushes. Close to the grove, she could see the pink and tail-wagging rear ends of two pigs, who were drinking from a trough. Piglets gambolled and clambered so briskly that she could not count how many there were. Another pig was lying in a large wallow, covering itself in mud. Someone was leaning over the fence into the field, scratching vigorously the back of a sow. Villa didn't want to intrude so she went a little further along the path, past the small stone cottage, to where a boar was snout down in the hard ground, digging up a long root that he presumably found tasty. Villa watching him go, a little uneasy at knowing that the boar weighed more than herself and her twin siblings together.

Villa stood for a few minutes, leaning on the fence post, soaking up the sun. Swifts and sparrows flickered like sequins against the brilliant sky, but everything was too bright to look at. Instead, she listened closely and wondered how she would find out what was making all the noise. Something made a mocking, rattling noise, something else cawed and creaked in the copses of trees that divided up the farm. In the far distance Villa heard short bursts of drumming, short, sweet trills rang from the hedges, and the sweltering grass all around her was chirruping and clicking.

The only thing she could recognise was the sound of the pigs, digging and drinking, and—she noticed after a few moments—giving voice to an unbroken stream of little grunts and chunterings. It reminded her a bit of her father, who was often teased by the family for his running commentary on everything. She wondered if it was the same with pigs, that even as she stood there the pigs were saying the porcine equivalent of *now where did I put my glasses, Gráinne darling are you there? Did you remember to talk to the Jacksons about Friday night? Oh, here they are how on earth did they get there I wonder, mustn't forget to pick up the blue jacket from the cleaners ooh and mushrooms, we're out of mushrooms.*

From beyond the fence into Home Farm field, she heard the sound of shed doors and the distant hum of a motor. Villa leaned against the rough wood of the post, and baked pleasurably in the sun.

Villa's attention was drawn back to the world around her by the sudden loud snorting of the boar, and the rapid grunting of the sows, all of them hurrying towards her, snouts bouncing and ears flapping like flags. Villa realised quite suddenly how fragile a barrier the fence looked between her and five briskly trotting porkers. She took a step back, and Lou was suddenly beside her.

"They'll do you no harm," Lou said, "big and all as they are. I thought you should be introduced. They have come over in the hope that I bring food. Meet Lucinda. Lucinda is a fine sow and very good-tempered. Minnie is her daughter, as mischievous a reprobate as you could hope to meet. Oscar here is mellow and happy, but he's a big lad, so keep out of his way. And this sow here, on the other hand, is a bit grumpy. Aren't you, Ophelia? And that is Ophelia's sister, Queenie. She's a sweetie, but a bit of a wanderer, we're always having neighbours call us to tell us that Queenie's with them, eating all around her."

Lou held a large metal bucket of apples, tomatoes and tattered cabbages, and began throwing these in for the pigs to eat. Villa, upon being offered the bucket, took a few apples, and was delighted to see first one pig then another make short work of her offerings. Emboldened by having the company of someone who knew the ways of pigs, she even joined in when Lou started scratching the pigs' backs.

She flinched from them at first. The sow nearest to her, Lucinda, was massive and hot, and when Villa tentatively reached in, her bristles were stiff and sharp, and her tough skin flaked. But Villa scrubbed valiantly, watching Lou and realising that vigour was the order of the day, and the sow wriggled, and snorted. Ophelia came over reluctantly, and permitted only a small amount of scratching of her ears.

"Why is Ophelia lying in the mud?" Villa asked, when Ophelia had gone, and Lou replied,

"Pigs have no sweat glands. In this sun, they'd

over-heat and get sunstroke. So, being the intelligent animals they are, they coat themselves in mud. Ray makes sure there's water in their wallow."

"Sunscreen," said Villa, surprised, but very pleased, to find such sense and logic.

Villa scratched sides of both Lucinda and Queenie, and they, leaning over to get their undersides scrubbed, eventually flopped on the ground. Lou gave Oscar a final pat, and said,

"Enough, you Sybarites. Queenie, go and feed your piglets."

As they turned away, Lou said, "If nothing else good happens today, at least you will know that you cheered up a fellow-creature's morning."

"Do you live in that cottage?" Villa asked, her mind already elsewhere.

"In a manner of speaking," said Lou. "We have some more pigs down near the river, if you've taken a liking to them?"

Villa wondered how anyone could bear to wear a coat and hat on such a day, but Lou did not seem at all bothered by the heat. The coat was a shabby item, pulled crooked by over-filled pockets, and the hat was a slouchy garment, with a deep brim that hid Lou's face. Overall, Villa was reminded of Paddington Bear, except it was hard to name the colour. Standing beside Lou was like walking into a dim room after bright sunlight. Villa guessed the clothes were some fancy-schmancy-technomancy farmers' clobber so that they could, when necessary, be hosed down. She wondered where she could get some—she was the bane of No. 6's life.

Lou was swinging the food-bucket, which seemed as full of food as ever, and was blissfully easy to talk to, patiently answering Villa's barrage of questions. Villa wanted to know what kinds of trees they were that grew in parallel lines down the field (walnuts, cherries, hazelnuts), what kinds of cows were grazing between them (Belties and Dexters, mostly, apart from the red-eared Matriarch), and what was growing in the four glasshouses that snuggled together just beyond a hedge-topped ridge and an orchard (herbs, gooseberries, and sure we'll look in on the way).

Meanwhile, Bridie had brought Flann down to Tubberlue. Surprised as she was to find that Bridie had a sister of essentially the same name, she was even more surprised to find that Bridget was considerably older than Bridie, old enough to be her mother, if not her grandmother. Bridie drew the car up outside the shop, where Bridget was sitting waiting for them, eating an ice-cream. Her shaved head glittered silvery in the sun, and in that it matched the rings she wore in her ears, on her fingers, in her nose, and through her eyebrows.

"She's a poet," said Bridie, as though that explained something. "She used to live on Cobwell, in the cottage by Home Farm Field, but she said she needed a change. Make sure to give her some lunch, Bridget. If it's daylight, the walk home will do you good, Flann. But only in daylight. Make sure you are home before twilight. Otherwise, it mightn't be good it does you at all."

"I'll just go home the same road we got here in the car," said Flann, puzzled. "It looked perfectly safe to me."

"It is," said Bridie, "it's the twilight that isn't. Out with you."

Flann clambered out of the rabbit-smelling jeep, and introduced herself to Bridget.

"Ice-cream?" asked the poet, and whipped an ice-cream out from behind her own ear, creasing up with laughter at Flann's reaction.

"Oh, that makes me laugh every time," Bridget said, wiping her eyes. "Come on, those books won't shelve themselves."

Tubberlue was divided into two by a green, thatched with a dozen stout beech trees that were crammed with corvids. Starlings crowned the roof of Bridget's house, and a couple of cats were sitting on her windowsills. One leaped down and started winding itself around Bridget's ankles, mewling, while Bridget opened the door, and even Flann had to duck her head going in.

Inside was bigger than she had expected. It was one very long room, divided by a very large fireplace and chimney-breast, and with a narrow wooden stairs on the wall opposite the door. All the walls were lime-washed stone, and the few pieces of furniture had been pushed all into one corner, to make room for the boxes. Flann looked about her, inching past the boxes to peer discreetly up through the stairwell, to the upstairs room.

"This will be great fun," she said politely, "but… ah…

where will the books go? There aren't any shelves."

Bridget beamed at her, and from the back pocket of her trousers she took an enormous, hard-backed book, which she slapped down onto the top of a box.

"That's what you think!"

Flann read the title: *Building Your Library*.

"Is this a book of instructions?" she asked, alarmed at the idea of having to build bookshelves.

"No," said Bridget, opening a box of books, "it's what's called magic realism. We'll look in this box first, see what we need."

Flann watched her in silence. Bridget took out the first few books she came across, each one a stout, square reference book.

"We need something to hold these," Bridget said. "Open up the book there, and have a look at the chapters."

Flann obeyed, bewildered. Immediately, her eye fell upon a chapter called *On the Housing of Stout, Square, Reference Books*. Disbelievingly, she found the page where the chapter started.

"Read it out!" Bridget cried. "We need to get going!"

Flann began to read aloud, with some difficulty as the print was very old-fashioned and elaborate.

> "The wise poet places reference books closest to the desk where the great work will be performed. This place may change according to season, availability of sunlight, or the preferences of pets. Thus, it is best to equip the shelves with feet, for greater

ease of movement. Once the feet have been created, let the supports in the upright position follow."

As Flann read the words, several boxes shuffled themselves to one side, and four wooden feet appeared, toe by toe, heel by heel, out of thin air. By the time Flann looked up, the feet had measured out a good distance between themselves, settled down, and sprouted long, smooth upright posts, each post equipped with flat little stumps at regular spaces.

"Take shelves of good wood, planed smooth. Let them be solid enough to resist bowing under the weight of learning. Rest them upon the flat little stumps. Thereon, place the reference books."

Bridget started putting the books onto the shelves.

"Well, cut off my legs," Flann muttered, borrowing one of Villa's sprightlier phrases, "and call me Shorty."

Seven

Lou brought Villa back as far as the oak tree in front of the farmhouse and then abruptly disappeared. Villa continued towards the house but as she passed the huge tree, she saw that one of its branches was so large that it rested on the ground at one point, before rising up again. The trees in Oaklake, all made by St. Maur Ker, were all the same size and shape, and none of them was climbable, because the St. Maur Kers did not need anything to climb their trees. She had never seen a tree of that size before, with such majestic branches, with so high a crown, and so wide a girth. *You'd need a packed lunch just to walk around it*, Villa thought, approaching it carefully.

Villa became suddenly very conscious of all the other trees around the farmhouse, some towering over it, some squashed together in irregular bunches. She could not have named them, except the oak, and holly, and ivy, and neither could she have named the animals and birds and insects scuttling among them as she passed by. Bridie's infirmary was locked up, and the wooden shutters closed over the windows, but there were voices, and singing, coming from the stone dairy.

Past these, and behind the house, there was a small stretch of garden, with flowers and musky-smelling shrubs. This patch was an escapee from the walled garden behind the infirmary, and sloped gently up to a low, thick hedge.

Unable to jump high enough to see over it, she crouched down, and peered through. She could see a narrow, white-gravelled path, with bright green grass in the middle, and a fringe of grass on the other side. The air was littered with butterflies, and dense with a smell she could not name: it was spicy, complicated, and both unfamiliar and comforting. Too impatient to look for the start of the path, Villa scrambled about to find a gap between the trees, and began to squeeze through.

At first, the trees seemed to resist her. It was not just that they grew close together, and that their branches were criss-crossed and plaited. It felt more like the trees were pushing, gently but very firmly, holding her at bay. Then, quite suddenly, she slipped through, between a little hornbeam and a crab-apple. Once in, she could no longer hear Cobwell.

> *She is poised, startled by being so com-*
> *pletely doused in silence. It is unnerving.*
> *There is a sound of wind, like a drawn*
> *breath. A boom, or a hoot, like a walrus*
> *belling. Trills and rustling, in a wave*
> *through the knotted branches, and she*
> *looks up, astonished at how high overhead*

they are. Something is chattering, little birds snapping and tapping their thin, sharp beaks. A frog, several frogs. A voice sings a staccato line of notes, and stops. Was it a warning? An acknowledgement? There is a cuckoo. Villa suddenly remembers about not disturbing nests, and she creeps forward, with infinite care. It seems like a very long time before she reaches the other side.

The white path, when she walked along it, began to curve around to the North, and the trees that lined it began to droop their branches down like awnings. Villa came to a neat stile, and there she stopped, and looked in.

The grassy lane continued past the stile, and vanished among the trees. Trees on either side of Villa were slim, their branches narrow, and their bark bright, but further along the lane she could see branches, wearing mosaics of lichens, knotting together like pythons. At first, the lane and the woods appeared to be empty of noise but as Villa stood looking, hardly even thinking, sounds began to accumulate like clouds on the horizon. Villa climbed up onto the stile, so as to hear more clearly. She was perched there, listening intently. A bird's voice unfurled a solo trill. Villa did not recognise the sound, and swung her legs over the post to climb down and investigate.

"Well," said Lou, inexplicably suddenly beside her, "aren't you a discovering sort of person?"

"Hi Lou," said Villa, her mind still trying to catalogue the almost-music, "where did you spring from? Did you hear that bird? Do you know what bird it was? Want to come exploring? How big is the forest? Will we come out the other side?"

"We don't really let visitors in there."

"But I only want to explore it," Villa said, "I won't do it any harm."

"No, you won't," said Lou, "but it's not the forest we're worried about. Now, since you want to explore, why don't you explore the house, instead?"

"Well, I did try to have a look around yesterday, when we got here, but a lot of the doors were locked."

"That is just so we have an excuse for not doing any house-work in there," Lou said blithely. "Here—this is a key that will open all the doors."

The key was very small, and seemed to be made of glass. Villa looked doubtfully at it.

"I wouldn't lie to you," said Lou. "Well, alright, I would, but I'm not, the key will work on all the doors, really. Lunch is ready, in any case. Come along."

Villa did not use the key that day. After she had eaten her lunch, Jolyon announced that the Graces would be helping to keep the house in order. With Flann in Tubberlue, Bram "still unpacking," and Raftery helping Mick and Bridie build a hen-house, Villa was on duty.

By supper-time, Bram had reappeared. He had, in fact, spent much of the day trying to find somewhere on Cobwell Farm that he could get a decent radio or phone signal. He did not want to draw attention to himself, in case someone asked him what he was up to or, worse still, tried to introduce him to farm work, which Bram confidently expected to be both dull and highly-scented. He was now looking pleased with himself, so much so that Flann, had she not been so preoccupied, would have pressed him for an explanation. But apart from Bridget's astonishing means for building her furniture, she had been distracted by Jolyon collaring her after the evening meal. She had complimented him on the nut roast, and he heaved out a large, tattered, book of recipes.

"We don't always just ask the cooker for food," he said. "This has been in Cobwell for centuries. Write down anything you want to add, and slip it in there."

Entranced and enchanted by the idea of a book that was never finished, Flann did so. To her astonishment, Villa had come to peer over her shoulder, though she hurried off with an air of unconcern as soon as she saw that Flann had noticed her.

In her room, in the half-hour before her bed-time, Flann let Mr. Wittgenstein know how her day had been.

Cobwell House
Cobwell Farm

Dear Mr. Wittgenstein,
Curiouser and curiouser, as Alice said as she fell down the rabbit-hole. Why would three sisters have the same name? And if Bridget the Poet is old enough to be Bridie

the Vet's grandmother, what am I to expect if I ever meet Britta the Blacksmith, yet another sister, Bridget tells me? Methuselah? A baby?

I tried to find out from Bridget about the river. I have an atlas with me, so I can see that the River Fass rises in the Sliabh Blouma, and that it runs to the Great River. But I can't see the map on the ground. Villa, for all her annoyingness, can. Show her a map, and put her in the place, and she's immediately pointing at some path or hill that looks exactly like every other path or hill, and saying 'that's the one we need.'

I tried to get Bridget to tell me in which direction I should follow the river to get to Dunmathew, because I bet I can get Dublinia from there. I find I have only the vaguest sense of how to get anywhere. This astonishes me. I have always thought I was quite well-travelled for my age. But of course, someone else always sorted out the details. And I can't bring myself to ask Villa. I think that to get to Prague, I will need to get to one of the ports in Breteyne—either Dover or maybe in Northumberland, and then trains, I suppose, to Prague. But Bridget was oddly evasive on the question.

I did not have to remind her to get food for lunch, a bit after twelve she said we'd 'pop' down to the village and buy some food, and what did I like? I said I didn't mind, but: vegetarian. Why, she says. I told her I thought it was wrong to eat animals.

"If it has eyes," I said, "you shouldn't eat it."

"Spiders have eight eyes," she said. "Does that make them four times as important as humans?"

But she wasn't teasing me, she asked me like it was a real question. I didn't know what to say. Happily, the shop wasn't selling spider sandwiches, so I didn't have to decide right away. Even more happily, the shop was selling the Boomco Burger; I rely a lot on this since becoming vegetarian. They're made from the fruit of the boomco tree, invented by the St. Maur Kers. Not just the burgers, I don't mean. The tree itself, the boomco. The phytotekt Mama works with, Mr. Decker, invented the tree, to produce both fruits and nuts, and even to harvest itself. They grow huge amounts of it now, in some rain-forest where they cleared out all the other trees. Actually, I hadn't thought I'd be able to get boomco burgers at Cobwell, because it's Granda who knew the people in Cobwell. Granda is a contrarian (according to Poppa) and a refusenik (according to Mama). And though Jolyon is quite easygoing and very sweet, Peg has a contrarian, refusenik, look in her eye. But maybe Tubberlue is different.

Never mind spider's eyes, though—I met Mr. Decker! Bram is sick with envy. He shoots his cuffs and says "of course I've met Dorian Decker—he asked me to call him Dorian—lots of times," but actually he is raging that it was me and not him. Bridget and me had just come out of the shop, and there was rattling and clattering like forks down a tin roof, and along came a very old-looking carriage, drawn by a mechanical horse. You don't see many of them, they are very expensive to make, Bram tells me.

The carriage parked under the shade of the trees, and an automaton got out. As soon as it approached the shop, I could see that its voice-box was still disabled. This never fails to anger me. People say they want their automata to be as human as a machine can be, but they don't want awkward things like, you know, being able to speak. "Automaton" means something that can act of its own will. Well, you can't act of your own will if you have been stopped from speaking. But while the automaton was in the shop, what do I hear but Mr. Decker calling my name from his carriage.

The fact that we had to go over to him made me expect someone frail, or ill. But he looks to be in the bloom of health, hanging out of the carriage so he could talk to us even before we had reached him. He is terribly elegant. He wears a cream-coloured high collar, and a stock, no less, with his dark hair curling over it, and a big ruby pin, and a dark-brown velvet suit. Bridget said later she didn't know if she should shake his hand or dig in with a spoon and I suppose he did look a bit like ice-cream and caramel sauce. With a cherry in the middle. His waistcoat was embroidered with suns. He has a very cherubic smile, and a deep voice like a flute but he called me 'my dear' so I can't like him very much. He and Bridget made small talk, which I am rubbish at, despite Poppa's best efforts, and Mr. Decker asked about Cobwell—smiling enormously as he did—and Bridget just said he'd be better off asking her sister.

After she said that, Mr. Decker immediately turned his attention to me, and said he knew I must be Flann Grace and that he had been 'so pleased' that someone as splendid as Mama had been available to take over from him while he was working. As if! The slightest chance Mama would have said no? She'd have put us in kennels if it had been the only way to get to Prague after the whole Villa debacle. But—he said that as a 'gesture of appreciation', if I wanted to visit High Tide House some day to enjoy the library, I was to just let him know and I would be welcome! Even Granda admitted he had heard that the library there was 'pretty good, I suppose, for something paid for by those blasted St. Maur Kers.' Which is high praise, really. I will have to clear it with Peg first but I'm sure she'll say yes. And if she doesn't—

Actually, that does mean I can't go hiking off to Prague quite as promptly as I had planned. But it wouldn't do to turn down a chance like this out of hand. The Klementinum's not going anywhere.

Half an hour after her bed-time, Villa was finishing filling in her log-book.

CALL SIGN: Good Ship Wilderness

HOUR: 22:00. Am supposed to be in bed asleep. Ha! Ha!!

WIND SPEED/DIRECTION: None. Not a breath of air.

TEMPERATURE: 30°C/86°F outside.

CURRENT POSITION: Cobwell Farm

INTENDED COMPASS COURSE: The Nearest Portal out of here.

SPEED OF TRAVEL: Midnight tonight.

FATHOMS: Unfathomable.

COMMENTS: A gibbous moon, nearly a full moon, so it'll be bright. Lou said that they don't normally let visitors see The Wilderness but I will just go a little way in. It can't be very dangerous. I mean, it's Hibernia, it can't have much in the way of sharks or cassowaries or deadly poison mambas or anything. When everyone else is asleep, sneak down the ivy on the back of the house.

Plan for future required. School was bad enough but I hate to think what gorgon-run prison Poppa and Mama will find for me now.

Current skills: Literate. Numerate. Can read maps. Sail a boat, catch and cook a fish. Fix things. Calculate the displacement of water by weight. Flann can't breathe unless she's welded to a book. Bram has to go through school and all the rest of it if he wants to have a shot at becoming what Granda calls 'a St. Maur Ker yes-man' which is his life's ambition. All I want to do is captain my own ship, so what more do I need?

When Mama asked Mr. Gabriel about whether Cobwell was near the boundary to the sídhe Mr. Gabriel looked very shifty. Maybe there's some sort of crossing-place, somewhere I could use to skip out of here. St. Brendan the Navigator was said to have gone to Tír na nÓg and all he had was a currach. There was a chap did that a few years ago, and sailed over to the coast of Newfoundland.

The starting point of my search will be The Wilderness, tonight, at midnight.

By midnight, Cobwell farmhouse was quiet. The adults had spent part of the evening reading aloud newspaper reports of, on the one hand, the drought having spread to Galicia and Gothica, and, on the other, unseasonal, wild, sea-storms churning the waters of the Hibernian sea and making the Corryvreckan Whirlpool not only unnavigable but lethal. Then they spent the rest of the evening wondering what it might mean. Raftery had persuaded Mick to read *The Legend of the Salmon of Knowledge* twice in a row, and was soundly asleep by the time Neachtain's Garden had flooded for the second time. Flann was dreaming of building a chocolate automaton that kept melting away. Bram had claimed to be so tired that he needed to go to bed early.

From under his bed he took out his EyeGram, now attached to a crystal-radio, and through which he had managed to hack into the telephone and radio system that he had seen at the O'Connell Beare's castle. He had been eavesdropping for most of the afternoon, on Magus Boitumelo, on Dr. Breck, and on the O'Connell Beare. Just before dinner, he had sent Breck an EyeGram message, and he was itching with anxiety and anticipation. Finally, Breck replied. Bram let out a yelp of excitement, and executed a brief, noiseless dance. Then he silently returned his machine to its hiding place, and switched out the light.

By midnight, the moon had risen to its height, and from its cloudless sky, it lit up as brightly as daytime the paths leading into the heart of The Wilderness. Villa slept on.

Eight

Villa was so annoyed with herself for having slept through her planned exploration of The Wilderness that she lay in bed for an extra ten minutes, berating herself. Filled with determination to do something especially useful with the day, she seized the unlikely-looking little key that Lou had given her, and vowed to devote the day (once she had visited the animals) to exploring the house. With the key in her pocket, she yawned her way down to the kitchen for breakfast, but stopped in the hallway, arrested by the sound of Flann's raised voice.

"I can't believe you did that!"

"Flann, I had to," Bram said, "you don't understand, I really—"

"You're right, I don't understand! What were you thinking? You can't do things like that! You could get into trouble! If the morals of it don't bother you, that should!"

"I won't," said Bram, sounding suddenly very cocky. "It worked. Well, nearly. They've agreed to meet me. Dr. Breck called me this morning."

Villa poised, one foot in mid-step, agog to hear.

"Come on," said Bram to Flann, "I'll show you."

He led the way out of the little utility-room at such a pace that both he and Flann passed Villa, still as a statue of an eavesdropper, without seeing her. When she trotted innocently in behind them, Peg was saying,

"…on earth would they want you to do?"

Bram shot his cuffs ostentatiously.

"Help them build the Rain-Maker. Of course, they have their own technomancers, but St. Maur Kers always encourage using apprentices. I spoke to them this morning, first thing."

Peg eyed him suspiciously.

"How do they even know about you?"

"Oh, I met Dr. Breck, and the Research Director, ages ago," Bram said breezily. "We met at the O'Connell Beare's castle, there was a meeting with the St. Maur Ker diplomat and the High King. We chatted about the Rain-Maker then. I heard that they were wondering what the best way would be to add amplifiers and a harmonica to the main engine of the machine."

"And you know about harmonicas," Peg said, disbelievingly, "and are an amplifier expert?"

"Well, not *expert*," Bram said, modestly. "And I don't have to make them, I just have to attach them and make them mobile."

He flashed a smile at Peg, and made his way jauntily over to the oven to get some food.

"So since we were on the subject," he went on, more comfortably now that he was away from Peg's stern eye, "she asked if I'd be interested in doing a little summer work with them."

Villa followed him to the oven to get her own breakfast, and when Bram turned back for the table, he was looking so inexpressibly innocent that she knew he must be up to something.

"How far is it from here to Dunmathew?" he asked. Peg was still looking suspicious, but Mr. Gabriel said,

"Well, you won't walk it. But someone from here goes in once a week to the market. I'm going tomorrow."

Bram said, engagingly,

"Can I cadge a lift?"

"No, you can't," said Mr. Gabriel, "but you can earn one. I have a busy day ahead of me today."

Bram's smile dimmed very slightly.

"Wonderful," he said tensely, "so kind."

After breakfast, Villa went back to her room to get the key that Lou had given to her, and then continued on up the stairs until she got to the third floor, where—after a bit of hunting—she found a narrow spiral staircase that led up into the attic. The top of the spiral staircase was closed by a door, but the glass key fitted perfectly.

Villa stood just inside the door, looking around. Every inch of space was cluttered with things that had been taken from the house, and were waiting, either to be repaired, or to regain usefulness. She inched her way past an armchair with a ripped cushion, a standing-lamp with a collapsing shade, and two big bags tied together, with ribbons and tangles of paper decorations bursting out. At one edge of the room there were some desks and chairs, school-desks, Villa realised when she examined them. The wooden tops had grooves for pens, and recesses for inkwells, and were bolted onto heavy iron frames with uncomfortable wooden seats. After an initial investigation, Villa sat down and took out a note-book.

Comments for Logbook: This room is like different countries, all in one place, all full of new stuff.

Old machines and bits of equipment and tools that I can't imagine what they were used for, like someone opened the door and horsed everything in. A big battery radio, a bit of iron gate, some buckets, a sewing machine, a model railway. Investigate further—fixing fun awaits.

Loads of wellies and big raincoats, rolled-up tents and bags of ropes and sleeping bags. Sand-bags (empty).

In the sun near the windows, chairs and paintings and cabinets full of stuff.

Currently sitting in what looks like a schoolroom from long-long ago. Desks in rows, wooden desks with tiny glass pots on them, a big board on legs behind me.

Opposite me a spinning wheel, and an enormous measuring tape hanging from the ceiling, and a gigantic shears beside it.

There's a piano near the far gable-wall, and a small harp with broken strings. The table has piles of stuff on it including what looks like—a ship's wheel? Really?

By the time she decided that there was too much to see in one voyage, and that she would have to make a plan if she wanted to explore Cobwell (before looking for a portal into the sídh), it was late in the morning, the attic was hot, and Villa was hungry. She put an object she had discovered into her pocket, closed the attic door carefully behind her, and tiptoed down the spiral stairs, just in case it turned out—as it often mysteriously turned out—that she was not supposed to have been there. She headed to the kitchen to see if she could scrounge some food. Peg had just made a pot of tea, and Jolyon was kneading bread. Lou emerged from Jolyon's work-room, and sat down. Mick pulled a stool up for Villa at the table, and poured her a glass of milk. Lou was making toast, and put a battered tin of biscuits on the table. Ray pushed over a plate of scones, and Villa stretched her other hand out for the butter.

"I've been meaning to ask you, Villa," Lou said, stirring the tea-pot, "why exactly did you get expelled? Your Granda mentioned it, and we've been dying to know."

"Really?" Villa was startled. "You've been dying to know?"

"Well, yes," Jolyon admitted, "but we didn't want to embarrass you by asking."

"I don't think Villa is easily embarrassed," Lou said.

"Embarrassed?" said Villa, "Are you kidding? I've been dying to tell someone. The parents said I wasn't to. But if you're asking… Right. It had to do with a rugby pitch, and a history class."

Immediately, everyone sat down at the table, looking at her with great expectations. Jolyon put the bread on the cooker to rise, and joined them, wiping his floury hands on his apron. Everyone took two biscuits to keep them going. Villa finished her scone, licked her fingers, and began.

"I really did it for some of my friends who play rugby. I don't know why they do, but that's what they do. They're on the school team. There's two teams in the school, one for the girls, one for the boys."

"Do all your friends play rugby?" asked Mr. Gabriel

"No. About three of them do. Jonny does—her name's Jonquil really, like the flower, we've been friends since forever, and she's very good at rugby."

"What position does she play?" asked Jolyon, who was fond of rugby.

"She's—" Villa thought deeply, "a fly-half. I hope you know what that means because she's explained it to me like fifteen times but I just—life's too short. Where was I? Oh, yes. The boys have a great big state-of-the-art building and a pitch with its own groundsman. The girls had a crummy little shed, and their rugby pitch has got all tree stumps and soggy bits in it. So, they asked the games teacher to, you know, sort it out. But the games teacher said she was forever asking the School Governors to sort it out but they said that all the money was being spent on the boys' game. Because the boys won lots of their matches, but the girls didn't. And the girls' team said, well, might that not be because the boys have better training and more kit and a proper pitch? Mightn't we win more matches if we had proper facilities? But the teacher said the Governors would only unlock the money-bags if something went radically wrong with the girls' pitch. She said she was blue in the face from asking."

There was a pause.

"What happened then?" Mick asked, buttering scones with great dexterity. "Here, have a buttered scone. Jam?"

"Well, that was that. But then we had a history class, about years ago when girls weren't allowed to go to school in case it stopped them having babies, and they weren't allowed to vote in case their heads exploded. And all these women across the world started having rebellions. They said they were sick of asking nicely, so they were going to take direct action. They got put in jail, and force-fed, and all sorts of dreadful stuff, and eventually, they got the thing done."

"And so...?" Mick prompted her, as he helped her to marmalade.

"Well," said Villa, "you see the Governors said they'd spend the money if the girls' pitch was badly damaged or something. So... I... well... I took direct action. I badly damaged it."

"What did you do?" Ray asked, toast poised.

"I... well, actually, to be completely precise," Villa said, suddenly unsure of how her audience would respond, "I blew it up."

There was quite a long silence. Then Peg said,

"How did you blow it up?"

"Glycerine," said Villa enthusiastically, "and some agate, and a bit of technomancy. I'm not good at much, but I'm not bad at those two, even though the teachers are starting to get strict about magic not being permitted. It made quite a noise. And there were bits of rugby pitch everywhere. And the girls' rugby team was delighted because they had to use the better pitch to train on. But none of the teachers were too keen."

She ate some scone, and added resentfully,

"Not even the chemistry teacher. You'd think he'd be glad that someone was listening in class."

"That's why you were expelled?" Mr. Gabriel asked.

"It was," said Villa, "though the two rugby teams made a guard of honour at the gate while I was being taken away. Jonny sent me one of her medals. And Jessica said I had *admirable spirit*. Unfortunately that is not what Mama said. Apparently being a rebel is okay only if you lived a hundred years ago. Otherwise, everyone just wants you to be a nice girl."

"What do they mean by *nice*?" Ray asked.

"I dunno," said Villa, "I barely know what they mean by girl. I asked Mama that, once. That was a difficult conversation, if you like."

"So you're not a girl?" said Mr. Gabriel.

"Well yes, but I thought all that meant was biology," said Villa, contemplating having some cheese, and deciding it could do no harm, "biochemistry. But… there seem to be rules."

"Are you a boy then?" said Lou, carefully pouring goat's milk into a glass.

"No," said Villa, "I'm a Villa. When I was little, that was alright. I was the *Good Ship Villa*. People didn't mind that I was my own ship. But now people want me to sail a different ship, and it's silly and made-up and not mine. I like my ship."

"I bet your parents loved that," said Mick.

"To be fair to my mother," Villa said, with the air of someone who did not say that kind of thing very often, "she did try to be helpful. I told her that if the rule was that girls had to be nice instead of useful, then I didn't think I was a girl. And she said, alright, okay, would you prefer to be a boy?"

"And what did you say?" said Bridie with lively interest.

"I told her the truth," said Villa, "I'd rather be a goat. I like animals more than people."

"And what did she say to that?" asked Mick.

"She said," said Villa brightly, "*For the love of God, Terence, get me a brandy.*"

Peg started to laugh, and said,

"I'd have paid good cash money to see that."

"You seem an enterprising sort of a person," said Lou, "but we don't need any revolutions started today. Why don't you come and help me check the wall of The Pot?"

Villa ate the rest of her snack with enthusiasm, and wiped her hands on her shirt while she followed Lou out of the kitchen into the shimmering sunshine. As they walked across the scrubby ground to the bank where the collar of The Pot rose up, she fished from her pocket what she had found during her morning explorations. She held it up and said,

"Any idea what this is?"

Lou looked at it. It was a faceted globe with one slightly flattened side, and about as big as Villa's palm. Whatever it was made of was as transparent as glass, with a smoky grey tint. It glimmered in the sun, but the interior of the globe was shadowy. Four thin, bony tubes protruded from the flattened side.

"I do indeed," Lou said, taking it from her hand. "That is a Blackstar. From the head of a whale. Do you know of the Blackstar whales?"

"Why is it called a Blackstar? When it isn't a star? Or even black? How did it get here? Aren't they extinct now? Didn't they live a really long time ago?"

"They were certainly alive a very long time ago," Lou said rather dryly, handing back the stone, "and might have lived on just as long again, had certain humans not decided that they could make better use of the Blackstar than could a whale."

"What is a Blackstar when it isn't attached to a whale?"

"The same thing as when it is," said Lou. "The whale uses the Blackstar for all sorts of things that whales need —travelling, hunting, keeping their pod together. They use it to hide. They are the biggest mammals on earth but because of the Blackstar, they can hide in the corner of your eye. They become a trick of the light."

Villa was silent for a moment, trying to picture a huge whale playing hide-and-seek amongst the fronds.

"Humans," Lou went on, "can use it for exploring the oceans—you cannot get lost even in fog, you won't disappear if you go sailing over the homes of monsters, or over places suitable for mysteries, where ships often vanish. Even if you are thrown off course in a storm, you will find your way back. Some humans, it is said, can use a Blackstar to hold open portals between worlds."

Villa was already aboard a sprightly clipper-ship in her

head, waves splashing over the prow as her crew followed a pod of whales, following them around the world. She hardly heard Lou saying,

"On all the blue Earth, the blue sea is the most mysterious of places and the Blackstar whales were the most mysterious of its inhabitants. And the humans were the only ones that couldn't share the ocean with them, and had to kill them all."

"Why were they killed?"

"Greed," Lou said curtly. "Everyone denied they had anything to do with it, of course. The first humans to kill the whales for their Blackstars used them to—"

"But if the Blackstar whales can hide in plain sight," Villa interrupted, "how did the humans ever find them and get the stars out of their heads?"

"That is a question," said Lou, "that has long puzzled us. But as we are not likely to answer it here, turn your attentions to The Pot."

"Are you not boiled, in that heavy coat? And a hat, and all?" Villa demanded abruptly.

"No," said Lou, "but thanks for asking. Now. If I can dangle you upside-down by the ankles, you can have a look-see down the walls and tell me whether there's any damage in the wall that needs attention."

Villa tucked the Blackstar back into a pocket and buttoned it safely shut. She clambered up onto the brick lip of The Pot.

"Ankles at the ready."

Nine

While Villa was being dangled down The Pot, and Bram was, to his increasing horror, helping Mr. Gabriel muck out the stables, Flann had found Peg in the hen-house, and asked for permission to visit Mr. Decker's library. Flann was unsurprised to find people in Cobwell unwelcoming towards the idea of her going to Hide Tide House. She knew they didn't think much of Mr. Decker, and she had prepared her arguments—practically a friend of the family, Bridget would be within a few minutes' walking distance—but she was surprised at the reason. They seemed grudgingly to accept that Decker was unlikely to try to cook her for dinner, or turn her into a dragon. They seemed infinitely more anxious about how she was going to get the short distance from Tubberlue to the edge of Littlefish Water.

Flann knew the path they meant: it was sheltered by a high bank on each side, with long grass, trailing brambles, and arching branches that turned the path into a shady tunnel that opened out, after a few hundred yards, at the white sands of Littlefish. It had seemed utterly innocuous.

"But why can't I go on my own?" Flann was puzzled.

"Because," Mr. Gabriel answered, "it is an... ah... private road. Someone already... authorised needs to accompany you when you first walk it, to establish your right of way. Otherwise, you'd need to, say, be a hierophant, or to have a melanaster, or—"

Mick cut him off: "Not many of them to the pound around here, Mr. Gabriel."

They could agree on no-one to accompany her. Bridie said she couldn't possibly, it was too risky, she had her sisters to think of. Mick said, "She's still a child, so I suppose I—" but Mr. Gabriel and Peg said at the same time that Mick, Ray, and Mr. Gabriel were 'obviously' out of the question. Peg would not let Jolyon go, Bridie wouldn't let Peg go, and no-one would let Flann go alone. Finally, Peg said,

"We could get the Cobwell Hound to go with her, but she'll have to wait a few days. You don't mind waiting a few days, do you, Flann?"

"Not at all," Flann lied, polite and furious, "a few days is fine."

"Good girl," said Peg.

Flann's sandals ticked on the sticky melting tar of the road. Her wide-brimmed hat sheltered her from the sunshine, but trapped the baking air around her face, and she wished she had brought a fan. The houses lining the road out of Tubberlue towards Littlefish Water dwindled away and the gaps between them were overgrown, with brambles twisting out like springs from a mattress, and blossoms gleaming in dark spaces. The path became narrow, and became a dirt track with grass growing up the middle and the sides pocked and broken by roots and hooves. Flann's sandals ground against stones, and twigs, unseen shells, crunched underneath.

Villa stumped along beside her, not seeming to notice the heat, her hair shining like green metal in the sun. The silence between them was awkward. Flann was officially still angry with Villa, but was uncomfortably aware that Villa was doing her a favour. Villa wanted to ask Flann a question, but—no longer being in the habit of it—did not know how.

She had just finished feeding chickens when she bumped into Flann marching angrily across the yard at Cobwell. Startled, Villa had followed her to the big oak tree, and asked her why she was marching angrily about.

"Good girl," Flann had growled, "*Good girl*. How patronising is that?"

Villa was not sure how to measure patronising, so she said,

"Who? Why? What's going on?"

"Dorian Decker said I could visit High Tide House, to see the library," Flann said, quickly, "and they," she jerked her head at the house, "won't let me go on my own. Apparently it would be just fine and dandy if I was a hierophant or the holder of a melanaster or, I don't know, a three-headed dragon. There's no-one free to come with me for a couple of days. A couple of days! He'll have forgotten by then! Bram can go to Dunmathew, but I can't go down the feckin' road on my own!"

Villa could not recall the last time she had seen Flann so openly angry. An angry Flann usually adopted a very cold manner—*dignified*, is how Flann thought of it, though Villa preferred *pompous*—and refused to speak. Now her chin was thrust forward pugnaciously, her eyebrows pulled down till they practically hid her eyes.

"What's a melanaster?" Villa asked, buying time while she cast about for a suitable response.

"Who knows? Isn't an aster a sort of flower, a daisy? It comes from the Greek for 'star'—the *melan* bit is also Greek, it means black. A black daisy, apparently, is what it takes to get rights of way on the path." She rolled her eyes, before adding vehemently, "This place is just too much."

Never mind your black daisies, thought Villa, with sudden excitement, *how about a black star?*

"I can go with you," Villa blurted out. "Look!" she said, fishing in her pocket. "I might not be an elephant or whatever, but I do have a Blackstar!"

"But—"

"Did they say you had to wait for someone in particular?"

"No," Flann said, "just that I couldn't go alone."

"Well, then," Villa said, "you won't be alone. And, sure, if that's not what they meant, you can always apologise later. That works for me."

They had set off immediately for Tubberlue, and Flann had bought ice-creams to refresh them for the path to

Littlefish. Branches and brambles grew suddenly higher, away from the houses, and reached to each other across the path, making a tunnel of it, with breaks in the roof, and the sun dappling the dirt and the puddles and Flann's skirt that swished the grasses as she walked. The light, fractured by the dense tangles of twigs and clustering leaves, was dazzling, and though there was no breeze to speak of, Flann began to hear the noises of the path, above the swish of her skirt and the crunching and rustling of her feet. It was whispering, the pattering of leaves against each other, or like water stirring gravel in a pool. There so nearly seemed to be a pattern to the sound that she slowed down, convinced that she could make out the words.

With a snap and a whirring of wings, a bird flew shrieking across the path. Like a rolling echo came the answering calls of other birds all along the towering hedges, and something—dry stalks? Wood?—snapped as something scurried, but as fast as she turned her head each time, the something was gone and Flann caught only glimpses here and there: bronze scales burnished and burning, a green and glassy snout, a neat cloven hoof gleaming and crimson, bounding out of sight. The thorn trees and the wild cherries crowded closer and closer, here and there the unexpected looming of an ash-tree, but somewhere, Flann thought, there must be willows. Willow-trees made those murmuring sounds, soughing with bated breath. She wondered if Villa had noticed.

A gate, tipping towards the horizontal and barely held in place with baling-twine, broke the dense darkness of the hedge. Flann stopped, excessively relieved to be able to see light not already cut to slivers by the leaves. She could see quite a long way through the gated gap, and the fields were bright as gold, and limes, and pearls. It would be a relief to sit on the gate—once it didn't fall down—and to take a break from the path, crowded in by the babbling hedge.

While they stood admiring the view, Villa said abruptly,

"Flann? Can I ask you a question?"

"Yes?" Flann said, doubtfully.

"You know the way you're a vegetarian?"

Flann stared at her.

"What about it?"

"I think I might be turning into one."

"What on earth do you mean? Turn into one? I'm not a werewolf!"

"It's the pigs," Villa blurted out. "Lou took me over to see pigs. And they had piglets, gorgeous little things with red bristles so they look like they're made out of polished copper. They were only a week old, and they were bounding around the place, swinging out of each other's ears and bouncing off their mother."

"And?"

"Did you know that pigs talk to their piglets when they're going to feed them?"

"And?"

"Sausages!" Villa cried. "Sausages! Pork chops! One minute I'm giving Lucinda back-scratches that she likes so much she falls over, and the next minute I'm eating sausages!"

Flann hoped Lucinda was a pig.

"Is that why you stopped eating meat?"

"No," said Flann, "the Philosophy Society at school had a lunchtime lecture on ancient philosophers who wrote about the ethics of eating certain kinds of food—meat, or tubers, or food related to the four elements."

"What four—oh, you mean water, earth, and…um…"

"Fire and air. I stopped eating meat because I'd never seen a pig. Or even a chicken. All I'd ever seen were packets of meat. How could I have an ethical opinion on something made in a tub?

Villa did not seem comforted. They walked on.

Finally, the hedges opened out again and the path became sandy, and a tension she had not known she felt sluiced away from Flann as soon as she heard sand and shingle under her feet as she approached the water's edge, dazzling on the eyes but with the relief of a light breeze. She stood still to let the cool air ruffle her clothes, her arms outstretched, like a cormorant drying its wings.

"Look," she said to Villa, "you could stop for a while, till you have time to think about it."

Villa looked mournfully at Flann. Thinking about ideas was Flann's hobby, not Villa's.

"You can't unthink an idea," Flann said firmly, "so you have to decide what to do. If those pigs were out in the wild—if there is any wild left—they'd probably be eaten by something. At least they get taken care of first, on Cobwell."

"Are you going to eat meat on Cobwell?" Villa asked, and Flann shook her head.

"But that's me, not you," she said, "and you'd better get back before someone wonders where you are."

"Thanks, Flann," Villa said rather sadly, and stumped away, back up the path. Flann went down to the lake.

Flann had seen the St. Maur Kers' self-sailing boats quite often, they were the only vessels permitted on the artificial lake in the middle of Oaklake. They were tight little cubes of polished metal, and Granda had once said he wouldn't know whether to climb into them, or pull them on and lace them up. They traveled only short distances and at a sputtering pace. Villa refused to sail in them, and Flann knew, but never said she knew, that Villa instead went whenever she could down to the other lakes, to Dairbrech or Uail, and there cadged trips in fishing-boats, currachs, and coracles. This St. Maur Ker boat was unmistakeable because it had the family's crest on its prow and a pennant in corporate colours drooping in the heat. Flann peered doubtfully into it, and climbed in uneasily, as it wobbled on the water.

The little boat was a great deal more salubrious than any other in which she had travelled. It was bigger, for a start; she could move around in it quite easily, and had a choice of seats. There was a dashboard with three very neat dials, between them showing the time, the longitude and latitude of Littlefish Water, and the depth of the water. There were two large brass handles, one on each side of the seat, each with a sign, one reading 'SAILS' and the other 'GO STOP'. Flann pulled the first to raise the sail, and pushed the second to get the boat going. It lurched, flicked its rear back and forth like a fish, and surged forward.

The bright blue water was as still as a plate, and under the glare of the sun it dazzled like glass, but the boat created a bit of a breeze as it sped along, and Flann dangled her hands into the cool water. There were three sails, though in such dead calm weather, the boat only moved thanks to the clockwork under the deck. Flann's eye was caught by the main sail, which did not seem to be made of the same material as the others. It was a little darker, but as it moved in the light, it had such rich colours, such subtle scarlets and blues, that not even the scorching sun could drain it.

Flann got up and went to look a little closer. The sail had an odd texture, too, covered in ridges and cracks, so that when Flann ran an exploratory finger over it, it felt like scales. With one hand on the sail, she looked above her head into the complex knot of rigging. It was not, as she expected, metal, and she thought at first it might be made of pearl, it was so white and gleaming. But before she could investigate further, the boat approached the shore of Eightfoot Island, crunching up onto the sand and gravel of the tiny beach.

Just as the boat settled itself, and Flann had turned to look up the sloping path that led to High Tide House, the breeze changed direction, and immediately Flann covered her nose and mouth with her hand and blurted out,

"Ye gods, what is that reek?"

The mix of stinks was crippling. The least offensive stench was of rotting fish, and Flann could find no proper comparison for the others—there was no form of ex-crement or decomposition that seemed quite up to the job. Flann set off scrambling over the sand and rocks, towards a set of steps cut into the rock, away from the smell. A tall automaton was waiting for her. It was one of St. Maur Ker's new 'Mrs. Danvers' models, made from some matt green metal and designed to take care of any (rich person's) home, from a castle to a manor-house to a ship.

The automaton beckoned to her to follow, and as they climbed up the deep stone steps, Flann wondered what would happen if she activated its voice-box. Her mother, Flann recalled, had found No. 6 singing in the kitchen, and had been very angry because, Flann thought now, Gráinne Grace expected her daughter to have better sense. Poppa had been infuriated because the automaton came with the house in Oaklake, a perk of working for the St. Maur Kers, and it really belonged to his office. Mrs. Danvers led her up a bright white path strewn with crushed sea-shells, with lush green lawns on either side, and beds of impossible flowers that Flann guessed were Dorian Decker's invention.

The house was not as big as Flann had expected. It had a great many windows, and all the windows had lots of tiny panes of glass, so in the sunlight it looked like it was full of flickering silver flames. There was a path of white stone and sand around the house and on the ground there lay two dogs of pewter, so hot that the air above them shimmered. The brick at the front of the house was thick with ivy. Flann could hear insects humming and rattling in it, and was surprised. The way St. Maur Ker ran things in Oaklake did not allow for insects, or things that didn't work for their keep.

The door was open and the hallway was wonderfully cool after the heat outside. The hall reminded her of the hall at home, big and bright, and with mirrors, and big vases of flowers, and places to hang coats. The automaton led her past the stairs and down a smaller hall and then down a couple of steps to one side of the kitchen. Finally, it opened the door and Flann was so taken aback that she actually stopped and stared, like, she later thought, a person in a storybook.

She was not expecting the beautiful courtyard that was behind the door, cool between the high walls. The ground had cobblestones, with moss and grass and lichens growing on them. On the other side of the walls there were big trees, covered in vivid orange and green leaves and lit up in the sun and with the blue of the sky between them, so that Flann thought they hardly looked like trees at all, but like some kind of exotic birds. To the right there was a long building that she thought might have been a stables, like on Cobwell, but there were no horses. The automaton seized the door handle and pushed open the door, and inside was the library.

Books from floor to ceiling, and a spiral metal staircase, and more books floor to ceiling, and some lovely deep chairs to curl up into, and desks with lamps on them. Flann had not thought the building tall enough to have such high shelves, but some were so high they needed ladders to reach the top. At the back of the room, beyond a long line of shelves, she could see a door and beyond it more books, and when she looked around she saw that there were lots of doors, all leading to more rooms of books. It did not seem quite possible and yet there it was.

Dear Mr. Wittgenstein,

...If I had the run of this library for the summer I would surely have caught up enough with Granda and Mama and Poppa to join in some of their rigorous debates —that's what they call it when they row about politics. They have such an unfair advantage, having started so long ago. I sometimes dream that I have come to the end of reading all the books in the world, and I finally get to go to bed, but when I open my bedroom door, there's an open stairway and I fall down it like Alice down the rabbit-hole, and what I am falling through is thick piles and piles of books and I realise I have only just started.

Of course, I couldn't stay too long, I worry about overstaying my welcome. But Mrs. Danvers stayed around, and it very sensibly brought me the catalogues and then went at an astonishing speed to get books for me. There was a bit of everything in that library. I know Decker can't have literally a copy of everything, but there was no book I could think of that the automaton couldn't find and it even brought me some I didn't know, like

Keating's *True History of Littlefish Water* or *Wilder Than Usual Life: A Cryptozoologist's Summer in Hibernia* by one Dr. B. Murphy.

But there was a very odd thing. When my chronometer rang to say I ought to be getting ready to go, I asked Mrs. Danvers to show me where Mr. Decker was, so I could say goodbye to him. Now, I know the St. Maur Kers say that these new models are infallible, but Mrs. Danvers made a mistake. She brought me up a small path from the back of the house, up a shrubby sort of sandy brae, and pointed at the building at the top. Then she went back to the house. But when I got to the building she showed me, Mr. Decker wasn't there at all. She had brought me to a laboratory.

As I was walking around to find the front door, I glanced through the windows, as you do. There was an automaton on the workbench, with some of the inner workings taken out. I've never seen that before, though I knew that they had to be repaired sometimes. But I always assumed that if you take out the gubbins of an automaton, it can't function. Well, this one could. It was trying to free itself, dragging at the straps that were holding it down, wrenching from one side to another, really struggling. It was horrible.

Ten

In the cool of the evening, Peg suggested that they eat outside. Murph had arrived up via The Pot, and Mick herded the four Graces into the bright gazebo that had astonishingly appeared in the yard, to meet their first púca.

"Bridget the Poet tells me you're a cryptozoologist," Flann said.

"What's that?" asked Villa.

"Someone who studies and searches for animals whose existence or survival is disputed," Flann replied.

"I'm a zoologist, strictly speaking," said Murph, "that's what I studied. But I have always had an interest in wilder-than-usual life."

"Like what?" demanded Villa, her fork poised. "What kind of thing? Where do you find them? Did you ever find anything really crypto? Where do you look?"

"Well, it varies. It depends on what I'm asked to look for."

"Where are you looking now?" Villa pressed.

"Um, well," said Murph, "I'm looking for a legend."

Raftery, busy with a boiled egg, looked up.

"Is it the Salmon of Knowledge?" he asked. Murph, astonished, darted a glance first at Lou and then at Bridie, and said,

"No-o-o-o! What made you think of that?"

"It's the only legend he thinks worth knowing," said Bram, and Flann said at the same time, "He thinks everyone is talking about the Salmon of Knowledge."

"Which one are you looking for, then?" asked Raftery with dignity.

"One that not everyone believes exists," Murph said, "but it is said that Eightfoot Island was formed when the Dagda—you've heard of the Dagda, right?"

Flann and Bram denied knowledge but Villa nodded.,

"Chief god, wasn't he? Controlled weather and time, and everything?"

"He was immortal," Raftery assured her, "with a magic harp and a bottomless cauldron."

"Bet he got invited to lots of parties," Bram quipped, then, catching the dry look his brother gave him, added, "So—Eightfoot Island?"

"The Dagda is said to have created Eightfoot Island," said Murph, "by dropping a chunk of the Pike of Phoenix into Littlefish Water. And it is said that there was a monster asleep in a hollow in the lake, and when the chunk landed, the monster was trapped beneath it."

"Not a very 'little fish,' then," said Raftery. "Is that what you are looking for? The monster under the island?"

"Well," Murph sounded a little defensive, "tales of wonder—fairytales, myths—even the wildest fairy tales

115

could have a connection, however vague, with a real thing."

"How do you go looking?" Villa said, having negotiated her fork.

"I have what's called a bathysphere," replied Murph. "Do you know what that is?"

Villa shook her head. Raftery did not expect that he was expected to answer.

"Some sort of vessel that will go down to a great depth?" Flann guessed.

"That's it," Murph nodded, cutting up some potato salad. "It's quite an old one but it does the job."

"You go under the water in a bubble?" Raftery said. Murph nodded again, smiling very brightly, as she had seen the humans do with young children.

"Where?" Raftery ate some egg.

"Well—lots of places."

"Can I go in the bubble?"

She looked at him in alarm, and said,

"Well, it is not really designed for many people."

"I'm little," he said.

"But—"

"I'm little and I'll be very quiet."

"But—"

"I'll give you my biscuit. Even though I'm little. And quiet."

Murph looked around uneasily, and Raftery reached into the biscuit tin for another bargaining chip.

"I'll give you both my biscuits."

"But—"

116

"And... and... I'll read you a bedtime story. Two. As well as two biscuits."

Flann said,

"You may as well say 'yes' now as wait until he wears you down by offering you the shoes off his feet."

"I can't take him alone," Murph spoke with distinct alarm, "I don't think Peg would agree to it."

"I can go too," Villa offered.

"You're hardly a responsible adult," Bram cut in, "you're only offering to go because you want to."

"And you're not offering to go because you don't want to," Villa retorted, "so same odds. Murph can be the responsible adult. Me 'n' Raftery will keep out of her way and look at the sights."

"I'm sure Murph has better things to be doing," said Bram smoothly, "don't you, Murph?"

Murph looked from one to the other, uneasily. Raftery took her hand and nuzzled his head against her arm. She started to laugh.

"You rascal," she said, "I had a pet goat one time, used to nuzzle me like that when it wanted something. Alright, I'll take ye for a spin under Littlefish Water in the bathysphere, just a quick look. It'll be a couple of days before I'm free, so don't be plaguing me about it."

Later, Flann opened her bedroom door when she heard Bram's steps on the landing, and beckoned him.

"When are you off to Dunmathew tomorrow?" she whispered, and he whispered back,

"About ten, Mr. Gabriel said."

"Oh right," she said, "I thought you might have been going really early. So I just wanted to wish you good luck."

Bram didn't know what to say. He mumbled,

"I thought you were still cross with me about…"

Flann stood back, and he came into her room, and perched on the edge of the window-sill. The room was warm and dim, and Flann, sitting by the desk, was a very shadowy figure.

"I think it is cheating," she said. "Poppa gave you that EyeGram so you could keep in touch with your friends, not hack the St. Maur Ker phones."

"I had to," Bram said, "I can't moulder away here for months! I'll get back to school, everyone will be talking about their summer—I was supposed to be the one everyone was jealous of! Off to Prague! On the Orient Express! Sailing in Sylvestra St. Maur Ker's yacht!"

"Other people's opinions don't matter."

"Yes, they do," Bram said firmly, "yes they absolutely do. That's how things work. Poppa is brilliant at his job but Cosimo St. Maur Ker's good opinion of him isn't chopped chicken. Mama's a brilliant botanist, but why is she replacing Decker? Because Decker had a good opinion of her."

Flann looked at her brother.

"God, I'd hate to be you."

"Well, I like being me," Bram retorted, "and I want to like being me even more than I do now. But I won't like being me if I'm stuck at school having to say to people that I wasn't next nor nigh Prague, I was on a farm in West Nowhere, shovelling horse—!"

"Shhh!" Flann flapped her hand at him. "Keep your voice down."

"So," Bram whispered, "I'm hoping to get Dr. Breck's good opinion by knowing what it is she needs to do, and being the one who can do it."

"Why don't you show them one of your model machines—"

"Flann, these people are expert engineers, technomancers. They are not going to be impressed with amateurish little efforts."

"You're not an amateur, you're fourteen."

"I hate being fourteen."

"Try being fourteen without everyone thinking your every fart is a powder-puff."

Bram was shocked. Flann was never vulgar.

"Who—"

"You make model machines that you won't show anyone that isn't family, and Mama and Poppa practically throw a party. I wrote an article on philosophy for the Gladdish Academy Newsletter and what happens? Mama has 'a little chat' with me about reading the wrong books."

"I can't sleep," said a very grumpy voice from the doorway. Raftery was mild-tempered except when he was tired, when he was like a scalded rat. His frown squashed his eyes out of sight, and his chin was out.

"Would a story help?" Flann asked. A story usually helped.

"No," growled Raftery, "I'm thirsty."

Bram got up. "Come on, Raffles," he said, "we'll go down and get you a drink of something."

"'nks," said Raftery, and as Bram took his hand, he added over his shoulder,

"A story might help afterwards."

Even unobserved, Flann rolled her eyes.

While Bram went into the kitchen to get some milk, Raftery stood yawning in the doorway, lifting his toes up and down, because the floor was cold. He heard voices from the sitting-room, and went to explore. The windows were open, and the curtains drawn back, and the sky was apricot, darkening slowly to a dusty gold. Several of the dogs were lying about, and one sat by the settee, leaning against Bridie's leg, looking up at her while she petted it. Peg and Jolyon were sitting in high-backed chairs on either side of the empty fireplace, drinking wine. Mr. Gabriel and Mick sat on a second settee, which looked bizarrely tiny, and Lou and Ray were standing by the open window, looking out into the rising twilight. No-one noticed Raftery, and as he came in, Peg was saying,

"…fierce storms up around Corryvrecken, isn't that the Cailleach's territory?"

"It is," Bridie said. "One of them, anyway. I told you before, I'm not happy about the Cailleach. She only collects the amount of firewood she needs to get through a winter. She could see out an ice age with what she was carrying home."

Lou said, "I think you're right to be worried. I've been watching those Storm Kelpies a while now."

"What do you think is causing it, Lou?" Mr. Gabriel asked.

"The feckin' humans, who else? This is getting serious."

Bridie said quickly, "Do you think this will harm the Salmon?"

Lou continued looking out into the fading twilight. Everyone starting looking at each other, to see if they were all equally uneasy at the silence. Finally, Lou said,

"I'm not willing to chance it anymore. If it comes to a showdown, if they make it a question of us or them, I will make sure that it's us. And I'll tell you something else—I think it's time to tell—"

"Boo!" said Raftery, popping up from behind the settee, and making Mick and Mr. Gabriel jump.

"C'mere, you rascal," said Mick, and hauled Raftery up by the back of his pyjama jacket, and put him in the middle.

"We'll take this up another time," Mick said to Lou. "Little pitchers have big ears."

"Is that the Salmon of Knowledge you were talking about?" Raftery said to Lou.

"What makes you think that?" said Mick, startled.

"I told you, he thinks any story about a salmon is about the Salmon of Knowledge," said Bram, behind them. He was holding a cup of milk, and staring at Lou; Raftery may not have been listening, but Bram had heard every word.

"Well, I can tell you the story," said Lou, "but this story may or may not have a happy ending. Come in, Bram."

"The last one ended in a salmon getting et by Fionn Mac Cumhaill," said Raftery, "so that wasn't exactly happy, was it? Not for the Salmon."

"A sensible way to look at things," said Lou. "Sit up here, so, and I'll bring you up to date. You may as well sit down too, Bram. Have some chocolate."

Raftery settled in beside Mick, and Bram found that the cup of milk he was bringing to Raftery had turned into two cups of hot chocolate. He gave one to Raftery, and he himself sat down on the end of the settee, beside Bridie and the dog.

"Why don't you tell us what you know of the Salmon of Knowledge," said Lou to Raftery. Raftery took a few sips of chocolate, and said briskly,

"Once upon a time, there was a beautiful garden, with a well so deep that the water in it came from the court-yard of the sea-god Manannán Mac Lir in the lands of the sídhe. Around the well there grew hazelnut trees, and one of these was the Tree of Knowledge. It would drop nine hazelnuts into the well, they'd be eaten by a salmon, and it would become the Salmon of Knowledge, until it died. Or got et. The goddess Boann was married to the man who looked after the garden, and he told her to never pick any of the hazelnuts from the tree."

Raftery refreshed himself with more chocolate, and added,

"But he wouldn't tell her why. Which was very irritating of him. People don't like being given orders, and not knowing why. I expect goddesses like it even less than normal people."

Mick hooted with laughter, then recovered himself. "Sorry, Bridie. Go on, Raftery. You tell a good story."

Raftery finished his chocolate, tipping his head back until the cup rested on his face, so as to get the last drops. Mick took out a vast hankie and wiped the arc of chocolate off the bridge of Raftery's nose.

"So, no surprise, Boann picked a hazel from the Tree of Knowledge, and all of a sudden, boom, the Garden flooded. The goddess was swept away, and the Garden—"

"And the cup-bearer," added Mr. Gabriel, "a cup-bearer was swept up as well."

"The stories never said about a cup-bearer," said Raftery, indignantly.

"I know," said Bridie, "she was very annoyed about that, too. She came back here, d'ye remember, Mick? She'd been turned into a water-spirit."

"I remember!" Mr. Gabriel said. "She was outside Cobwell, shrieking abuse at us, and then she tried to get in. It was a job to be rid of her."

"Come all the way in, Flann," said Bridie, getting up to close the curtains. It was dark now, and the moths were starting to fly in to scorch themselves on the lights. Flann, having come down to see why her brothers were taking so long over a glass of milk, had hovered in the doorway, not wanting to interrupt. She pulled upon a stool. Villa dodged in behind her, and perched on the arm of the settee beside Mr. Gabriel.

"Anyway, the Garden was swept away," Raftery went on, "and the nuts of the Tree of Knowledge were swept away, nine of them. Except a salmon et one, and became the Salmon of Knowledge, and Fionn Mac Cumhaill et the Salmon and he had all the Salmon's knowledge."

"Not exactly," said Lou, and Mick said,

"Fionn got a burn on his thumb from the hot fat of the salmon he was cooking. When he needed knowledge, he put his thumb in his mouth. That tiny bit of fat had enough knowledge in it for him to be famous for his wisdom, rather than for being a semi-immortal with a thumb-sucking habit."

"The fruit of the Tree of Knowledge hold all the knowledge of the world," said Lou, "but not in the way people usually mean. They didn't just hold knowledge *of* facts. They didn't just hold knowledge *of* anything. They hold knowledge itself."

"How does that work?" Villa demanded.

"If you put potassium into water," Lou said, "what happens?"

"It skids about," said Villa, "and the hydrogen ignites. Like tiny lightning strikes."

"Right," said Lou. "That's knowledge of what happens. What the fruit of the Tree of Knowledge holds is what is in the potassium and the water to make it happen. The knowledge of what is embedded in seeds so they turn into plants, in roots so they signal to each other, in weather-systems and ocean currents. All the complic-ated systems of the natural world, all ticking over."

Neither Villa nor Raftery said anything, but continued staring at Lou, eyebrows up, eyes and mouths in perfect circles.

"So where are these hazels now?" Flann asked.

Bridie said quickly, "Lou, are you sure we should?"

Lou laughed.

"Raftery will know shortly, won't he, Mick?"

Mick blushed, and muttered something about Raftery being *right there* when Kit landed.

"Who's Kit?" Villa said under her breath to Mr. Gabriel, but he just shook his head, and said, "You'll find out when it happens."

"They were all washed away," Mr. Gabriel said then, to Flann, "so the god of the seas, who was there at the time, was able to save the Well, if not the Garden. Then he sent the Salmon to bring back the hazels."

Bridie snapped her fingers twice, and Villa had a mug of cocoa, and Flann a mug of warm milk with nutmeg sprinkled on it.

"They're out there now?" Villa said, enchanted. "In the oceans? And the Salmon of Knowledge in pursuit?"

"It'll take a while," said Raftery, kicking off his slippers and curling up. "What happens if it can't find them?"

"That is not likely to happen," said Lou. "There is very powerful magic behind it."

"But some people say that there is magic behind the drought," said Raftery, "that the St. Maur Kers are using big magic to make the drought happen. If all the water dries up, the Salmon can't succeed, can it?"

The twins looked at him, and at each other. Raftery was acting like a different person. They had not expected him to know what was being said about the drought.

"What would happen," Villa said, slowly, "if the Salmon failed to find them?"

There was a definite silence. Villa was suddenly not enchanted at all. She said,

"Everything would unravel, wouldn't it? Nothing would know how to work. Nothing would grow, seasons wouldn't change. Everything would come apart, like a rope fraying."

"The Salmon has its own currents," Bridie said quickly, "the currents of enchanted water from the Well, through the waters of the worlds. This kind of drought would have to last a very long time to stop the Salmon returning to its spawning-ground in Cobwell."

"What about winter, though?" Raftery said. "You said the Cailleach had enough fuel for a thousand winters. An Ice Age."

"If it came to it," said Mick, "if these reports of the Storm Kelpies and the Cailleach are true, the Salmon could manage millennia of ice easier than heat and dust."

"No, we could survive drought better," Bram said, "because the St. Maur Kers are making the Rain-Maker. We have no protection against extremes of cold. If it really came to it, drought would be better for us."

There is a long silence.

"What?" Bram asked, looking around.

Then Flann said,

"I think they might be wondering who you mean by us, Bram."

Bram looked at Lou. *I will make sure it's us.* Lou said nothing. Bram said impulsively,

"There's no proof that St. Maur Ker is causing the drought, anyway."

"No," said Lou, "but there will be. We are all tenants here, in this world as in every other. The St. Maur Kers are no different, not them, not any of the other families, the elite, the ones with their private armies, their private corporations. But the St. Maur Kers are trespassing on the landlady's patience. They all are."

"What happens if either the heat or the cold becomes a threat to this salmon?" Flann asked hastily, seeing that Bram was developing the rare flush he got when he was angry. Her question failed spectacularly to act as a diversion. Bridie answered bluntly,

"What would happen is that we in Cobwell would have to help the Garden to shrug. Cobwell would have to shake off everything—and everyone—that stops the Salmon coming home. Everyone causing the drought, everyone causing the winter."

Raftery squashed up closer to Mick.

"You're scaring Raftery!" Bram said indignantly, but—Flann thought—sneakily, since he wanted less to protect Raftery than to make Bridie feel bad.

"Where and when did this drought start?" Bridie demanded, and Bram retorted,

"I don't know— it started— somewhere out in the Inca Empire. Haiti, I think. They've had it over a year, actually."

"And you don't think," she said, "that 'somewhere out in the Inca Empire' there are a great many Rafteries, all scared, not because of a story of what might happen in the future, but because of what is happening outside their window? Everything turning to dust around them, rivers drying out? Are you sure it was an accident that it started there? The Pharaoh's Courtiers were very angry at the Inca Empress, weren't they?"

"Yes, well, that was because she wouldn't give permission to one of the Courtiers to take over the schools on the island he lived on."

Bridie said nothing.

"But how could we survive an ice-age?" Bram demanded, then.

"I don't mean to be unsympathetic," said Bridie, "but the Salmon was sent to recover that which was lost, and without which nothing will survive. It was only the humans who started mucking about with droughts and Cailleachs. Youse are not the only things that want to live."

"So it's the Salmon we're concerned with, here on Cobwell. Not humans," Lou said. "Just so we all know where we stand, if it comes to it."

Then seeing the look on Bram's face, Mr. Gabriel added hurriedly,

"But, of course, it won't come to it."

"I'd rather know," Raftery whispered to Mick, "than be lied to."

"Are you sure?" Mick whispered back.

"Why are you telling us now?" Bram was suddenly struck by the thought. "Why not when we arrived?".

"We didn't want to involve you," Lou said, "we didn't think it was safe. But you're kind of involving yourselves, one way or another. On one side or another. So it's best we know where we stand."

"In case it's a question of *them or us*," Bram repeated what he had overheard.

"Exactly," Lou said, mildly. "Everyone will need to know who is *them* and who is *us*."

Eleven

To Villa's surprise, the promised trip in the zoologist's bathysphere actually came about, the following day. She had not quite believed that Murph had really meant to let Villa come with her down into the depths of the lake. It seemed so much more likely to be the kind of thing offered to the twins. But sure enough, the day after the late-night hot drinks and frayed tempers, Villa came back from helping with the pigs to find Murph in the kitchen at Cobwell, with her hip propped against the kitchen sink and a cup of tea in her hand.

The table was laden with dishes and plates of food, and Mr. Gabriel was pouring out tea for Bridie and Ray. Mick was helping Raftery with the serving spoons, and the labourers were passing along dishes of vegetables and plates of cheese.

"I'm not kidding!" Murph was saying to Mick and Mr. Gabriel. "There was an honest-to-goodness sounder of eels inside in the back of it, twanging away on the strings with their tails! Oh, there you are—the very girl."

Villa eyed her suspiciously—'the very girl' was a phrase

she often heard, usually followed by 'would you like to explain how this happened?'

"You have not, I hope, forgotten your agreement to come down in the bathysphere with me?"

"I have not!" Villa said. "When? Now? Right away? Do I need to bring anything? What do you wear in a bathysphere? Is there oxygen and everything? Where do you buy a bathysphere?"

"To answer your questions in order," said Murph, "now, yes, yes right away, no, whatever you like, yes and I didn't buy it, it belongs to my employers. I had one but it—broke."

Villa nodded—another phrase she knew, usually from using it herself.

"Can I go as I am?" she asked and Mick said,

"Not before you've had a bite of lunch." He cut some bread for her, deftly dished out some coleslaw and tomato slices and then paused, a fork poised above a plate of sausages, and said,

"How many sausages can you cope with?"

Villa eyed the sausages. Normally she'd eat four without thinking, but Cobwell's food seemed to fill you up for longer and besides… there were the pigs. The happy squealing of the piglets had not quite faded in her mind, nor had Flann's advice.

"Give us two," she said. She would think better on a full stomach.

The bathysphere entirely filled the mouth of The Pot. The hatch was made from plates of very thick glass that appeared to be held together with wide bands of bright corals and colourful lichens. It was attached to the body of the bathysphere by four large brass key-screws, and these Murph undid. Once unscrewed, the lid popped opened with a little sigh, and four silver rods pushed the hatch up far enough for Murph, Villa, and Raftery to climb in. Murph grasped a large silver handle in the middle of the hatch, pulled it shut behind them, and then tightened it with another four brass key-screws. She pushed the handle back into the hatch, where it fitted neatly around an eight-sided socket about the size of her fist.

Murph was opening a drawer in the dashboard, and from it she took a large sapphire.

"Now," she said to Villa and Raftery, holding up the massive gem, "what do you use sapphire for?"

Both looked blankly back at her. Murph looked from one to the other, astonished.

"Sapphire?" she said, just in case they had not heard her. "What do you use it for?"

"Hanging around your neck?" Raftery hazarded, recalling his mother getting ready for a party. Murph looked appalled. She lowered the stone. Villa, a dim recollection suddenly coming back to her, said,

"Wait now, you mean magical properties?"

"Well of course I mean magical properties!"

"Something to do with water, isn't it?"

"Something to do...?" Murph repeated. "I thought you'd have them all on the tip of your fingers! Goodness knows, humans have so little magic, I would have thought you'd take all the help you could get."

"Well, we're not really allowed," Villa protested. "I used to, when I was little, but once we moved to Oaklake, we weren't let. They don't allow it in school either, magic, or technomancy."

"Not allowed," said Murph after a long pause. "That's... astonishing. They'll be rationing oxygen next. The St. Maur Kers can use magic, and technomancy, and all the rest of it, though? How is that?"

"That's... different," said Villa, and stopped, at a loss as to why it was different. She and Raftery looked at each other. Murph seemed quite disturbed by the news, but she pulled herself together, and said,

"Right. Let's get this show on the road. Villa, hop up there, and put this sapphire into that octagon. Raftery, come here to me. Will you release the brake?"

With her hind hoof, she pressed a switch that caused a small stepladder to emerge, and Villa climbed up, and jammed the sapphire into the socket. Light pulsed briefly through the gem, turning it so pale a blue that it was almost white, and then died down again, until there was just a dim, pale glow in its night-coloured heart. Raftery grasped the handle Murph pointed to, and pulled, releasing a long, clanking iron chain. The bathysphere lurched left, then right, as it came away from the brick lip of The Pot. It sank down past the jagged rocks where the water was still bright and clear, down further, through a green twilight, down further, where the water was becoming lightless, and then it took off.

At first glance the bathysphere looked like nothing so much as a gigantic transparent eyeball, and what had looked like bands of coral and lichen on the outside were in fact brightly-polished silver on the inside. Four narrow seats, each facing a different direction, allowed one person to drive the bathysphere, and others to keep watch on the water. The battered wooden control-deck took up most of the space on all sides and it was covered with dials and levers, handles and buttons, switches and cogwheels, ratchets and keys and spirals of gleaming copper ribbon.

Murph showed them how the bathysphere worked, where to sit, and how to keep their balance. She demonstrated the telescopes, periscope, binoculars, and the magnifying glasses that dangled from chains above their heads. She explained how the engine had been devised—by whom, Murph would not say—to make sure the machine could travel both above and below water, and that it would not buckle under the pressure of the water even at great depths.

"I can't show it off properly," Murph said, her eyes sparkling, "not unless we are in open water. But it's fast as a dolphin when it gets going underwater, and you want to see it skipping along on the surface, too."

"Like a dolphin," Raftery said, staring about him.

"It must be pretty tough to go so far underwater," said Villa, looking around a little uneasily at the great walls of rock, and the depth of the water above her.

"It's tough as a rock," Murph assured her, "it's heat-proof too. Not long after I got it, I was in Boiling Lake, looking for firebirds—right up beside the underwater volcanoes. Not a crack did it get."

The vessel slowed down, and Murph, muttering something about being sluggish lately, tapped a few buttons on the control-deck. She didn't seem to quite like the sound, so she took out a spanner from under her seat, whacked it across the lever so it shifted another few centimetres, and the bathysphere gave a shudder, and picked up speed immediately.

"Villa," she said, "you see the key in the floor at your feet? Take hold of it and wind it up. We'll be into Littlefish Water in a minute, and we need a steady speed."

Villa looked. There was a flat disc of metal at her feet, with a handle sunken into it. She pulled the handle upright, and started turning it.

"Not too hard, now," said Murph, "we don't want the ship at storm-speed."

"What's storm-speed?" Villa said, slowing down her winding until Murph nodded. "Why can we not go at it? What would happen? Why does it have storm-speed if you can't go at it?"

"That's enough winding," Murph said. "We don't want to go so fast that we can't control the ship. We have storm-speed just in case we bump into something that is worse than an uncontrolled ship."

The bathysphere surged forward from the caves under Cobwell, and out under the crystal clear, emerald-green of Littlefish Water.

CALL SIGN: Good Ship Littlefish
HOUR: 22:00. Am supposed to be in bed asleep.
WIND SPEED/DIRECTION: None. Not a breath.

Temperature: 31°C/88°F outside.

Current Position: Cobwell Farm

Mental Compass Course: Our trip to Littlefish Water

Speed of Travel: Immeasurable

Fathoms: Unfathomable.

Comments: I have been saving my pocket-money, and money I get for doing odd-jobs on the boats at home, so as to buy my own boat. But maybe if I saved it all and never got into trouble no more maybe I would have enough to buy a bathysphere.

Littlefish Water was amazing. Beautiful. Like a jewel. Wild-life on every side. I thought Raftery was going to burst with excitement. I could hardly bear to face in one direction for fear that I would miss something in the other.

The very first thing I saw was a great big pike, a sort of greenish-yellow colour like it was made of gold but had been underwater for a long time. At the same time Raftery was waving at a tiny silver octopus and then all of a sudden the light dimmed a little bit and when we looked up there was a huge sea-snail going overhead, it was pink as roses with the sun behind it, and the spiral of its shell marked out in violet.

The lake was much more deep than I thought, there must have been miles of water above us. Murph said she'd show me how her instrument panel works on another visit. The floor of the lake was weird—at least, not what I expected. I thought it would be flat and stony, like the shore. It was hilly—high hills, that you'd have to walk up. I thought there were trees but Murph said that it was kelp, Raftery said it was a few baubles short of a Christmas tree. There was cloudy-looking algae and just when you thought there could not possibly be anything swimming in it because it was so thick, out would pop a big striped eel or a trout that really was all the colours of the rainbow. Murph was as quick as anything—look here at this lad! And you'd hardly have time to think why is there a sea hare in a lake? before she'd be dragging you over the other side, saying I bet you've never seen a moon-fish before! A marvellous fish, a big one with eyes as big as your fist and lovely garnet-red and emer-ald-green stripes on him over a dark-brown undercoat.

CONCLUSION: That's not any ordinary lake, and even as I write that I have a feeling that I should have known. It's one thing having all that kelp and the algae and a lake so deep that it began to get a bit dark because the sunshine couldn't reach so well. But there were things in there that—well I don't know.

There were things that would make you wonder how on earth it got there. There was an enormous antler, with moss hanging off it, and a huge sort of pitchfork with one of the tines broken and the rest of it all studded with barnacles. Raftery saw what he said was a hoop-forest but I think it was a ribcage, though of what I don't want to think.

Murph said we couldn't stay under for too long, not on our first trip and she started bringing the sphere back up again. I asked her if she knew of any crossing-places with the sídhe because I had always heard that where there's water, or bog, that's where you'll find a way to get in. Murph looked very disapproving and said You don't want to be thinking like that, what would you be doing, amongst the aos sídhe. Anyway, she says, you can't just wander over when you feel like it. They are magically protected. I said, so we're safe from the aos sídhe getting in. There was a long silence and then Murph said, that's one way of looking at it.

But then this happened: Just as Murph was saying we should go home, the ship bumped a bit, like it stubbed its toe on a rock, and I looked up. It looked like a cloud at first, a cumulus thundercloud, but then it sort of separated, and there were three—well. They were awful things, all crevices and greeny purple shadows, big domed heads on them, and these massive eyes that sort of pulsed. One of them stretched out like it was going to touch the bathysphere, and another one let its jaw flap down and its mouth was all full of spines. It was a terrible thing to see.

First Rule: take care of your crew. So, I grabbed Raftery and turned him round so he saw nothing, and I can't say I was sorry to turn my back on those things. Murph saw them, she let this hoot out of her and said pedal to the metal. I hope I never see what would make Murph use storm speed if those yokes didn't. But we were off out like an otter into water. Murph wouldn't tell me what they were. "Put it out of your mind, alanna," she said. As if. There are plenty of things I learned—the rules of tennis, how to make a cake that looks like a pair of shoes—that I would happily jettison to make room for a proper account of those monsters. Funny—you see the word "monster" and you think you know what it means. Then you see a monster, and that wasn't what it meant at all.

How can I find out what those things were that I saw? Not just those spine-mouthed things. Everything. Who would know? Murph? Lou? I will write a list before I forget, and ask.

- A sequinned squid. It has huge red eyes.
- A coral tree with crystals hanging from it
- A starfish that looked like it had a constellation in its inside
- A thing that looks like a canoe, but looks like it is made out of wooden lace
- Something that looks like a hank of lilac wool, but has eyes and can swim
- A chorus of yodelling clams
- Things that look like a pterodactyl lost its shadow
- A fish the size of a baby shark (so Raftery tells me) made from glass and its innards made from silver and emeralds
- A dark green horse with a really long red mane flowing behind it like seaweed
- Something that looks a bit like a fighting-fish, and a lot like a huge, huge moth, and a little bit a very long, gauzy rainbow.

Twelve

A night of broken sleep had awaited Flann after the parley she and her siblings had stumbled upon, worrying about the drought, and about the Cailleach. She had breakfasted alone, helped feed the chickens, and to round up some sheep that had broken out of their field, all in a sour gloom. She was at odds with everything, unable to find anything that didn't annoy or worry her. Bram was helping Mr. Gabriel pack crates, and Villa was nowhere to be seen. Eventually, on her aimless wander about the hot farmyard, Flann spotted Raftery in the open door of Bridie's infirmary, playing Happy Families with shimmering little figures that appeared to be made of wood. They were too busy to notice Flann, and, on impulse, she wandered inside. Mindful of the frequent warnings not to disturb any of Bridie's patients, Flann walked slowly, and as lightly as she could, through the dim passageway.

Some patients were out and about. A duck with a bandaged leg was hopping cautiously along. Foxes hunted elsewhere often took refuge in Cobwell, and there were two here, nursing the marks of their escapes. Flann crept along towards the closed door of the pharmacy, but along the way she could not resist sneaking a look into one of the larger dens. At first she saw nothing in the darkness, then there was a flash of violet, red-rimmed spark of colour. Four more sparks, then eight, then eighty, and she was struck by a gush of hot, rank air that sounded very much like it had been blown through something that flapped. Tentacles, perhaps. Flann backed away fast. It had never occurred to her that the visitors had been warned away for their own safety, not for the tranquillity of the patients.

"That you, Flann?"

Flann hurried across the passage, following the sound of Bridie's voice.

"It is," she said.

"In here."

Flann looked around the stall-door, and came face-to-dripping-snout with a bright brown heifer, who licked Flann's face in a friendly, rough manner. Bridie was at the far end, with the cow's tail in her hand. Her other hand was not visible. She was staring off into a corner, concentrating. The cow waited placidly. After a moment, Bridie looked triumphant, lunged, and the heifer gave a startled moo.

"Got it," said Bridie. Flann, with the sudden appalled realisation that she knew where Bridie's other arm was, said falteringly,

"Got it?"

"This cow has a habit of jumping over the moon," said Bridie, withdrawing her arm, and turning to sluice it down from the bucket behind her, "ends up eating stuff she shouldn't eat."

"She jumps over the moon?"

Bridie dried her arm, and patted the cow affectionately on the rump.

"It's just a phrase," she said. "It means she falls through crossing-points into other worlds. Brings back all sorts of stuff in her insides. Sometimes they get stuck."

"Oh," Flann said faintly. Bridie held out her hand and held out a small clump of large, angular blue seeds, glittering in a slimy chunk of orange curd.

"I think I know where these are from," Bridie said, "but we'll get Mick to check."

Then she looked sideways at Flann.

"Squeamish?"

"No," Flann lied, rallying, "just… you know. I don't know many vets."

Bridie laughed. She gave the cow half an apple, scratched her between her horns, and said to Flann,

"How is your day going?"

"Oh," Flann replied, looking around casually, "you know."

After a moment, Bridie said,

"Do you know what you should do? You should go away down to Tubberlue, drop in on Bridget. She's bound to have more books looking for a shelf of their own."

"Mmmm."

"The walk would do you good," Bridie added briskly, "and there's no use moping about here. We didn't mean you to hear what we were talking about, but it doesn't help anyone to let it eat away at you."

"Things were simple in Oaklake," Flann blurted out.

"Mmmm," Bridie sounded disbelieving. She gave the other half of the apple to the cow, and led Flann out of the stall.

"Well, they're not simple now," she said, pulling off her boot, and picking straw out of her sock, "even if they ever were, even in Oaklake. You'll just have to remember that what doesn't kill you, thickens your neck."

"I'm not sure I want a thick neck," Flann muttered.

"You can't be sure you won't need one," Bridie replied, "you might be grateful for it yet. Lookit, I know it was a bit of a shock and all, finding out about the Cailleach. But lurking here worrying about it won't help you. Go on down to Bridget. Books will settle your nerves for you."

Flann sloped off, grumpily. She sat for a short while in the resting branch of the oak tree, enjoying the shade and watching the chickens scratching up the ground. Abruptly, she lost patience with herself and her mood, and she stood up with a feeling of great determination, though determination about what, she did not know. The chickens scratched on. Two doves got into a spat in the branches overhead, and a small shower of broken twigs, feathers, and leaves fell on Flann's head. As a last resort, she took Bridie's advice and started out for Tubberlue.

Tall beech and short holly shaded the path from Cobwell farmhouse to the road. A donkey came trotting up to the gate on her right, so Flann stopped to say hello. Birds gossiped and chattered around them, blackbirds making erratic plunges out of the hedgerows, shrieking their alarm-calls, every time a cat or a horse went by. The dogs were variously helping move the sheep or running about subjecting everything and everyone to a thorough sniffing. Through the perfectly still, blazing air came distant sounds of a tractor, of hammers and saws, and a gurgling tide of voices. The hedgerows were just beginning to show slight signs of the turn towards autumn; blackberries were too ripe to pick now, rosehips were flushing from orange to red, and clusters of hazelnuts were turning from green to ripe brown. Flann gave the donkey's snout a parting pat.

No-one passed her on the road. She walked slowly, ambling along as she had seen donkeys and escaped sheep do, stopping now and then to admire a honeysuckle, or to watch a ladybird scuttling along the branch of one of the many blackthorns in the hedge. Twice she saw plants that she had only ever seen at Cobwell, one an upright stalk studded with round orange berries, the other an emerald-green vine with vivid red ovals, both plants poisonous. Oaklake did not have poisonous plants. It was only now that she wondered why.

When she reached Tubberlue, and saw Bridget sitting outside the little shop reading a newspaper, Flann was still thinking about the point of poisonous plants. She sat down beside Bridget, and fanned herself with her hat.

"How did you get on in Decker's place?" Bridget got up, folding the newspaper. "Good library?"

Before Flann could answer, there was a great clattering of hooves and rattling of wheels, and a pair of sprightly grey horses cantered up to the village green, pulling a wagon filled with vegetables and plants. Perched among them was Bram, looking faintly alarmed, but otherwise very cheerful. As the wagon rattled through the village, Bram waved at Flann, and Bridget remarked,

"He looks happy, anyway."

"He's on his way to Dunmathew," Flann said, "he's expecting to be taken on as an apprentice, to work on the St. Maur Ker Rain-Maker."

"Does he have any reason to expect it?" Bridget said, tucking her newspaper under her arm and opening her front door. "Or does he just hope it?"

"It amounts to the same thing," Flann said. "What he hopes for he gets. He falls on his feet."

"Or people turn things upside down, so that he lands the right way. Come away in. Let Bram be Bram."

The castle at Dunmathew was not very big, as castles go, but it was decorative, with trees set about as though the castle had been built in a wood, a small clear river gurgling past, and a large walled garden to the rear. Mr. Gabriel drew the wagon up at the foot of the bridge that crossed the river to the grassy bank of the castle grounds, and Bram clambered out. Once over the bridge, Bram was just debating whether to try the nearest door, or to go all the way around to the front door, when he heard his name being called. Dr. Breck was approaching. Bram straightened his tie, and smoothed his shirt.

"We were just having a mid-morning break," she said, waving her hand to indicate a picnic-table amongst the trees, where half a dozen people still sat, "but I'll get you settled in before I introduce you to the others. Good to see you again, Bram."

She smiled at him, shading her eyes with her hand. Bram felt a rush of relief, and realised that he had been anxious about this meeting—whether Breck would remember him, whether he would be dressed properly, whether she was pleased or irritated about having a new person to deal with. But she seemed happy enough to see him, and everything seemed quite relaxed. Breck wore a dress, not a suit, and had her hair tied loosely up on the back of her head. The sun twinkled on little silver decorations on her sandals as she led him to the back door.

"I'll show you where we work," she said, "and then maybe you'd like to see the Rain-Maker itself?"

"Brilliant!"

The back door led into a big square foyer, full of sunlight, where coats and boots and outdoor gear were hanging up. There were random bits of furniture, too, a double-doored wardrobe, and a large wooden trunk. Three shallow steps led up into the main hall. It was very cool and dark and wood-lined, with an arc of bay windows letting in the sun on one side, and a wide flight of stone stairs on the other. It smelled faintly of beeswax. Breck trotted easily up the stairs, Bram keeping pace with her, and then along a corridor to the last room on the left.

"We work in here," Breck said, opening the door and letting him look in. The room had four long work-tables laden with equipment and bits of dismantled machinery, but before Bram could look more closely, Breck set off again, up another, narrower flight of stairs.

"The workroom is in a tower," Breck said. "More windows, you see, so more light. The Rain-Maker is in the top of the tower."

They reached the door as she finished speaking, and Bram followed her inside.

Bram had seen pictures of the original machine, the model built by the O'Connell Beares from centuries ago, and had thought it looked bulky, and awkward, and rather unimpressive. The St. Maur Ker version was magnificent. The frame was made of a crimson wood with a metallic sheen, and moved on wheels, two large wrought-iron wheels at the back, to carry the weight, and two neat silver wheels in the front, for direction. The machine itself comprised three vast tubes, with flared mouths like trumpets. These were made of some white material that seemed to absorb the sunlight, and radiated a faint white shimmer like a pearl. Bram went closer to it, and with a shock realised that it *was* pearl; the three trumpets were all made from single pearls. He wondered uneasily about the size of oysters. The bolts attaching the trumpets to the frame were gold, as were the levers at the back that tilted the machine in whatever direction the technomancers required. The levers had handles of opal, and the tubes that carried lubricant and cooling fluid to the operating parts were clear, like glass, but as flexible as the stem of a flower. These tubes ran alongside the levers, and then hooped underneath the trumpets, where there was a dense mass of wiring, so twisted and knotted it looked more like a medieval manuscript illustration than a piece of machinery.

"This is the bit you will be helping us with," said Breck, and Bram followed her around to the other side of the Rain-Maker. She was standing beside the glass harmonica, that Bram had heard her describe when he covertly eavesdropped. It was smaller than he had imagined, being composed of twenty glass bowls of increasing size, all fitted together on a spike. This glass kebab was held up by a wooden frame—the same crimson wood as the machine's frame—and on each side of the bowls were two large metal tubes that were perforated along one side. Bram peered at them. Breck said quickly,

"Those are for another component, to be added later. Here are the amplifiers."

The amplifiers were small silver dishes, thick at the base, but in a thin filigree around the rims. She showed him where the harmonica was to be attached underneath the Rain-Maker, and Bram saw at once that it would be very tricky indeed—it was not just that the frames had to be joined together, but the amplifiers had to be secured to both the harmonica and the wired underside of the Rain-Maker, and everything connected to the tubes, in order to run smoothly, and not overheat.

"Think you can do it?" Breck asked, and grinned at him, as though it was a playful question, expecting the answer *of course*.

"Of course," Bram said, and Breck grinned more widely.

"Good," she said, "I'll show you the work-room."

He followed her back down the stairs, and over her shoulder she said, casually,

"The two magi are here today—want to meet them?"

Bram straightened his tie. This was what he called a good day.

When the twins came downstairs for supper that evening, Peg said rather awkwardly,

"Come in here for a minute. We want to talk to you."

Everyone was sitting or standing in a semi-circle in the sitting-room: Jolyon, Mr. Gabriel, Mick, Ray, Lou, Murph, and Bridie. Flann was wondering if she ought to be worried, Bram just wondered.

"I don't know if Villa said anything to you about what she saw on the trip today," Murph said, and each twin shook its head, Bram thinking rather guiltily that if she had tried, he would probably have growled at her.

"Well, we don't want to be alarming you," said Peg, "but Villa and Raftery went for a spin with Murph, took the bathysphere down, in the caves between Littlefish Water and The Pot. And they saw something—well, something unexpected. Even Murph didn't expect this."

"When you say 'unexpected', you mean…?" Bram asked, and Murph said,

"We mean terrifying and dangerous."

"Oh right. That's good to know."

"But easily avoided, once you stay away from the water, except on Cobwell," said Mr. Gabriel. "You'll come to no harm, then."

"What are they?" Flann asked, and everyone cleared their throats a bit, until finally Jolyon said,

"Have you heard of the Fuath?"

Flann shook her head, but Bram, to her surprise, said, "Yes, I have."

Catching Flann's expression, he said,

"It was in a story I was reading to Raftery. They're kind of a mythological water spirit, aren't they?"

"They are," said Murph. "A malevolent, baleful, being that thrives on hatred, fear, and viciousness. And not as mythological as we might like."

"Oh," said Bram rather blankly, but then he rallied, and said,

"I thought they haunted the northern waters? Somewhere in Scotia—don't the Sutherlands or the Mackays or someone…?"

Glances were exchanged all around the room. Bridie discreetly turned a newspaper face-down, so as to hide the headline about storms raging down the coast of Hibernia from Scotia.

"Usually, yes," said Mick eventually, "but of course, you know, it's open water. It's not like there's a border patrol in the sea. The Fuath follow trouble."

"They can't come into Cobwell," Peg said firmly, "so don't fret yourselves about that. But be careful once you're off Cobwell, don't be swimming in the Fass or the Creak, or anywhere else, until we find out what's happening."

She gave Flann a particularly close look as she said this, and Flann looked as unconcerned as she could, thinking of her postponed plans.

"Anyway, we didn't know whether to tell you or not," said Mr. Gabriel. "We don't want to frighten you, but you ought to know, so you can be careful."

Thirteen

Cobwell, being where it was, had the stars of more than one world in its sky. That night, the waxing moon became full. The spinning world moved further through the Pleiades, and the worlds to which it was attached spun through their constellations. What also happened, which rarely happened, was that on the same night, three other moons were full, and three worlds moved the same number of degrees through their last autumn constellation, at exactly the same time.

Villa woke up.

The moon made her room unfamiliar, and it took a few moments to recognise in the jagged shapes on her chest-of-drawers the outlines of her telescope and her books. She lay still for a moment, wondering why she had woken up, then remembering with a rush of delight: The Wilderness.

The night was cooler than the day, but still very mild. The ivy-vines were rough, and the leaves cool and smooth. Everything under the moon seemed so silent that Villa climbed very slowly down, afraid that any slight sound would be loud enough to wake the sleeping. Once down, and across the gravel path to the gap in the hedge, she ran.

The path between Cobwell and The Wilderness was white as ivory. Villa slowed down, briefly afraid that she would not be able to find the entrance again. But it was not hidden, and the smooth edges of the posts and the steps glimmered. Villa clambered up onto the step, and held on to a branch over her head to keep her balance. There was complete silence, and Villa had the heady realisation that there was no-one to observe, or to even know, if she went in. But she would not go in, not properly, she would stay by the stile.

Or with just one foot over the stile, on the forest side. The left foot. That way she could balance properly, and look around her.

The moonlight made everything very stark: very black, velvety shadows of trees and bushes, very bright path, grass and leaves black here, splashed with silver there. There was no colour. A rough circle of grass and shrubs lay between the stile and the path into the denseness of trees.

Then, almost without thinking, the right foot, over the bar of the stile. Villa perched. The air felt peculiarly dense.

The trees and brambles to left and right were so thick she could not see through or past them. If she just went a few feet beyond the stile, she could see better. The air was tangible, like water. The moonlight was splintered through the slim branches and narrow trunks of saplings, but gleamed off the trunks of the bigger trees. The grass was so short and the ground so dry that Villa made no sound at all, tiptoeing quickly through the clearing towards the path. The silence was so absolute that it seemed impossible to remain unbroken, and Villa stopped every few yards to listen for a sound she was sure would soon be made.

Finally a sound: a sudden crashing of paws over dead wood. Villa, one foot still in mid-tiptoe, stopped, and felt her entire head filling with the pounding of her heart. The sound had come from a few yards to her left, and she turned just in time to see a badger, with a wallowing gait, run across the path. Villa took a deep breath, thrilled at the sight, and pressed on.

The badger seemed to have set something in motion. It had disappeared among the trees, but the smashing of the dry wood still echoed in some distant way.

> *Water is gushing, gurgling through narrow rocky spaces and crashing down falls. Wasps and woodworm are chewing noisily at the interiors of fallen trees. Mice and shrews are trampling through the undergrowth like elephants. From the other side of The Wilderness, beyond the trees and into the Wild Meadow, comes the roaring of grass being ripped out or chopped down by grazing cattle and horses. Villa falters—from a silence as deep as The Pot, The Wilderness*

has burst into what sounded like an improvised drum solo. She hesitates at the edge of the path.

The roaring and rushing was cut through by a clear, guttural, sound, a bray, a belling. Villa jumped, twisting round to the direction of the sound, and through the trees straight ahead, she saw a human figure running towards her. The trees swayed out of the way, the moonlit air seemed to part. The figure was shaggy with leaves, and from its head sprouted ten-point antlers. It rushed towards her. Villa was frozen to the spot, unable to put into action the clear, pressing instructions in her brain.

The antlered figure rushed up to her, leaves flying, birds twittering, and skidded to a halt. Villa looked up—and up it seemed—into an ivy-covered face and large eyes that had a blade of gold through one brown iris. Her limbs finally getting the message from her brain, Villa bolted, racing for the stile and scrambling up and over in less than a minute. She slipped on the top bar and fell, bounced off the step, and lay winded for a few seconds. She could hear nothing. Slowly, she clambered to her feet, and dusted herself down. She took the long way, by the path, back to Cobwell Farm, because she couldn't face climbing through the hedge.

As she turned onto the path that led into Cobwell's yard, she caught a very faint whiff of a stink, but it was gone too quickly for her to pay it much attention. She was so weary that she considered sleeping in a barn, rather than climbing the ivy-covered wall to her room.

Finally, wearily, she struggled up the last few feet of ivy, and dragged herself over the window-sill. She tumbled into bed, and lay for a couple of hours, thinking about what she had seen. Then, very abruptly, she fell asleep.

The Fuath could not cross the River Fass to the Cobwell side, but they could see far enough to watch Villa go over the boundary into The Wilderness. They could see, which she could not, the moonlight glinting on the domes, planes, and metal of the Glasshouse. They saw the horned figure bounding from the direction of the Glasshouse, and disappear in among the trees. They saw Villa toppling over the stile. They slid back into the depths of the river, and glided back to Littlefish Water.

Villa slept until after nine the next morning, and when she did wake up, she was groggy and befuddled. She stumbled about, trying to find her shoes, and when she did find them, she sat looking at them, unable to remember what should happen next. Yawning, she lurched downstairs, and went into the kitchen. Bram had already left for Dunmathew, and Flann was having her breakfast, reading as she ate. Villa looked into the cooker, but it was empty. She could not think of anything she wanted to eat. Flann was shocked.

"Not even a sausage?" she said, when Villa sat down, breakfast-less.

"Sausage," Villa groaned, rubbing her eyes. "No."

Flann put down her fork, and closed her book. Jolyon came out of his workroom to get some more tea. At the same time, Bridie came in with a wren with its wing in a minuscule splint.

"Scrambled eggs?" Flann said, and Villa groaned again. "Toast? Porridge?"

Villa shook her head.

"What's up?" Jolyon said, reaching for milk, and Flann said, still shocked,

"Villa's not hungry."

Bridie finished tucking the wren into a tiny nest in the corner of the cooker.

"Are you not well?" she asked, coming over to take a look, and answering herself. "You look very peaky. Stick out your tongue, till I have a look down your maw."

Villa obligingly stuck her tongue out, and Bridie peered in, shaking her head. "Fever?" Bridie muttered, and placed the back of her hand on Villa's forehead, but then whipped it back with a yelp, and Villa recoiled too, sparks flying and crackling.

"What have you been up to?" Bridie demanded, and before Villa could protest that she was innocent of wrong-doing, Bridie flexed her hands, and tried again to test Villa's forehead with her hand. This time, nothing happened, apart from a couple of last sparks, and a bit of fizzing.

"No fever," Bridie said, and seized one of Villa's eye-lids, and pulled it up. She said nothing for a while.

"You'll be alright," she said, "whatever it is you're not telling us."

"Villa?" Flann said sternly.

"I've done nothing!" Villa protested, and Jolyon said,

"Don't worry about Villa, Flann. She's not your job."

There was a short, uneasy silence.

"Tell you what," Bridie said briskly, "I'm over to see my sister Britta today. Why don't youse come with me—I don't expect you want to see a smithy on a hot day, but I'll bring you to the Callows. Lovely and cool, you can relax, paddle in the river, do you a world of good."

"It sounds like a doctor's prescription," Flann said, and Bridie replied,

"Well, I am a vet. And Villa wants to be a goat."

"It's a great idea!" Jolyon said. "I'll go and get Peg."

Villa would have loved to see a smithy, but realised that what Bridie really meant was that they were not invited. Besides, Raftery would be delighted with being near a river. She said,

"The Callows will be lovely. Thanks."

Fourteen

*The Callows near the Great River
(the Sionnan, but Cobwell always
calls it "the Great River").*

Dear Mr. Wittgenstein,

Even with occasional stops as Bridie brought her patients
back to the bog-holes, trees and ditches that were their
homes, it did not take long to drive to the edge of the
Callows. Lou joined us too. The road after the village was
very bumpy. Bridie said there was nothing you can do
with a bog road, and Lou laughed and said, the Prince of
the Deer had tried everything. Villa asked why he was
called the Prince of the Deer. Mr. Gabriel said that it was
just the title of the local lordship, like being called the
King of Sweden or the Prince of Wales. Thousands of years
ago there was a tribe that called themselves the People
of the Deer. It's funny to think of so long ago. The Court
doesn't like things in the past. Corporations borrow their
names from ancient times but they say 'historical' or
'traditional' like it is a medical condition.

There were no road-signs or anything, just lots of orange, stunted trees and scrubby bushes. The road stopped being a proper road once we were out of the only village on the way, and was more like the path up to Cobwell. Then for no apparent reason, Bridie stopped the car and the doors popped open. I don't know why here rather than anywhere else we passed, everything looks exactly the same. We got out rather doubtfully because we didn't know what we ought to be looking at.

I suppose it was because none of us—none of us Graces—knew what to expect that we were very tentative when we got out. Even Villa.

The ground was very soft, and we followed Bridie and Lou and the others through the trees and the clumps of grass and reeds. It was quiet, but not absolutely silent even though you couldn't see anything that was making noise. It was still very hot and shimmery, but like the farm, not quite as hot as everywhere else. We walked on a bit further, and then the trees cleared and you could see the river.

It was like your eyes adjusting to the twilight.

Twilight: the soft, diffused light occurring when the sun is just below the horizon.

At first you think there's nothing to see and then quite suddenly you can see a lot of things. The water was shining like silver and was very still in big pools separated from each other by grass. So at first it looked as though the river was very small, but then you realised that the river was stretching so far beyond the vegetation that you had thought it was sky. To our left was a huge stretch of very green grass. It has been a long time since I've seen so

160

much grass and so green. Everyone's lawns at home are drying up and turning yellow. But here there's miles of green. Mr. Gabriel said that we could not walk through the Callows itself, but that if we followed him we could go to the wetland, over to the right.

"We're less likely to kill things by stepping on them," he said.

I waited while the others picked their way past me. Everyone was speaking very softly. I was looking at the river and as I was looking, a heron flew over. It was flapping its wings very slowly, like it hardly mattered, and its feet trailed behind it like a scarf. I don't know where it came from, because I hadn't seen it in what seemed to be an empty sky. It was just quite suddenly there, already busy, already in flight. It disappeared off over the Callows. I was left looking at the bright, still water and at how you couldn't really tell where the sky ended and the water began. No wonder people think the sídhe are just out of sight.

CALL SIGN: Edge of the Great River
HOUR: 14:30. Just finished lunch.
WIND SPEED/DIRECTION: 4 knots; West/South West
TEMPERATURE: 31°C/88°F outside.
CURRENT POSITION: The Callows
DAYS TRAVEL: Between Cobwell Farm and the Callows
SPEED OF TRAVEL: Eye-watering. There's never nothing on the roads when Bridie is driving.
FATHOMS: The deepest point in the Great River is five fathoms. I think.

COMMENTS: The Great River is the longest river in Hibernia, and the rivers near Cobwell—the Fass and the Creak—are tributaries of it, as well as the Deelagh River that flows through Dunmathew, that flows into the Fass. The Callows are like the flood-plain of the river, on its east bank, so it's sandy and muddy, and has pools of water, and lots of grass and trees, but in high weather (as Lou calls it), it's all water, the river takes all the land back. The Great River is so wide that from the Callows, it looks like a sea, stretching clear to the horizon, and then you can't tell the difference between sky and water, it's all the same, blurry, dusty blue.

Even after The Wilderness, I've never seen anything so gorgeous in my whole scrappy life; if Cobwell is magic, the Callows is magic with sparkles on. The Wilderness looks huge and magnificent but the Callows is bright, and cheerful, and serene (Flann's word). It was not possible to be sad, or unhappy, or even tired there.

I was mostly with Raftery and Lou. Flann was walking around like she was in a daze, not so much looking as listening. Lou seemed to know everywhere amongst the pools and the grasses, where you could walk without getting soaked or killing anything. We nearly lost Raftery who went chasing after a dragon-fly as big as your hand but Lou seems to have really long arms and managed to catch hold of him before he disappeared into the grass.

Sometimes what we saw was not what I expected from the name. We saw a thing that Lou said was called a jewel-winged damsel-fly and I hadn't actually expected its wings to be made of hundreds of little bits of topaz and emeralds. Then there was a butterfly that looked exactly like Painted Lady which I've often seen but this one kept changing colour and patterns.

We saw iris and bulrushes and marsh-marigolds and dog-daisies and when we were in amongst the grass and stuff Mr. Gabriel pointed out what he said was a reed-bunting and Raftery had to be collared when we found frogs. I asked if we could look for leeches just to see if they really drink your blood but Mr. Gabriel said he didn't think there were leeches but we could go looking for beetles if I liked, so we did.

As we were trudging back to the car to go for lunch (Mr. Gabriel carried Raftery because he was very tired but I'm too old to get lifts) Lou stopped me and said Look at this. And it was the most bizarre yoke I've ever seen. I didn't think it was an animal. It was about as long as my little finger and it was covered in little bits of sand and stone and tiny snail shells and slivers of pearl and gold, all stuck together. Lou said it was called a caddisfly larva and it protected itself by making a case out of debris. I don't care what Bram says about St. Maur Kers and the Academies. No-one could make a larva-case better than a caddisfly can.

The Callows were very beautiful. The sound was astonishing. I had never thought about the sound of the hot summer until I was standing in the Callows. At home there was always noise in the distance, but every-one nearby was too hot to move. Here, there is noise all around, with things rustling and creeping, and things whistling and shaking themselves and walking in water. Far away everything seemed very still and shimmering. Shimmering is another word of Flann's. She says it means 'shining with a soft, wavering light'. Normally, when she uses a word I don't know—which is most of them—she is very sniffy about it. *Fancy not knowing that! For goodness sake, Villa, how do you even speak?* But today she told me what they meant, no fuss.

Still very weary from her night's adventure, and a little queasy from the bouncing drive to the Callows, Villa left Raftery in the care of Bridie and some frogs after a picnic lunch, and wandered away. The ground was thick with shining grass and damp sand, and it was difficult enough to walk over it. But there was a faint, cooling, breeze from the river, and though the water was low, there were pools for her to splash in. She could hear voices, Raftery exclaiming over something he found, Flann or Lou or Mr. Gabriel calling to each other. Now and then, Villa looked back, and thought that it looked like a painting or a photograph, with bright colours, and people running about. The river was low, and too far away for her to walk to it, and she decided that she would walk as far as the next clump of trees, and then turn back. When she reached the trees, she stood among them for a minute or two to cool down. They were young, slim-trunked birch trees, with bright, creamy bark, and bright green leaves that shimmered in the sun. Standing a little further down from them, out on its own on the bank of the river, was a tree she did not recognise.

It was a tall, sturdy tree, for one growing in a sandy river-bank. The bark was a dark, metallic red that shone hotly in the sun, and leaves like emerald and gold scimitars showered down. Villa scoured her memory, but could not call to mind ever having seen such a tree before. She walked around it a few times, part of her mind focused on trying to place the tree, and a little part of it enjoying the shade from the sun. She leaned against the trunk, and was startled, hearing water lapping, as though there was a wind, as though the river was high. She stepped quickly out, to look around. The sky was still clear. She could tell by the glittering light that the surface of the distant river, and the pools and puddles that glittered near the low-tide mark, were ruffling and rippling. But she could not hear any water lapping.

Glancing back up along the river bank to make sure she could still see the rest of Cobwell, she saw that there were other visitors to the Great River—one visitor, at least, who evidently had been taking a swim, as they were streaming with water, and the sand around them was dark and shining. The figure reached around its own neck, grasped a huge hank of greenish-black hair, and started wringing it out like a wet sheet. Then it strode forward, and Villa—who had been carefully advised about talking to strangers—was torn between knowing she should really go back to her siblings and Cobwell, and being goggle-eyed with curiosity. The figure was a little taller than

Villa, wearing a long, tattered, shapeless gown, of some clear, emerald-green cloth. As it came closer, Villa saw her skin looked frosted, like the sea-glass Raftery had in his Cabinet of Marine Curiosities, and was from different angles as green as it was blue. Light seemed to glint on elbows and ankles.

"That's an unusual tree," said the bather to Villa, and Villa said,

"I've never seen one like it before. Who are you?"

The figure looked at her, as though the question was a tough one. Her eyes were very pale blue, and opaque as pearls, and the long, long hair was tangled and branched like corals. Looking at her was like looking up at the sun from underwater.

"Sorry," she said then, realising how long it was taking to answer, "I've had a fair way to swim, and I'm a bit dazzled in the sun. My name is… Keer. Who're you?"

"I'm Villa," said Villa. "Properly it's Somerville, but I only use Villa. I'm staying at Cobwell Farm, we came up here on a trip."

She waved her hand in the general direction of her siblings.

"Cobwell," said Keer, and the voice suddenly sounded low and, Villa thought, oddly gluey.

"I heard tell of Cobwell," said Keer, "but it was a long time ago. I've been away a long time. And look what I find as soon as I get… home—such a tree as this!"

"What is it called?" Villa asked, "What kind of wood is it? Does it have fruit or nuts? What lives in it?"

"Slow down there, sparky," said Keer, "I'm not a botanist.

I last saw a tree like this a long way away from here. It's beautiful, though, isn't it? That lovely sheen it has, it looks magical. And those gold leaves—like something from a fairy-tale. A gateway to another world!"

"I'd love to find a real gateway," Villa said without thinking, "a portal, from here to the sídhe, or to the Isles of the Blessed or somewhere!"

"Be careful now what you wish for," said Keer, and laughed, "you never know when the sídhe might be eavesdropping."

"You're not one of the sídhe, are you?" Villa demanded, "By any chance?"

"No," said Keer, quite firmly, "I am not. You're not one yourself, no?"

"No," said Villa.

"Are you sure?" asked Keer, peering at her.

"Of course," said Villa, thinking Keer must be very dazzled if she thought a person might somehow forget that they were *of the mound*. "I wish I were, it would be much more exciting."

"Hmph," said Keer, "don't believe everything you read, kid."

"Don't call me 'kid'," said Villa, "you can't be that much older than me."

"You'd be surprised," said Keer, and Villa, recalling The Wilderness, and recalling that Cobwell housed a púca, grunted. Keer said, with a conciliatory air,

"Do you want to see a sea-centaur? Come on—you can do that from the shallows, I won't let you drown."

Fifteen

A couple of days later, Flann walked down to the village to get some ink for her fountain-pen, and Bridget was in the shop, buying food for the cats. Flann was tempted to go over and talk to her, but did not want to impose her company on Bridget, so she hovered behind the stationery shelf while she decided. Bridget made the decision for her, waving across the heads of the others in the queue, and then coming to find her.

"Well met," she said to Flann, "I wanted to ask you if you'd help me with one last box I need to put away."

"Of course," said Flann. "I can't today, because I promised Mr. Gabriel I would help him fix a back window, but I could come down tomorrow."

"Not planning to sneak off to Prague just yet, then?" said Bridget unexpectedly, and shot out a hand to catch the bottle of ink that Flann, in shock, let fall. Bridget laughed.

"Sorry," she said, "couldn't help it. Bridie guessed."

"How?"

"You were asking about the river. It was her guess you

were planning to use the river to guide you to Dunmathew, and you'd take a train from there."

"How did she guess?" Flann was quite indignant. Bridget smiled.

"That's how your Granda ran away to sea," she said, and Flann wondered again about the ages of the sisters.

When they left the shop, they saw that Decker's carriage was drawn up outside the post-office. He waved at them cheerily, and the automaton got out, and went inside, with a bundle of letters in its hand. It moved slowly, and was, Flann could see, considerably dented around its arms and legs. Suddenly angry, she said to Bridget,

"I hope to trespass on his generosity. Excuse me a second."

She strode up to the carriage. Mr. Decker was as friendly and charming as before, his dark hair shining against his spotless clothes, and his smile even broader than before.

"It was so kind of you to let me use your library," Flann said, as suavely as she could, telling herself to pretend she was Bram. "It encourages me to hope you might be persuaded to let me visit again—just once more. There was a book I didn't quite have time to look through, if I could just pop in to get the name, I'd be out of your hair before you know it."

"Charmed, my dear," he said, and Flann kept her smile pinned determinedly to her face. "I am going to be away a couple of days, but by next week I'll be back, and I will be delighted to host you."

While Flann and Villa both helped Mr. Gabriel fix the window, Raftery was helping Mick repair a gap in the hawthorn hedge. Ever since Murph and Villa had brought back a report of the Fuath, Mick, Ray, and several other farm-hands had been scouring Cobwell's boundaries, looking for gaps and weaknesses. Mick had found an old blackthorn that had been damaged by something—the goats were looking suspiciously innocent—eating away the bark. Mick, in a glimmer of sapphire shimmer, stepped over the high hedge in order to work on the other side, and the dogs appeared in force beside him, patrolling up and down, scanning the river and the opposite bank.

Raftery was not permitted on the outside of the hedge but, being small, he handed saws and blocks of wood out on request. When one of the blackthorn's branches had been repaired, and was once more a sunny, neat whole, Mick suggested that they take a break before starting the next job, and dispatched Raftery to a nearby oak, assuring him that some bottles of goat's milk and a package containing scones would be found keeping cool in the lower branches.

When Raftery returned, hunched and panting with the strain of carrying the wire basket without dropping it, he found Mick in conversation with a soggy cyno-cephalus who clearly had just emerged from the river. Being a reader of tales from strange lands, and from under the sea, Raftery was less astonished than he might have been at the sight of a dog-headed man. The dog's head was that of a liver-spotted springer spaniel, and the human body was lean and muscular, and Raftery was particularly curious to see how a person with a dog's head spoke, dog's mouths not being adapted for human speech.

"Raftery, this is Kit," said Mick, "Kit, Raftery. Kit and I worked together a long time ago. Kit, I heard you were dead. Gone in that last invasion of the sídhe."

"Raft'ry, great to meet ya," said Kit. "No, takes more'd'n a wee mill to get rid of me. Great scrap, it was, but I got lifted as a POW."

"Prisoner of war," said Mick to Raftery, and Kit said,

"Got thrown in with a load of the sídhe and sold off to St. Maur Ker for their machines. That man Decker is a—" here Kit glanced at Raftery. "—He's due a good kicking, that man, and I'm at the head of the queue. If he charged us a penny a puck, he'd make a fortune."

"Where were you?" Mick asked, "Want a scone? Drop of milk, maybe?"

"Ah, go on, then," said Kit, and while Kit made short, crumbly, work of a scone, Mick turned one of the bottles of milk into a bowl, and Kit lapped noisily.

"That's the stuff," Kit said, "first bite of decent food I've had in two hundred years, rats and drowned seabirds not, in my opinion, being a balanced diet."

"Where were you for two hundred years?" Raftery said, equally pleased to note that the scone had been well received, and that the same number of them remained.

"Thrown into a great pit of a trench between Hibernia and Scotia," said Kit, stretching out, leaning up on muscular forepaws, "all in cages, south of the Corryvrecken

Whirlpool, and the Straits of Moyle. Then, not long ago, we were all moved, all jumbled together in a big cage. They brought us close to Corryvrecken. Only just got out."

"How did you escape?" Raftery asked, reaching for a scone.

Kit looked at him, and at Mick, and said,

"That's why I came back this way. I thought I'd warn you. I didn't exactly escape, you see, but there was this storm. Never saw anything like it. Thought my hour had come. The sea was so high and rough that we got washed out of the pit we were dumped into, cages broken, chains and all in smithereens."

"A storm," said Mick thoughtfully. "We've been hearing reports of storms. Bridie thought it might be…"

"Storm Kelpies," said Kit, ears twitching. "Yes. It was. They're not messing about, I'll tell you. This is what I was told: someone's stolen the Cailleach. Whipped her out of the Whirlpool when she was aestivating."

"When she was what?" Raftery said, spraying crumbs here and there.

"If someone sleeps through winter, it's called hibernating," Mick explained, "and if they sleep in summer, it's called aestivating. Who'd want a Cailleach?"

Kit sat up, scratching its ear vigorously with its foot.

"Not in front of the child," Mick hissed, giving Kit a dig, "cover yourself up. Man alive, Kit."

"Sorry, there. You do forget your manners after a couple of centuries in a pit. Who'd want a Cailleach is whoever has been collecting all these semi-immortals, and aos sídhe, and mythological beings, to make their accursed machines. That's where you'll find her."

"Where could they hide an immortal like the Cailleach?" Mick wondered, but was not expecting an answer, so was much surprised when Kit said,

"I know they put her on a ship—enchanted, of course, sailing underwater and all the rest of it—and it was heading south-west from the Whirlpool. I didn't follow it, I turned off at Malin Head and came inland to get home. But I'll just remind you that Sylvestra St. Maur Ker owns Inishcanara Island, in the sea beyond Lough Farderg. My guess is, they have the Cailleach in—or near—Inishcanara."

"That's class," said Mick, "we'll let the Bridgets and Lou know."

"One other thing," said Kit, "since I'm told Murph is here with you. I was one of a job-lot of sídhe and semi-immortals that were being traded as elf-parts for the St. Maur Kers. But you will remember Ciarnat? The cup-bearer to Boann, who was swept away and supposedly drowned when the Well of Knowledge flooded? She was in there with me, and broke out with me. I have a feeling she's headed this way. I'll be off now—thanks for the grub—bye!"

Kit had been trotting down to the river, and on the last word, dived in, and paddled off at the rate of knots.

"Was that the Kit that Lou said I was going to meet?" Raftery asked. "When you said I would be right there when Kit landed?"

"It was," said Mick.

"Who is Ciarnat?" Raftery asked, taking a deep breath after a lengthy drag at a bottle of milk.

"Ciarnat was a human child," said Mick. "Remember, Lou talked about her the other night? Stolen by the púca and presented to Boann as a cup-bearer in the Garden of the Well of Knowledge. When the Well flooded, Boann was swept away, but so was Ciarnat, along with all the hazels that fell from the Tree of Knowledge."

"I remember. And Boann became the River Boyne," Raftery remarked, wiping away a milk moustache.

"She did," said Mick, "but poor Ciarnat wasn't a goddess. The same enchantment that has so far kept the hazels safe meant she didn't drown. She became a sort of water-spirit. She was rare mad about it."

"Flann says you can learn to accept anything."

"Yes, well, no-one stole Flann away and forced her to be servant to a goddess," Mick said sharply, "and then let her drown, and forgot all about her. Ciarnat was just an ordinary person, she didn't get a legend, or her own river. Anyway, Ciarnat came back here, to Cobwell, trying to get in, calling down curses—very inventive curses—on all of us."

"Where did she go when she was washed away?" Raftery asked. "Where did the hazels go?"

"The waters of the Well of Knowledge flow from many worlds," said Mick, "so we don't really know. The Well itself was a portal to many worlds, including that of the sídhe. The hazels went everywhere in the water of the Well, scattered into rivers and streams, across the worlds, into gutters and drains, bottomless trench and puddle."

"Lou said if they were lost, Nature would unravel."

"Yes," said Mick, "but remember, Lou also said they are virtually unlosable. Lou sent the Salmon after them, and bound them to the water of the Well. Once the binding remains, the hazels are safe until they are all collected, when the Salmon will return to the Well. That will be many, many years in the future, and I can think of nothing that can stop the Salmon."

"Except if the seas dry out," Raftery pointed out, "or freeze."

"Well—yes," Mick admitted, "that is true. But we're not there yet."

"The St. Maur Kers have the Cailleach," Raftery pressed, and Mick said decidedly,

"That's true too. But the Salmon has Lou. And all of Cobwell. We mightn't be as flash to look at as the St. Maur Kers, but we're not nothing."

"My grandmother gave me a book, *Maps of Impossible Places*, for my birthday. Would the places the Salmon is going be in that book?"

"I don't know," replied Mick. "Why don't we have a look at it this evening? But right now, I have to tell Lou and Bridie and the others what Kit told me."

Raftery said,

"You said the Salmon is under an order from Lou. You said Lou was there when the Well was flooded. I said the St. Maur Kers, and you say 'Lou'."

"Eh…" Mick dithered, "um…"

"What is Lou?"

There was a long silence, and Mick finally answered.

"I'm not really supposed to tell anyone. It was one of the rules when we—me and Mr. Gabriel and Ray, the Bridgets—agreed to help out on Cobwell. All I can tell you is that Lou is the reason that Cobwell is here."

Sixteen

BRAM: It was even better than I had expected. Of course, I had been to the castle before, but they have set up their workshop under the west tower and it is amazing. They moved the original model of the Rain-Maker in, and set up all the work-benches around it.

RILEY: *What does it look like?*

BRAM: It's really heavy, battered looking, and looks a bit like a nautilus shell but with trumpets sticking out of it. I don't know what metal it is made of, I think it's iron, it weighs a ton. I mean, literally a ton.

RILEY: *Not literally trumpets, though?*

BRAM: Practically—they're funnels for making a really loud blast, because back in those days, they thought that loud noises would shake the clouds and make it rain.

RILEY: *But not these days?*

BRAM: No, they still use a kind of vibration, but it needs more than just noise to make it strong enough. That's where modern technomancy comes it. The St. Maur Ker model is really slim and streamlined beside it, really elegant. Gold and pearl.

RILEY: *Tell us what you're doing.*

BRAM: Obviously they have some of the best technomancers in the world working on this, but they have me and a couple of other apprentices working on a glass harmonica. Back when they built the original, no-one could control the pitch of the sound that was made. So now they are going to attach the harmonica to the trumpets and to the amplifiers. That's the bit I'm doing.

RILEY: *Is it difficult to attach them all together?*

BRAM: It's very delicate. Lots of moving parts, and all of them tiny. But not difficult, no.

RILEY: *You'd say that anyway, of course. You'll never say anything is difficult.*

— LONG PAUSE —

BRAM: It really isn't difficult to attach

them. I mean, honestly. Just slow, and lots of close, tiny steps. Besides, if they were difficult, Dr. Breck and the Research Director wouldn't be letting apprentices make them, would they?

RILEY: *Well... I suppose not.*

BRAM: They're fiddly to make, the moving parts. So, you have to be handy, and know what you're doing, and be able to read the technical drawings. But it is more like building a model aeroplane than inventing something.

RILEY: *You always pretended that you didn't use kits to build models.*

BRAM: Well... hum. Hmph. Well. I suppose I thought it was a bit babyish. But Dr. Breck, the technomancers—even the apprentices... They really know so much that they don't mind saying that there are things they don't know.

RILEY: *I suppose saying that there is something you don't know is easier if one of the things you do know is that you've brains to burn. Why don't you show them some of your mod—*

BRAM: No. They're not family. They're not obliged to be impressed.

Dear Mr. Wittgenstein

I really don't know what to do and there is no-one I can ask.

When I found out that Mr. Decker was going to be away from High Tide House, I decided that this was my best chance to see what he was up to. So I figured that if anyone questioned me, I could just pretend I had forgotten he said he was away, but in the end, no-one asked anything. I went down to see Bridget, and asked her if I could borrow her bicycle, and she kind of eyed me like she thought I was up to something, but she said okay. Her bicycle is like nothing on earth, a big, clunky thing, but it has a dynamo on it, so you can build up a bit of speed. I figured that if I was whooshing along the road to Littlefish, nothing that might be lurking in the sides could lure me away. I don't know why Lou and the others said someone needed to come with me to Littlefish—Villa got back in one piece and she was by herself. Bridget has the bike painted purple, with circles with three legs coming out of them on it. I set off with a bit of wobbling, but no accidents occurred, and I got to the water without mishap.

The little boat was there, which was good because otherwise the whole plan was off, and when I got over to the island, Mrs. Danvers was there. I told her Mr. Decker gave me permission to come back, which was true and no lie. It didn't say anything, just led the way up the path, and into the house, and disappeared. I sneaked out the back way, and started off for the laboratory that I had stumbled across on my last trip. Half-way up the incline I was overcome with terror, that someone could see me, and at the same time this feeling that if I didn't look around, then no-one was watching. If I couldn't see them, they couldn't see me. Logic flies out of the window when dread comes in at the door.

When I got to the laboratory, I could not open the door, but I could peer in through the windows. I don't know what to do now. He's a terrible, terrible man. Those poor—whatever they are. Sídhe. Sea-creatures. I don't know. But he has them in jars, and some of them are slumped on the floor, all joints and wings, and some of them are fighting to get out, and some of them have given up. But they are alive, and he—

The work-bench he had the automaton on had a bit of a machine on it, and a dead fish, a big one, a pike, I think. It was slit open, and the guts were in a pile beside it, and the sides of the fish were held back with wire and pins. There was a piece of an engine beside it, very slim and streamlined and elegant. I couldn't see terribly clearly, but there must have been a thousand tiny parts to it, and all around the fish were levers and cogs and bolts and things, tiny and glittering like eyes.

But on the end of the work-bench, there was something else, very dark and gelatinous. I don't know. A very long snout like a crocodile, all strapped up with wire. Huge dark fins, with little lights at each joint so it looked like a constellation pinned out on the table. A very short, thick tail, but wrapped in a nasty-looking cloth, so maybe it used to be a long, thick tail. There were scalpels and pins around it, and an incision in its chest—

It was still alive, it was panting, and moving its head around like it was hoping to spot a way out. I couldn't look. I ducked down so that I would not catch its eye. And then when I stood up, there was Mrs. Danvers, looking at me. I could have died of fright. And then I was really angry, and I whipped out my screwdriver, and before either of us it knew it, I had reconnected her. The first thing she said to me wasn't thanks or anything, it was,

"You've seen now. You can't do nothing."

What I did do was run—down the slippy sandy slope, through the gardens, down the rocky steps to the water, and into the boat. Half-way across, I looked again at the sails, and how knobbly and rough they were, and I couldn't bear to think of what they might be made of.

I don't know what to do. I want to burn down his house.

CALL SIGN: Adventuresome

HOUR: 22:00. Am supposed to be in bed asleep.

WIND SPEED/DIRECTION: Amazingly, a breeze, first inland breeze in months. About 1 knot is all, though.

TEMPERATURE: 21°C/69°F. It would usually be thought of as warm, but after being broiled in a drought for months, this feels suddenly cold. Contemplated jumper. Rejected.

CURRENT POSITION: Cobwell Farm.

DIRECTION OF TRAVEL: To The Wilderness. More precisely, towards the Glasshouse, and what the Captain thinks that the Glasshouse contains.

SPEED OF TRAVEL: Cautious. The Wilderness is not kidding

about being a wilderness. It's not somewhere you go and look at wild things.

FATHOMS: Unknown.

COMMENTS: Possible addition to crew: Keer.

Keer seemed very interested when I told her I was staying on Cobwell. She used to know it, a long time ago. When I mentioned my interest in finding a portal Keer said, "Did you never think there might be a portal on Cobwell, if that's what you're looking for?" And I said "no," which was true, and she said, "maybe I should call down to Cobwell someday, and we'll see what we can find."

And this is what I think, I think it's The Wilderness. I think that's why Mr. Gabriel and Peg and the rest of them don't want us to go there. They're afraid we'll fall through to somewhere else.

We went looking for sea centaurs in the edges of the Great River, but we didn't see any. Keer said she had seen them when she got caught up in a storm, and I asked, "what storm? We've a drought, how could there suddenly be a storm?" And she kind of laughed, and said, everything changes. And until today, there was no sign of any storm. When we were on the Callows, the sky was blazing blue and everything so bright you can hardly see. Today I was in Tubberlue and the breeze was quite brisk. There were even clouds, away on the horizon. I haven't seen as much as a mare's tail cloud since April, and there was a very low, pale bank of cumulus clouds to the west.

Everything changes.

As Flann curled up in her window-sill and glared at the moon, and Bram disconnected his EyeGram, as Villa dug some squared paper out of her drawer and began to draw a map, and Raftery slept, the Cobwell grown-ups were downstairs, standing around the kitchen table. In the centre of the table, newspapers were fanned out, just showing the headlines.

Ballinpooka Bugle
DROUGHT HOLDS BUT STORM RAGES
Storm Kelpies Raging— Linnenshee Floods

Papa Stour Sentinel
DANGERS FROM THE DEEP!
Storms Resurrect Haunted Ship

Gairloch Guardian
CAILLEACH MISSING!
Storm Kelpies Rage as Whirlpool Goes Nuts Altogether!

Thule Trumpet
HIGH KING IN LOW TIDE
Hibernia's High King Stranded in Thule. Emperor Arranges A Bit Of Craic as Storms Damage Royal Row-Boat.

"Ah, now, lads," said Lou, "this is bad."

Seventeen

There was no change in the weather in Dunmathew when Bram went over for his day's work that Friday, except that—as he would have seen, had he been up as early as Flann—the dawn sky was rosier than usual and the sun itself was a red-rimmed orange. Bram's desk in the castle work-room was near to the window, and he opened it immediately. For once, he was the first to arrive, and he spent a few quiet, pleasurable, minutes snooping at the workbenches, admiring the craftsmanship, and imagining himself being the boss of a technomancy workshop. It was a delightful image. Then he recalled himself to the present. The room was already getting warm and the sun was shining on his desk, so very shortly, his companions would arrive. Bram hurried to his desk, and got to work.

A little later, he realised that he did not have enough metal to finish what he was doing. He was making a very fine frame of bars and rings, that in Dr. Breck's drawing looked like a very stylized fruit-tree. It had to fit over the perforated funnels alongside the glass bowls of the harmonica. He was not quite sure what was the purpose of this, and Dr. Breck had been extremely vague about it. To join all the straight bars of this frame together, and secure the tiny rings to them at the exact distances apart, he needed a lot of thin gold filaments.

All the supplies were kept in a separate room in the opposite tower, and though Bram had not been there before, he was confident he could find it. He opened a few incorrect doors along the way. He found a large room in which a dog was eating all the cushions on a chair, one in which two coats of armour were playing chess, and one in which two apprentices, sitting with their backs to the door, were using electrodes to startle a captive weather-imp into creating lightning.

Closing the door on their giggles, Bram was startled in his turn to find that a door, along the passageway to his right, was open, the keys still hanging in the lock. Through the open doorway he could just see a tall cabinet of glass, containing a machine of some sort. Instantly curious, he took a few steps onto the threshold. The room was narrow but with a high ceiling, and it was entirely lined with shelves. A door to Bram's left opened into another, larger room, and he could hear someone moving about. The machine in the cabinet was about the size of Raftery. and it rested on a carved and varnished wooden base. A transparent coil came out of the top, and went into a flat metal disk. Above the disk was a set of metal bars and glass globes that Bram was surprised to realise he knew was called an orrery, a model of the solar system. He took another step, puzzling over the orrery. It did not quite look familiar.

As Bram watched, the globes began to move, each globe beginning to spin on its axis, and each metal bar that carried it beginning its circumnavigation of the central axis. Colour began to flush their pale sides, and a twist of glittering blue liquid eased down through the spiral. As soon as the spiral was full, the blue and shining gold started to pour, slowly, like tar, over the machine below. First it flowed into four large channels, or tubes, and then into innumerable channels of diminishing size. The engine was encased in a network of channels and tubes and capillaries so fine it looked like it was wrapped in lace. Then the machine, or engine, or whatever it was, suddenly shuddered so violently it shook the cabinet, and the glass rattled.

Bram took a step into the room, and then three swift steps back when the frame of the glass cabinet suddenly thrust out a sinewy neck and a glistening snout with long, thin hairs, that seemed to be seeking, alert for a scent or a motion. Bram stepped slowly, his heart pounding, out of the bright patch of sunlight, into the shadows of the hallway. The guardian sank back into the wood of the frame. Bram backed into the shadows of the hallway, breathing shallowly. At the same time, Dr. Breck hurried out of the room, and looked up and down the corridor. Without thinking, Bram ducked out of sight, into a niche beside a statue.

That there were mechanisms too sensitive, or even too advanced, to be attended to by apprentices, or by anyone except the most experienced technomancer, was not surprising. That Dr. Breck should be tending a machine in a locked room was not, in itself, a cause for alarm. Nonetheless, Bram scuttled noiselessly back up the hall down which he had just walked. He took some deep breaths, and when his hands stopped trembling he set off walking again, stepping so firmly that his shoes made quite a lot of noise.

He perfectly faked surprise when Dr. Breck, locking the door behind her, called his name. He greeted her cheerfully, and told her he was on his way to get filaments. She commended him on his dedication to the job, and suggested he should have lunch with her one day next week, and he could tell her about the model machines that his father had told her about. Bram, flustered by the suggestion, continued on his way.

The last door that he opened was the door to the stock-room. Bram took out a box of filaments, and took a box of grommets while he was at it. He was about to leave when one of the chief magi, Boitumelo, strode in.

"You can't leave a tool down in this place," she said, "without someone runs off with it. Where do we keep the drill-bits? The silver ones?"

"Here," said Bram, opening another press, and lifting down a box of silver drill-bits of different sizes. He was terrified that he would drop it, but Boitumelo slung it around as carelessly as a bag of cabbages.

"You busy right now?" Boitumelo asked, and when Bram shook his head hopefully, she beckoned to him. "Lend me a hand."

All she needed was someone to lift some outsized sheets of wood off the carving table and onto the sluicing bench, but Bram didn't care if she had asked him to pull the wings off flies. She had the charming tendency to talk to everyone as if they were her closest colleague and not a random summer apprentice, and Bram was glowing with delight.

"We were lucky to get the use of this place," she was saying now as they carried the wood to the bench, "it's not the only place that has an early model of a rain-maker, but it is the oldest working one. The other one is in Lithuania, but the drought's worse there. And they have quite the hub of conspiracy theorists."

"What is their problem?" Bram sided immediately with authority. "Why do all these people insist on trying to blame the St. Maur Kers for the drought?"

"They're an easy target," Boitumelo shrugged as she spoke. "One, two three, lift. Easier to find someone to blame than to figure out a way to fix a problem."

"Still," Bram went on, "it isn't as if it would even be actually possible for St. Maur Ker to cause a drought. I mean, they don't just happen for the asking."

"And why would they want to?" Boitumelo said, grasping the second board. "One, two three, lift. Who benefits from a drought? Researchers, maybe, we get to try out cool new ideas. But that's all."

Bram was about to agree, but in the back of his mind he heard Mick's contemptuous voice, *so they can sell good weather back to us.* He took refuge in his own comment on the impossibility of manipulating a drought, and Boitumelo's agreement. As they positioned the last frame on the bench, Boitumelo said thoughtfully,

"Although, of course… it isn't actually impossible, I don't think. Technically, it's possible."

"What?"

"It's a thought, you know. Here—lend us your Eye-Gram."

She started punching letters into the keypad.

"Don't 'Yo, bro' me, I'm your mother," she said crisply, when she had made contact. "You know that conspiracy theorist friend of yours? No, not her, the other one, the clever one? Loves opera? Who's that? Donald, that's it. What was his theory about how St. Maur Ker could be causing the drought? No, not the one about the alien cats, the other one. Some claim about the jet stream."

She listened thoughtfully.

"Thanks, doll. Don't forget to do the laundry, and walk the dog. No, you can't get your sister to walk the dog, she's grounded until she finds a way of getting tar off a peach velvet coat. And pick some beans for dinner, your da is making that thing with cheese."

"You see," Boitumelo handing the EyeGram back, "some are less bizarre than others. Donald would believe anything, bless him, but this idea he picked up is that St. Maur Ker are using magic, enhanced technomancy, to change the way deep-ocean waves move, create an anticyclone to make a stationary area of high pressure, then breaking up the jet streams one by one."

"Why would anyone do that?" Bram exclaimed, wanting to re-capture a former certainty. "Is it even possible?"

"It would take some powerful magic to do it," Boitumelo answered after a few seconds, "but, yeah, if I was trying to make a drought, that's the way I'd do it. I mean, a real, world-changing, drought, not just a little bitty, one-season, harvest-wrecking drought. As to why—"

The phone on the wall of the work-room rang, and Boitumelo went to answer it.

"—and as to why," she said, when the call had finished and she was picking up her bag and her keys, "if you can make an anticyclone, you can make a Rain-Maker to fix it. If you can make bad weather, you can sell good weather, and you can make a lot, a lot, a lot of money. You can make a Habsburg Emperor very happy. You might impress another Emperor. And us humans, we do throw flowers at anyone who's got the moolah. Trust us to lionise the wrong people, every time. Come on, I've got another meeting."

Bram picked up his boxes, and Boitumelo locked the door behind them.

"Thanks for the help," she called over her shoulder, turning away towards the stairs. "Who knew being a magus and a researcher would be meeting after meeting after meeting after..."

Her grumbling faded as she went up the stairs. Bram retraced his steps to his work-room. He wondered if perhaps he should have listened more closely in geography class. Anticyclone? Jets? He would ask Flann. But would Flann know? If he wanted to know what Pliny had written about weather, yes probably. Translate Boitumelo's words into plain language? No, probably. For that... as he reached his workroom and heard the voices of his fellow-apprentices as they arrived, the dismal thought struck Bram. For that, he would have to ask Villa. Villa, imaginary Captain of the good ship *Endlessly Annoying Sister*.

Eighteen

Since her adventure at the full moon, Villa had not been back to The Wilderness, so when she met Keer again, it was on the slopes of the Pike of Phoenix. This saw-edged hill was on the very edge of Cobwell, so the slope up which Villa walked was less searing-hot than the opposite slope that faced out into the parched farmlands around Tubberlue. She walked around to the hotter side, and stood for a minute, looking at the clouds. Above the western horizon, there were thin, bright clouds, curved like hasty pencil-lines. But even with the slight gusting breeze, she decided it was too much like walking over a frying-pan, so she returned to the Cobwell side, and sat at the edge of the little round lake, taking in the view. She could just see The Wilderness from there, and the stretch of road leading to Tubberlue, and a little bit of the shaded path that led up to Littlefish Water. The water itself was shining like a mirror under the blazing sun, and was so bright that when Villa looked at it, she could see red and yellow after-images for a long time afterwards.

The water in the Wild Meadow gleamed only here and there, like the panes of glass in the Glasshouse, between the trees. Birds were perching all over some of the tall trees, so that the round crowns of the beech and the ash looked like they had been decorated with dark baubles, unmoving and stark against the cloudless sky. From a long way away came the grating call of a raven, and Villa felt a rush of excitement. She had never seen a raven, had assumed that, like the wolves and the bears, they had been pushed out of the way to make room for humans. She had said something of this nature to her father years ago, and he had told her that farmers didn't like ravens—"they eat lambs, you know." *So do we,* Villa thought now, *we just wait a few months, and we roast it, first.*

The lake behind her was small and perfectly round. It was tucked into a hollow in the side of the Pike, overhung by the peak of the Pike, and looked to be nearly as deep as The Pot, though the jagged green bottom of the pool was just visible. It was sheltered all around by the rocky sides, which caused noises to echo faintly. So, when Keer rose to the surface behind her, the rush and trickle of water was repeated, over and over.

"How did you get there?" Villa exclaimed, even before *hello.* "How deep is that pool?"

"Deeper than you might think," Keer replied, hauling herself up onto the edge of the water. "There's caves all around here, you know, between the Pike and Littlefish Water. I told you," she added, seeing that Villa was staring at her, "I used to live around these parts."

Villa hadn't forgotten. She was staring because—despite her parents' endless reminders to be kind, and not judgy—she could not stop thinking about how odd Keer looked. There was no getting around it. She looked even odder than she had on the Callows. Her skin was a little bluer, her eyes a little pearlier, her hair even more like coral. She was brighter than before, shining.

"That's not a portal, is it? A portal to another world?" Villa asked, suddenly inspired. "Have you ever used a portal? Are there any near here? Where could they lead to?"

Keer laughed. "This isn't a portal, no," she said, "and yes I have used them. I used one to get here."

She stretched, sighed, and looked around. The Pike was not very high, but they could see the farmhouses skirting Cobwell with golden cornfields that stretched behind them, and the path that led to Littlefish Water.

"What's that?" Keer pointed, "The lake at the end of the path?"

"That's Littlefish Water," Villa told her. "The little dot is Eightfoot Island. Mr. Decker lives there."

"Who," Keer's voice was cold, "is Mr. Decker?"

"His name is Dorian Decker. He works for St. Maur Ker's Research Academy. He's a tekton. Makes animals and plants for the St. Maur Kers. He invents all sorts things, and he makes them come alive."

"Oh, does he," Keer said, and Villa turned in surprise at her strained tone. Keer seemed bigger, trembling all over, so bright she glowed. Seeing Villa looking at her, she struggled to control whatever emotion had taken hold of her, and finally smiled. Relieved that she did not have to worry about Keer's feelings, Villa asked, in her pouncing manner,

"When used you live around here?"

"Oh," Keer was vague, "it was a long time ago. I'm older than I look."

"I think probably nothing is as it looks at Cobwell," Villa observed, and Keer laughed.

"I think you're right. But it doesn't seem to worry you."

"I like it here," Villa mused, "I'm in the way at home, knocking things over, and saying the wrong thing. I fit in, here. There's room for me. Or it's the right shape, or something."

"I remember," said Keer, looking away, "when I was here before, that there was a thing called a Blackstar lying around somewhere."

"Oh, there was!" Villa exclaimed. "I found it!"

She unbuttoned the pocket of her shorts, and held up the Blackstar. Keer snatched it out of her hand, but as soon as she held it, she went very pale, and handed it back. Villa, a bit surprised at Keer's rough grabbing, took it. The Blackstar felt very slightly warm, and, like Keer, bright. Keer's unusual usual colour began to come back.

"Sorry. I—I remember—at least, I remember the story —that is, being told the story, of how the Blackstar whales were killed. It upset me."

"Lou said humans killed them to take the Blackstar so that they would never get lost," Villa said, and Keer darted a gloomy glance at her and muttered,

"Lou, now, is it? Will I tell you the story?"

Without waiting for an answer, she drew her knees up and wrapped her arms around her shins.

"Great islands of animals they were, tails bigger than a ship's sail, and right at the centre of their heads, the black, glittering thing of magic that gave them their name. Their skin was green as the deep sea and their eyes were like suns, bright and golden and welcoming. It was said that their Blackstar allowed them to navigate the seas of other realms, using the stars of the Otherworlds."

"Lou said that they used the Blackstar to never get lost," Villa was awestruck, "nothing about them being able to swim from world to world."

"They were the biggest living thing in the oceans," Keer went on, "three or four families travelled together, sailing their roads through ocean miles as humans walked the spaces between rooms in their house. I encountered them in the waters of the Pacific Ocean."

"What were you doing in the waters of the Pacific Ocean?" Villa asked, and Keer said impatiently,

"I was swimming, what do you think? I'm trying to tell you a story, not give you a police report. Stop inter-rupting."

"Sorry."

"I heard them before I saw them," Keer resumed a dreamy voice, "I was swimming, and I heard the most entrancing sound. It was a hollow noise, the whale voice, a peal not of bells but of echoes, some star-sound dimmed by distance. They let me swim with them."

Villa was too agog to say anything. She could picture huge green whales speeding ahead of her ship, but to be down amongst them, a speck between vast, rough sides, swimming in the swash of the whales breaching, flukes crashing like landslides.

"I began to understand them a little," Keer went on, "the rattles and blows, the squeaks and snorts and sighs, the belling and the booms began to sound familiar. I could tell which peals and bass notes spoke of place and movement, or which high claps or rolling honks were greetings."

"Why did you ever leave?" Villa asked her. "If that had've been me, I would be there yet."

Keer gave her a sidelong sort of a look and to Villa's horror, Keer's eyes filled with tears. Villa never knew what to do when people start crying. But Keer went on,

"I didn't want to leave. But there was a terrible attack. I don't know if you know that there was a big battle, right on the boundary between the sídhe world and this one."

"Yes," Villa nodding, "when the sídhe tried to come over to this side. Lucky that St. Maur Ker were able to keep the border safe."

Keer managed a derisive snort.

"No," she said, "the other way around. The humans went knocking on the borders of the Otherworld, looking for a weak spot."

Villa, about to speak, was so shocked that she forgot what she was going to say, and left her mouth hanging open. What had Lou said? *The first humans to kill the whales for their Blackstars used them to...* but the sentence went unfinished. The humans planned to invade, using the Blackstar.

"How would anyone be able to find the borderland?" she asked, gathering her scattered wits. "It's not like there's sign-posts, there are no maps. Isn't everything all hidden, unless you get an invitation from like one of the sídhe?"

"That's why they wanted the whales," replied Keer, and a sparkling tear glittered down each cheek, "their magicians and their mavens claimed the Blackstar in a whale's heads would provide a guide to the waters of the wild. Not content with taking one, they took them all. The water was full of dead…"

She let go of her shins, and rubbed her eyes vigorously. She nodded towards Littlefish Water.

"That's your Mr. Decker for you."

Later, about one in the afternoon when Villa returned to eat her dinner, she found the kitchen table covered in newspapers, and a discussion raging.

"I'm not exaggerating," Lou was saying as she came in, "you could fit a couple of elk in there and still have room to lasso them. They didn't build that just for pig-iron, they are planning something significant."

"Do you know for certain that it was the St. Maur Kers?" Peg asked, and Lou said impatiently,

"They didn't have their insignia on it, if that's what you mean. But you will remember that even the humans were wondering, thirty years ago, why St. Maur Ker were going to such trouble to secure their claim to a tiny little remote island like Inishcanara. That family have huge estates in at least three empires, homes in every major city, why did they make such a fuss about their claim to a guano-covered rock out on the edge of chilly Hibernia? They maintained it was because their ancestors had built that gigantic astrolabe. Now we know better what they are up to."

The silence that followed this was uncomfortable. Villa moved as quietly as she could so that she would not interrupt as she got her food. She was torn between wanting to ask outright what it was we knew now, and the feeling that if no-one noticed her, she might overhear a lot more.

"It wouldn't be the Fuath?" asked Jolyon, and Lou answered tersely,

"The Fuath follow, they don't lead. They take advantage of the toxic situations that other people create. They are parasites, that live off the damaged remains when systems fail, and civilisations fall."

Mr. Gabriel sighed.

"The newspapers aren't lying about the drought being ramped up," he said, pointing to the *Trômso Tribune*, the *Galway Gazette*, and the *Tubberlue Sentinel*, "and yet we seem to have winter on the way as well."

Villa looked over Mr. Gabriel's arm. As well as headlines shouting of the immense height of waves crashing down on seaside towns, and of long-sunk shipwrecks being flung up onto land, there were pictures of smashed boats and flooded houses, and of restless sea with dark clouds boiling above them.

"So," Peg was brisk, "there's no point in hiding from it. If we're at the tipping point, we have to know what it is necessary to do."

"Peg's right," Jolyon agreed. "Lou, what do you think St. Maur Ker is up to, on their little island? What are we looking at?"

"I could not get close enough to see," said Lou, "because whatever it is, they had some serious defence hardware around it, and I am pretty noticeable, you know, so I didn't risk going close."

Noticeable? Villa wondered, *Short and shabby and half covered in hat?*

"What I saw was this—it's not what's on the top of the island that worries us, it's what's under it. They have used the ancient astrolabe as a framework, and they have hacked it. They've made the astrolabe part of something they built right in the heart of the island. I don't know what mechanism they are using to make it work, but whatever—wherever—that mechanism is, it has started to work. Do you know what I think they are doing?"

"Don't string it out, Lou!" Bridie exclaimed. "This isn't a story-telling competition! Stop racking up tension, just spit it out."

Lou laughed a lot, hawked loudly and moistly, and spat on the table. A miniature Lou sprang up and in a disproportionately loud voice, announced,

"They are re-creating Zeus!"

Then it disappeared. There was a long silence.

Nineteen

"Zeus?" Bridie repeated

"Yep. Ever met him?"

"Never," Bridie retorted firmly. "Repulsive character, ought to be on an offenders' register."

"Well, happily it isn't his personal life they are recreating," said Lou and Villa, before she could stop herself, exclaimed,

"Zeus was the ancient Greek god of the weather! He controlled all the weather. Like the Dagda."

Everyone turned to look at her.

"Got it in one," Lou agreed, "and the St. Maur Kers have their eyes on the same prize. They are not using the astrolabe to understand the heavens, it's part of their machine. They've built a steam-god. It looks like a human, and acts like an immortal."

The enormity of this idea silenced them. A machine the size of an island, even a little island, was quite a mouthful. Villa thought of the models that Bram had made, and of the automata that cared for the houses in Oaklake. But they were normal-sized, domestic-sized. She could not picture what Lou was saying any more than she could picture, really, the size of a dog or a bull in a myth, compared to one in real life. *Real life*, she thought, and laughed, *St. Maur Kers planning to steal weather and sell it.*

"The drought was a test," Lou said. "I told you they had bigger plans. Start with controlling the deepest ocean currents. Freeze them, boil them, dry them out, at will. Now it's whole seasons."

"They couldn't," Peg objected, "literally, they couldn't. They don't have that level of magic, they rely on trapping the sídhe even for minor things that, ye gods, I could do myself. No little semi-immortal could make a steam-god work."

"Who," asked Lou, "said they were semi-immortals?"

Peg was startled. Everyone (except Villa) realised what Lou meant, and there was a rippling murmur of anxiety.

"Kit," Bridie explained to Villa, "was talking to Mick about the Cailleach. She has been carried off, that's why the Storm Kelpies are losing their reason. She's a full-blown, honest-to-gods immortal. And she's a weather divinity, at that."

"Like yourself," Villa remarked, still chewing on a chop. The silence suddenly became profound, and she stopped chewing. Then, putting two and two together and for once getting four, Villa added in dismay,

"Oh! If they want their steam-god to be the same as the Dagda, or Zeus, they'll have to pack it full of weather immortals! Not just elves or the sídhe or púcas or semi-immortals. They'll need the full Gaia—deities from each season! And you Bridgets are summer."

"We are," Bridie agreed, grimly, "and we balance the Cailleach—she sleeps while we rule, we sleep in winter. If she wakes now, trapped, where does that leave us?"

"Maybe she isn't yet awake?" Villa suggested, not quite sure of what Bridie meant. For answer, Bridie took up another newspaper, the *North Nuuk News*, and laid it on top of the others. The front page was filled by a photograph, of a choppy sea with its waves frozen stiff.

"Oh, she's awake, alright," said Bridie, "and she's not happy. So we have that to think about as well as the question of what effect will this have on Cobwell?"

No answer to Bridie's question had been vouchsafed by the time the farmhands started coming in for their evening meal. Bram was left back to Tubberlue by Dr. Breck, and he met Flann there, and they walked together to Cobwell. Bram was so full of chatter about the Rain-Maker that he did not notice that Flann was silent about how she had spent her day. As soon as the evening meal was finished, everyone left except the tenants of Cobwell, and the Graces. Bram started,

"Villa, there's something I wanted to ask—"

To his unutterable astonishment, Villa said at the same time,

"Peg, are you not going to tell the twins?"

Peg sighed, and rubbed her eyes so hard Flann was afraid that they would burst.

"Lou?" she said. There was no answer from under the hat, for quite a long time, so long that Raftery got up to go and have a look under it, in case Lou had somehow slipped out and left just the coat and hat behind. Lou ruffled Raftery's hair—which he usually hated but he let it go this once—and said,

"We're all in it together, I suppose."

"All in what together?" asked Bram, with a horrible, creeping feeling that he really did not want to know.

In this, he was quite right. When Lou explained what seemed to be happening in the centre of Inishcanara, the island that the St. Maur Kers had gone to such trouble and expense to secure, Bram at first flatly denied that this was the truth. Then he denied the possibility that such a thing could be done.

"Where would they—where would anyone—get enchantments like that?"

"Don't be such a muppet!" Villa snapped. "They steal it. It's not their magic. They use, you know, the sídhe. Semi-immortals. Immortals, even. Mick was talking to a cynocephalus taken prisoner after Decker invaded the sídhe, and would have been sold to St. Maur Ker for making enchanted machines. Raftery saw it too."

"Why on earth," Bram demanded as disbelievingly as he could, "would they do it?"

Even as he spoke, he could hear Magus Boitumelo saying *us humans, we do throw flowers at them that has the moolah*. Bram looked at Flann.

"What does 'lionise' mean?"

"To give approval, praise, public attention," Flann told him. "If you built a steam-god to mimic the power of the Dagda, just as an example."

"And you don't get to call me a muppet," Bram growled at Villa, "you're just determined to disagree with everyone, you want to be *different*, so you just believe anything anyone says against the St. Maur Kers, and you know nothing, nothing about them!"

"The point is, what are we to do?" Mr. Gabriel butted in hurriedly, while Bram simmered, and Villa cast about her for a return insult. "This is a change of scale. Cobwell could survive without difficulty anything that St. Maur Ker could throw up. But if they are harnessing the powers of the immortals…"

"Our job is to make sure the Salmon returns to Cobwell," said Bridie. "Even if the oceans freeze, the Salmon can swim them. But if the waters boil, if the ocean floors are dry, the Salmon can't hunt, and it can't find its way back to its spawning ground."

"Hang on a second," said Bram, "we have—we practically have—the Rain-Maker. With a Rain-Maker, drought can be fixed. We have no defence against eternal winter."

"Humans might not," Lou pointed out, "but Cobwell will."

"But Cobwell could use the Rain-Maker and—"

"You don't get it, Bram," Peg interrupted, "you're missing the point. You're missing the scale."

"What point?" Bram snapped, "What scale? What's the point? Who matters?"

"Cobwell matters," Jolyon told him, "and the Salmon. Everything else relies on them. They aren't single things, one place, one species. They are all places, all species, and everything that connects them."

"You can't just abandon everyone, for Cobwell!"

"You want to abandon everyone, just for your own

species," Mick snapped back. "Humans are not the only things that want to live. The problem for you, is that you think this is your choice. Not any more, it's not."

Bram was trembling with anger. He looked at Flann, who was frowning fiercely at the milk-jug, and recalling their grandfather's favourite dismissal of an argument: *if you want a simple answer, don't ask a complex question.* He looked at Villa, who was scowling at her plate, and digging a groove in the table with her knife. Raftery slid out of his chair and came over to pat Bram's arm, but Bram wrenched his arm away and Raftery retreated, offended. Able to bear neither the silence nor having upset Raftery, Bram took an unprecedented action—he left his food untouched, and he marched out of the room, slamming the door so hard that all the delph in the dresser rattled like castanets.

CALL SIGN: Battle-stations

HOUR: 22:00. Am supposed to be in bed asleep.

WIND SPEED/DIRECTION: Beaufort Scale 4 / South-South-East.

TEMPERATURE: 19°C/66°F outside. Baltic inside. Everyone is furious with Bram. Mick (who had to comfort Raftery) muttered about sending Bram back to Oaklake, he said, 'let his damn automata look after him', and Bram is returning the fury with added extras. Bram is never angry. He's the most even-tempered person I know, he's the one can get arguments settled, even

Poppa calls him 'The Negotiator.' I went to Flann and asked what had rattled Bram so badly. Flann always speaks up for Bram, manages to make things not his fault. This time she just shrugged, and said that these days, the inside of Bram's head was *terra incognita* ('unknown land'). I don't know how people work but I do know that Bram doing this summer work with Dr. Breck means he is exposed to St. Maur Ker without a break. Maybe it isn't good for him.

CURRENT POSITION: Cobwell Farm

COMPASS COURSE: Set for The Wilderness.

SPEED OF TRAVEL: As fast as possible.

FATHOMS: Unfathomable.

COMMENTS: Bram is being such a little monster that I can't find a portal quick enough to get away from him. He's the one that everyone says is great, that everyone says is going to be such a success when he grows up. If he is what succeeds, then I'd rather be a failure. But it would be even better if I could find somewhere that being me wasn't being a failure. Keer dropped hints like clangers that there were portals somewhere on Cobwell, so I think I'm right about The Wilderness.

But then, yesterday. All those headlines. And Lou being worried about Cobwell. Bridie. All along, everyone has said Cobwell is safe. Cobwell can't be touched by St. Maur Ker, Emperors can't harm Cobwell, Cobwell can take care of Cobwell. And now, maybe the madness that is that horrible family and the rotten Court, and what they say is 'the way things are' is so big and so contaminating that not even Cobwell can steer clear. It seems wrong to think of leaving. Though what can I do if I stay? I can't even tie my shoelaces properly.

Bram worked without distraction on the Rain-Maker for the whole next morning, and only when he had the last silver loop in place did he so much as look away from his task. He was in the tower with the new Rain-Maker, and he was lying on the wooden floor, fastening threads of gold to points on the frame of the glass harmonica. He had finished the frame of bars and loops, attached them to the parallel bars of the frame in which the harmonica rested, and then came the exhausting task of attaching each separate filament, of which there were hundreds, to the glass cups at one end, and to the tubes of cooling fluid on the other.

He wriggled out from under the harmonica, and rested, rubbing his aching neck, stretching his cramped arms. He still did not know what the frame was for, though it reminded him of something he could not quite place. He had had to line up the loops very exactly over the holes in the wooden tubes of the frame, and attach them so that the bars remained still but the loops could move up and down. He reached over, and pressed his finger against one of the perforations in the wood, felt the silver loop depress.

Flutes. That's what the frame looked like. It looked like two long wooden flutes, with silver keys. As soon as he thought it, Bram remembered Dr. Breck telling him that the glass harmonica was played by hand, by running damp fingers over the edges of the turning glass cups. So the tubes he had just attached would bring water running over the cups, and something could extend through the flute-like keys. But where would the player sit? Not inside the frame, it was far too tiny—

Sitting in a rectangle of sunlight, Bram felt suddenly chilly. The St. Maur Ker Academy did not use elf-parts. They would not imprison some living thing, some aos sídhe, in the tiny, cramped flute-thing that Bram had just built, they would not force something's fingers through the perforations, run water over them, make them end-lessly play the harmonica—

Bram got up. The St. Maur Ker Academy did not use elf-parts. He would go and take a break now, he was later than the others, but he could sit outside in the quiet and the sun, and all uncomfortable suspicions would wither away. He pulled open the door, and outside stood Dr. Breck. They both exclaimed in shock, and she started to laugh.

"Sorry about that, Bram! I was coming up to get you for a break, you can't be let overwork. Can I take a peep?"

Bram stood back, and let her in. She went over to the patch of sunlight and stood in it, with her hands on her hips and the sunlight making her hair shine like a halo.

"My," she kept saying, "my, my, my. I had no idea you were so close to finishing it."

Bram could not help smiling. It had been worth the discomfort, the frustration of the tiny filaments curling up and having to be coaxed into the right spaces.

"That's impressive, Bram," she said, "I don't mind telling you. Come along with me now," she added, taking his arm, and leading him out, "I have a feeling you can help us with something even bigger. How would you feel about that?"

Bram did not want to gush, so he said, "That sounds interesting."

"I will tell you about it over lunch," she suggested, and Bram realised in astonishment that it was much later than he had realised, "I think this warrants lunch somewhere nice."

They went downstairs. Dr. Breck looked out of the window,

"It seems funny to say it, after all this drought, but we'd better bring jackets."

She pointed to the barometer and the thermometer that hung, side by side, on the wall, the bright brass fittings gleaming dully. Bram had not looked carefully at this part of the hallway before, and it struck him that Villa would have loved it. All sorts of meteorological equipment, of all ages, even a very old lightning detector that looked like the insides of a radio. Dr. Breck gave Bram his jacket, and pulled a tapestry shawl around her own shoulders. The clouds were not heavy, but the day was dull, and faintly chilly, with a misty feel to the breeze, as though it might rain later. Dr. Breck led the way out of the castle grounds towards the town.

"Have you been to Lough Farderg during your holiday in Cobwell?"

Bram shook his head.

"Do you know of Inishcanara," she asked then, "the island beyond the mouth of Lough Farderg? Ever heard of that?"

"I know of it," Bram replied, "of course. Charles St. Maur Ker, Cosimo and Sylvestra's grandfather—"

"Great-grandfather."

"—great-grandfather, bought it. Set up some sort of astrological machine on it."

"He built an orrery," Dr. Breck told him. "Do you know what an orrery is?"

"It's a model of the planets in the solar system," Bram replied, and Dr. Breck smiled, and asked,

"But which one?"

"Which one what?" Bram was startled.

"Which solar system?" she repeated. "Ours? Or... somewhere else?"

Bram did not reply. *The orrery in the locked room*, he thought, *that's why it looked odd. Not our solar system.*

"Would you like to see?" Dr. Breck said quietly, and Bram started at her, his heart rate rising.

"You'll have to not say anything to the others," she warned him, still speaking very quietly, "we don't want jealousy. But you are unusually gifted in this line, Bram. And I think... I think... no, I'm sure," she ended with happy confidence, "I'm sure we can trust you. And that you can help us."

Bram was too astonished to say anything, and was still silent when she led him into The Cherry Orchard for lunch. It was a very ornate and extravagant restaurant, run by three Hyperborean sisters and their uncle, Vanya, and it was very expensive. A supercilious waiter flicked linen napkins into their laps, and handed them the menu.

"I think this constitutes a celebration," Dr. Breck said. "Sylvestra will be pleased."

Dear Mr. Wittgenstein,

I don't know what to do. I don't know that even reading all your books would tell me.

I don't care what Mama or anyone else says, there is no pretending that Dorian Decker doesn't use elf-parts. He does. He has a work-room full of trapped elves, and they are all missing parts. He is not a real magus. He's a liar and a cheat. He calls himself a theriotekton, a maker of creatures. There is no such thing. It's a fancy word for a vivisectionist.

But I don't want to be the one that says it. I want to be in Prague, in the Klementinum, spending my days welded to a book, which is Villa's expression. I don't want to be a contrarian. I don't want to cause trouble, to disrupt people's lives. I want to be left alone, so I can read and become wise, and you can't become wise through mess and worry and not knowing what to do.

I will go to sleep, and will be able to think about it calmly in the morning. It isn't my job to fix adults. If the St. Maur Kers pay Decker to be a technomancer, or to make plants, or animals, it's their job to know how he does it, not mine to tell tales on him.

I knew writing to you would help,
Flann.

PS. Technically, it is morning now. It's about 3 a.m. I've just woken up from a terrible dream—that poor thing with its chest open.

I have a horrible feeling that I do know what to do.

Twenty

Despite having been up very late, Bram left the house very early the next day, dodging down for breakfast in the brief lapse of time between Cobwell getting up and out to work and his siblings waking. He walked down to Tubberlue, cadged a lift from a brewer delivering barrels to Dunmathew, and was in the castle so early that the guard-elf had to come down from its breakfast and let him in. The first thing that he did, before he went about his legitimate work, was to go to the small cupboard in which he had found a piece of clockwork guarded by a bristle-toothed dog. He looked at the clockwork for a long time, then he shut the door, and he went back to his amplifiers.

When Villa arrived in the kitchen, Raftery was eating breakfast with Mick, showing him Bram's old specimen case, from which he had removed the bits of model machines he had kept in it, and which he had newly painted in Raftery's favourite colour, of greenish-blue.

"Look," Raftery announced, and slapped a piece of paper onto the table in front of her, so that she could read Bram's one line apology, while Raftery read it aloud, too.

"Well, it's something, I suppose," Villa observed grudgingly. "You've always liked that specimen-box."

"I want to find things here on Cobwell," said Raftery. "It could be a Cobwell museum."

Villa was too busy eating to respond, and Raftery got to show Flann both the note and the case when she arrived. Flann looked at the note for a long time.

"You know, that might be the first time in fourteen years," she said, "that Bram has ever apologised for anything."

"He might want to get used to it," Villa said tersely, "if he's planning to join up with St. Maur Kers."

They ate in silence. When they were finished, Flann intercepted Jolyon, who emerged from his workroom in search of a cup of tea.

"I'm going down to Tubberlue if that's okay. I won't be long. I'm going to see if Bridget is settling in alright."

Without thinking, Villa asked,

"Why don't me and Raftery come too? We will see if we can find some specimens for the display case?"

Raftery was delighted. Flann was less pleased, as she was not exactly telling the truth, but Villa's offer to help Raftery was so unexpected that she did not want to overturn it. Besides, it made it easier for her to ask Villa for a favour. As they got ready to go, Flann caught Villa's arm.

"Villa," she said, "can I borrow the lend of your camera? And can you show me how to use it?"

"I'll get it, said Villa. "What do you want pictures of?"

Flann looked uneasily behind her.

"Don't tell anyone," she said, and whispered in Villa's ear, "High Tide House."

The lane between the edge of the village and the shore of Littlefish was indeed very quiet, and they did not dare comment on the newly-strange sight of clouds gathering in the blue sky, or the frisking of wind in their hair. (Well, Flann's hair, there wasn't much chance of frisking in the forest of green spikes on Villa's head). When they reached the sandy shore, Flann climbed into the boat, and Villa suggested that she and Raftery would walk the shore looking for interesting things.

Raftery was a meticulous seeker, and as he turned over every stone and leaf Villa had ample time to look around. The sky was quite grey now, and though the lake was sheltered, the wind was brisk. Each time he paddled into the water, she held his shoes in one hand and his hand in the other, so that he would not accidentally stray. She had brought a bag with her to carry any specimens he found, each carefully wrapped in tissue. As they reached the farthest part of the shore, where the lake water met the low, rolling hill, Villa saw that the hill was cracked open here and there, and that there must be caves. With a thrill of excitement, she wondered how deep they might be, how far back into the hill did they go. Most of the cave mouths were covered by water, but one or two opened out onto the sand. But before they got that close, she heard her name being called. Keer was walking along the shore, splashing in the water.

"I was exploring the cave," Keer called to them, "I thought I recognised your voice. Nice to see you. Who's this?"

Villa introduced Raftery, who instantly persuaded Keer into helping him search for shells. Keer was obliging, even wading further into the water than Villa would let Raftery go, and coming back with some remarkable shells and shaped stones. After a while, Villa suggested that they sit and eat something, since if Raftery got too hungry, he became very grumpy. They sat on a flat rock by the lake and no sooner had Raftery drunk some milk and Villa had split a scone with Keer, than they heard the hissing of the boat across the water, and saw that Flann was returning. She was about halfway across when they heard a second, more violent sound, some metal rattling and crashing, and heavy drumming, muted but getting louder and louder.

Villa leaped up and rushed along the shore to help Flann get the boat in, and as she ran, she looked up the lane to see what was making the noise. It was a metal horse, with a very well-padded saddle, and on it was Dorian Decker, his hat gone, and his shining curls flying in the wind. Keer ran into the water, and took such a deep breath that Villa though she would inhale the grass off the ground. Then she blew out a wind that ruffled up the water so much that the boat turned, and it and Flann were brought thumping up on a further, rockier part of the shore. Flann clambered quickly out, and up the col-lapsed stones over into the field that ran alongside the lane. Villa had stopped, staring at Decker and his diamond-eyed horse. The horse skidded to a halt, and Decker, about to hail Villa, caught sight of Keer. His eyebrows rose up and up, his eyes so round with astonishment that he looked like a cartoon of shock.

"Hello, dearie," said Keer, "slaughtered any whales lately, you murderous wee bastard?"

Without a word, Decker yanked the horse's head around, and set off back up the lane.

"Off with you," Keer ordered Villa, "not a minute to lose, into that field after your sister, or she's done for. I'll explain later. Go—*go*!"

Villa did not hesitate. The sand slipped horribly under her feet but she made good speed to the heap of rocks, scrambled over them with scant regard to safety, and plunged into the grass after Flann. Flann might spend her days welded to a book, Villa thought admiringly, but she sets a cracking pace. Flann was charging through a hawthorn hedge which slowed her down almost enough for Villa to catch up with her, but also enough for Decker on his horse to spot her, and urge the horse forward over a gap in the high hedge.

Racing up to the barrier, Villa slowed down only enough to make sure she didn't lose an eye to the haw's long spikes, and then shoved and wriggled her way past the finger-length thorns and the twisted, knotted branches. She exploded out onto the other side like a cork from a bottle, at the same time that Decker's horse landed, its iron hooves gouging deep furrows and flinging up clods of red earth.

Villa, poised in the hedge, stopped dead.

The moment the horse's hooves touched the ground, it was a different world. Huge, gnarled trees were thick on the ground. The grass was gone, the ground was a sodden, trembling mass of moss, sand, and lichen, the dark green a patchwork with great splashes of pink, yellow, and red. The sky was dark, everything the sooty sort of blue of a late winter day. Everywhere Villa looked, shadows slipped by, red or yellow eyes gleamed out from crevices or from high branches. The scents of yarrow and meadowsweet and dog-roses were gone, and their places taken by a repellent stench, like something dead and rotting and dragged from a moist grave. Villa saw the flash of Flann's pale tunic, and knew that if she did not start to run now, she would be too frightened to move. She flung herself out of the hedge, slipping and tripping over roots, and grabbed hold of a fallen branch. With this tightly grasped and ready to strike away anything that came near her, she raced through the trees, straining to keep track of Flann.

The horse slewed around, sending a couple of trees flying, and Villa pressed on, her lungs burning, her legs starting to shake. She couldn't see Decker or his horse, but the stench occupied all her senses, and in her mind's eye she could see the fearful shapes that had loomed over the bathysphere, the dull, pearly glow of their bulbous eyes, their yawning, bristling mouths, and the shadows that shivered in the hanging folds of their limbs. She sped on, her breath roaring in her throat, her neck aching, temples throbbing, lungs straining. Flann heard her, turned, Villa grabbed her hand. The hooves thundered, drummed, came closer and closer. Villa barely had time to register the dimming of the stink when the shrieking of breaking trees shook the air.

Flann and Villa looked around, stared at each other.

There was no time to say anything. Decker and his horse were upon them. The horse, red froth flying from its nostrils, crashed through the crowns of the trees, splitting the ground where it landed, sinking up to its shoulders while Decker flogged it on. In a moment, it was out of the trench it had created, and directly facing Flann and Villa, its speed hardly diminished by its thunderous crash into the earth. As soon as it was clear of the trees, though, the horse suddenly swerved, threw up its head, galloped a few stretches, then, without warning, stopped.

Decker, on the other hand, kept going. He flew in a beautiful arc over the horse's head, his limbs flailing, his cloak snapping like a kite behind him. He sailed over the heads of the astonished Graces. His curls flickered in the dim light, and the jewel in his jabot fell out. He came to land with a loud cry and an enormous thump. Flann and Villa stared at him open-mouthed. Decker, sitting up and looking around, bewildered and appalled, just had time to wail,

"Oh this isn't fair!"

before, with a loud bang, like a sonic boom, and a sparkle of gold like a fire-work,

he

turned

to

dust

Villa and Flann stared at the Decker dust, then at each other. There was a rainbow of coloured dust in a little ridge on the ground, a rough outline of a person's shape. In the middle were some ivory buttons and a fob-watch on a gold chain. To the sides were some opal cuff-links and a couple of gold and sapphire rings. At the foot-end were the steel caps from his boots. At the head-end there was a fine set of ivory dentures and an earring. Flann and Villa looked back at each other. The horse was nibbling young leaves from a branch that it had cracked free of its parent trunk.

"Does this seem to you, Flann," Villa asked hoarsely, "to be a good time to get out of here?"

"It does, Villa," Flann assured her, sounding as if her lungs had been rolled up like a tube of toothpaste so all her voice was squeezed out in a thin stream. They began to inch their way past the horse, which ignored them completely. The Graces were torn between wanting to get back as quickly as possible to somewhere that they recognised, and being too astonished to move.

"Thank goodness the stink has gone," Villa said, hoarsely, and Flann wondered aloud where everything else had gone. The field was exactly as it had been when they had walked heedlessly past it that morning with Raftery. There were even birds singing, and a couple of crows chatting to each other as they poked about for worms. There were the same few scattering of trees, but no glistening or furtive figures, no bright and hostile eyes. The ground was solid again, grass grazed down here and there, up to Flann's shoulder near the edges. They reached a gap in the hedge, and climbed through. Flann sat down suddenly.

"I haven't run so hard since…"

Villa flopped down beside her.

"I've never run that hard."

There was silence. Each sister wanted the other to give an explanation for what happened. Neither wanted to ask, and thereby to hear that the other did not know. Flann said,

"We had better get back. Raftery."

They got up, and set off, so shaky after their burst of effort that they staggered, and stumbled, and Villa started to laugh, and Flann followed her. By the time they reached the shore of Littlefish Water, they were wiping their eyes and singing about going on a bear hunt. Keer and Raftery were waiting for them, Keer perched on a rock and Raftery beside her, arranging his specimen bag.

"You look like a pair of drunks," said Keer. "Come on, we had better go."

Twenty-One

"What happened?" Villa demanded, suddenly recalling that Keer had said, *I'll explain later.*

"Here, Raftery, you'd better go with Flann now," said Keer, and Raftery trotted to Flann. Keer clapped her hands very briskly. The boat dislodged itself from where Flann had abandoned it, and sailed over. Keer turned to Villa.

"Did Decker happen to turn to dust, by any chance?"

"How did you know that?" Villa demanded. "Tell me what happened!"

"I'll tell you on the way," Keer replied. "You're coming with me."

She stood up; up and up, she was as high as a hill now. She glittered dully, and her pearly eyes had a blueish sheen. The little self-sailing boat ground up onto the sand and made them jump.

"You won't fit in that tiny boat," Villa objected and Keer made no reply, but grabbed the prow of the boat in both hands and yanked vigorously. The boat lifted up for a moment, then seemed to snap from the centre, and bobbing on the water was a larger vessel, with a wooden frame covered with hide, a small cabin, and two sails bellying out without a breeze.

Flann was quicker to realise what was happening but was hampered by not wanting to frighten Raftery. Keer reached out, and Villa was so busy staring at the boat that she did not notice until the shadow of Keer's hand fell on her. It took Villa a few moments to realise Keer's hostile intent, but Keer gripped her so tightly that she was choking. Villa struggled in her captor's fierce grip. Her kicks and her flailing fists made no impression on Keer, who with nothing more than a couple of 'ows', heaved Villa over the side of the boat, and climbed in.

"Stay here," Flann whispered to her brother, and started to run, but Keer saw her, and with a sweep of her hand brought a wave up out of the lake that knocked Flann off her feet. Far from being frightened, Raftery retaliated, and Keer was pelted with a stinging hail of pebbles from the beach. Gleaming and glowing-eyed, Keer dodged them easily, and with a snapping of fingers she bundled all the pebbles together and aimed the rock at Raftery. But she hesitated, looking down at his furious face. Keer dropped the pebble-rock harmlessly on the shore but seeing Flann running, squelching, to Raftery, she set the boat sailing and the water of the lake thrashing so high that a wave crashed down on Flann, drew her under the water, then flung her back out onto the shore, hard against the pebble-rock. Flann lay very still where she fell, and Raftery looked from her to the boat, speeding over the lake, and vanishing into the caves.

The waters calmed. Alone on the shore, Raftery saw a

long, dark, fluttering shape rise from the lake's depths to just below the water's surface, and follow in the wake of the boat. Another rose, and followed, and another, and another. Then he was alone. He went over to Flann and called her name and shook her, but had to conclude that she was so fast asleep that he could not wake her. He looked about. For want of something to do, he made his way over the slippy, difficult sand, and picked up his specimen bag. He was sitting beside Flann, hoping to wake her up by telling her where he had found each object in the bag, when he heard footsteps crunching along the shore.

"Where are we going?" Villa asked. They were far into the caves by now, but the sunlessness did not seem to trouble Keer, nor slow the boat down to any degree. Whatever the sails were made of seemed to include some sort of bio-phosphorescence, so they were not travelling in utter darkness, but they were at such speed that even Villa could only think that they were out of control. To her surprise, Keer answered her. In all the adventure stories that Villa had read, the hero always asked the villain that question, and the villain would not reply, or would merely sneer, or would make some cryptic threat. Keer had clearly not read the same stories. She answered,

"We are going to Dunmathew. I have a job for you."

"Why Dunmathew? What's there? Who do you know in Dunmathew? Do you mean the castle? What job? What are you doing? Why me?"

"You do ask a lot—"

"And while we're at it," Villa ploughed on, her fear fermenting into a form of anger, "what happened to Decker? How did you know about the dust? Why did the field turn all weird and scary and then turn back again? What's going on?"

"Give me the Blackstar," said Keer, "and I'll explain everything."

"No," retorted Villa, who couldn't take an order to save her life, "I found the Blackstar. I won't give it to you. But if you don't tell me the answers, I'm going to drop the Blackstar into the water and you'll never find it."

As she spoke, she unbuttoned the pocket of her shorts, took out the Blackstar, and held it out over the edge of the boat.

"Don't be such a numpty! Alright, alright, alright—it makes no difference what you know."

Keer sat out of reach, and held up her hands to show she was not going to try to get the Blackstar.

"That's the answer to some of your questions," she said, pointing, "the Blackstar. Where did you get it, by the way?"

"Upstairs in Cobwell," Villa answered, "I found it. Lou told me what it was. You told me about the Blackstars, and how they were killed."

"Decker killed them."

"But it happened hundreds of years ago. Decker wasn't hundreds of years old."

"You're living at Cobwell," Keer pointed out, and laughed, "you ought to know better by now."

Villa quietly put the Blackstar back in her pocket and buttoned it.

"Tell me, then."

"If I had a harp," Keer said unexpectedly, "I could tell you a great story. That's what I wanted to be when I was your age, Raftery's age, even. A poet. A teller of tales, a singer of songs."

"I'm going to go out on a limb, and say that it didn't work out like that."

"Salty little thing, aren't you?"

"I'm not a *little thing* at all," Villa snapped, "but I am cold and hungry and frigh— and I'd like a feckin' answer."

Keer wrapped her arms around her shins. The boat sailed on.

"I had been drowned a long, long time when Decker first started to work for the St. Maur Kers," she went on, "in their early years, of finagling their way into the orbit of the Habsburg Emperor. I was swept away when a stupid, arrogant goddess stole a nut from a tree, and the garden where the tree grew flooded. We were swept away, she and I."

"Ciarnat," Villa whispered, "you're Ciarnat, that Mr. Gabriel told us about. The cup-bearer."

"When I was little, I was Keer," Keer/Ciarnat told her, "but Boann insisted that, in the Garden, I was called Ciarnat. There was another deity there when the garden flooded, a very powerful one, who could have saved me but didn't, too busy trying to save the damn garden, let me drown. But you can't drown in enchanted water.

That is how I got to live with the whales. But when Decker invaded the sídhe and failed, he brought back with him a host of the aos sídhe, púca and elves and what have you, semi-immortals, including me."

"Why? What did he want you for?"

"The reason he invaded the sídhe at all was because the St. Maur Kers steal magic by trapping it in their machines."

"Why do they need to do that? They are powerful magicians."

"Do you believe everything you're told?" Keer mocked. "Everything is a trick. The St. Maur Kers trapped aos sídhe in machines. Then they told everyone that the machines worked as magnificently as they did because St. Maur Ker were such great magicians. And everyone believed them, and let them do what they wanted."

Villa didn't speak.

"You know those first flying machines they made, the ones shaped like dragon-flies?" Keer said. "Each one of those has bits of dragon's liver in it. See the sails of this boat? Made out of elf-skin."

"You can't fool everyone," Villa protested, "someone would have noticed."

"Not really," said Keer. "All St. Maur Ker have to do is to keep all the ugly stuff, the hunters raiding the borders with other worlds, the captives, the bits and pieces of elves, out of sight. Then they could go on giving the humans what they want. Everyone is happy to believe what they think they see."

"Like the Emperor's New Clothes," Villa said, faintly, "the fairy-tale. Everyone pretends to see them, for fear of being a fool, even though there's really nothing there."

"Humans never learn," Keer retorted. "This time it is the St. Maur Kers who benefit. And Decker isn't much of a magician but he's smart enough a human to know how to rise to the top of the St. Maur Ker pile. He has his eye on the Pharaoh's Court. He decided he would make his fortune by creating an endless supply of captive sídhe."

"Because if he had all the captive sídhe," Villa guessed, "the St. Maur Kers would buy everything they needed from him."

"You see?" snapped Keer. "See how quickly you worked that out? You're a human too."

"I worked it out," Villa said loftily, "I didn't say I'd do it."

"Where do your parents make their money?"

Villa opened her mouth to retort, and then shut it again. She didn't see how a botanist or a lawyer would use bits of elf, but she did not want to find out.

"So," she said uncomfortably, "tell us about Decker."

"Decker thought a single raid would be enough for him to have a permanently-open portal into the other worlds," Keer said. "It failed. He hadn't understood that some portals lead to more than one world, so an attack on the sídhe was an attack on other worlds, and all the worlds retaliated. But having been over to the other side, he wasn't quite the same when he came back. Time slips unevenly between worlds."

"Was that why you were still around when Decker came back?" Villa asked, and Keer nodded, and said, "When he came back, it was two hundred years later, and he knew enough about the sídhe to know that once he did not step on human soil, he would never die."

"Everyone said he always stayed in his carriage," Villa remarked, "like the myth of Oisín in Tír na nÓg, and he had to stay on his horse when he came back."

"Poor old Oisín," Keer said, but Villa ploughed on,

"But does that mean the field me and Villa were in was on the human side or not?"

"That lane, between Tubberlue and Littlefish, was created by the flooding of the garden," said Keer. "When Boann picked the nut, the garden flooded and released a burst of enchanted energy of such magnitude that it blew the side off of the Pike of Phoenix. There were lumps of the Otherworlds flying everywhere, and one of them gouged that lane out so deeply that it was partly in this world, and partly in the sídhe. When Decker chased Flann into it, he—being of the sídhe, and being on a horse inhabited by a captive aos sídhe—tipped it over from being both to being just sídhe, and being that part of the sídhe that he had invaded, and laid waste to."

"Then why did it change back again?" Villa leaned forward. She had never heard such an exciting story.

"Because of you," Keer told her. "You flipped it back again, to the human side. A portal, or a world-crossing, only stays open a couple of seconds. You use the Blackstar, or the Blackstar uses you, to keep them open and stable enough to cross, for a long time. That's how I found you."

Villa said slowly, "You found me. On the Callows, you mean?"

"I had used a portal in the sea to get to the Callows," Keer said, "it was just chance you were there. Remember the tree? You asked me—"

"The red one, the crimson one?" Villa was outraged. "Are you telling me I was standing beside a portal, and *I didn't know it?*"

"I could see that you couldn't see the portal, but you could see past the portal, you could see a tree growing in a world that brushed your world. I knew you would be invaluable to me."

Villa did not know what to say. Fragments of what Keer had told her fluttered in her mind like cut bunting and she did not know what was most important. She needed time to think, and she looked into the water, so that she would not have to look at Keer. *Invaluable.*

Villa realised that the water was becoming lighter. They were nearing the end of a cave. It was also becoming considerably smellier.

"You still haven't told me why we are going to Dunmathew."

"There's a portal there that leads to more than one world," Keer said, "in the castle. If Decker could be King Rat through providing St. Maur Ker, and maybe even the Court, with an endless supply of captive sídhe, why shouldn't I? I'm sick of being the butt of tricks. I'm sick of being the one others make use of. I want to be Queen of the Heap, even if it means behaving like a human. You are going to hold the portals open for me."

Villa stopped staring at the water and stared at Keer instead. She could understand the words Keer was saying, but she could not make them mean anything.

"I'm afraid that requires you to be incarcerated for the rest of your life," Keer said, "but you'll get used to it, I expect. I got used to being a cup-bearer."

Before Villa could answer, the stench intensified, the boat rocked badly, and out of the water rose the huge domed head and the bulbous eyes that Villa remembered from the bathysphere. *The Fuath. This day gets better and better,* Villa thought to herself, *at this rate I'll be eating my own feet for supper.*

Keer looked startled at the appearance of the Fuath, but listened as they spoke. Villa heard only a grating murmur. Desperate to hear, but terrified of alerting Keer, Villa slid with painful slowness out of her seat, inching her way down the boat. The fact that the Fuath were leaning on it meant that Villa's movements did not disturb the boat, but as soon as she was within earshot, she stopped.

"...hopes that you will lead us. We heard you speaking to the human child, and we think that we can be of service to you. Dunmathew has a portal as you say, what they call an entrepôt portal, it opens into the sídhe, into Muinbeo, Narnia, some others."

"I don't need you to tell me it's an entrepôt," Keer said, and the Fuath said,

"Yes, but what if we could tell you of a bigger entrepôt? Before our late dear leader's demise, our eyes were turned to The Wilderness on Cobwell. That is where there is a big prize."

"Cobwell?" said Keer, and at first she sounded puzzled, like Cobwell was the last place she would have expected to find a portal. Then she repeated the name again, *Cobwell*, in a tone of wonder, as though a great light had begun to shine.

Without thinking beyond the next few minutes, Villa crept over to the tilted side of the boat, and slithered over the edge into the cold water. She had no idea where she was in the caves, so she swam for the light, and hoped for the best.

Twenty-Two

When Flann came to her senses, it was with a mirror pressed to her face. She moved, and Raftery shouted,

"It worked! She's not dead!"

The mirror was removed. Flann could see, blurrily, Raftery's face.

"Good lad, Raftery," said another voice, "take it handy, Flann, don't flail around so much. Raftery, will you go to the kitchen and see if Mrs. Danvers has rustled up a bite of food."

Raftery vanished, and Flann tested out the possibility of being vertical, which, when taken very slowly, worked out well enough. When she was upright, she was looking into the face of a stranger, but not an unfamiliar one. Though the hair was dark-red and straight, and the eyes brown, there was enough family resemblance for Flann to be able to say,

"Are you Britta? The third Bridget?"

Britta smiled.

"I am. I see your brains aren't too rattled, if you can still put two and two together and get three."

She held out a very large hand, and Flann shook it, saying,

"Enchanted."

"You're not wrong there," Britta agreed.

"Why did Raftery announce that I wasn't dead?" Flann asked her. Her voice sounded thick and distant, as though she was talking through a cushion.

"You weren't dead," Britta said, "but we couldn't stop Raftery from fretting. So, we showed him how to see your breath by holding up a mirror to your face. He thought we meant that the mirror would keep you breathing, and we couldn't get him to put it down."

"He's very determined," said Flann, wondering if she was going to vomit, and realising at the same time that she was terribly hungry. "How did you get landed with me?"

"An automaton," Britta replied, "or, rather, one of the aos sídhe who got used to hanging around in the interior of an automaton that someone reconnected."

"Mrs. Danvers," said Flann.

"She saw what happened, from High Tide House. Saw Decker chase you, saw him get dusted, and, when they had finished celebrating, they were down the garden just in time to see Ciarnat sail off with your sister and leave you in a pile on the sand."

"Who's Ciarnat?"

"Keer," said Britta, "the human child stolen by the púca on the wishes of Boann, and who was drowned when Boann caused the Well of Knowledge to flood."

"How could she still be alive?" Flann asked, cautiously

swinging her feet onto the floor. She sat very still until her head stopped spinning.

"Same way Decker was, I suspect," Britta said. "Enchantment."

"What does Ciarnat have to do with the Cailleach?" Flann wondered. Now that she was able to look around, she saw Mrs. Danvers carrying a tray of food in from Bridget's kitchen. Raftery followed with another, smaller, tray.

"Nothing, as far as we know," said Britta. "Sit up here and eat this, it'll be good for what ails you."

"What ails me?"

"You got a slap across the head from a very angry semi-immortal," replied Britta. "People have died from less. Eat."

Flann, with help from Raftery on one side and Britta on the other, sat at the table. Mrs. Danvers sat opposite.

"Raftery told me how Kit explained to Mick that the St. Maur Kers used a marine trench to house all their captives," Mrs. Danvers said. "When the Cailleach was taken from the Corryvreckan Whirlpool, and the Storm Kelpies tried to stop the abduction, they caused such storms that all sorts of stuff was dragged up from the sea-bed. Everything that St. Maur Ker had kept imprisoned under the sea was released."

"Including poor Keer," said Flann, through mouthfuls of soup. "She can't catch a break, can she?"

"She hasn't had a say in her own life since she was about ten," Britta mused, "maybe that's what she's trying to do now. What we don't know is how."

"But not using the Cailleach, we know that," said Flann, hoping to goodness that there was something we knew.

"She had nothing to do with the Cailleach," Britta assured her, "that's the St. Maur Kers."

Mrs. Danvers clanked out into the kitchen.

"How did you get here?" Flann asked, scraping up the last of the soup. She did not know what it was made of, but it was so delicious and soothing and invigorating that she did not really care. "You are not normally at Cobwell."

Britta drew a deep breath in, and sighed it out.

"No," she agreed, "I'm not. I am in the smithy up near the Callows. But my sisters are... not well."

Flann put down her spoon. Mrs. Danvers took away the soup-bowl, and put a plate in front of Flann.

"Not well?" she repeated. "In what way not well?"

Britta hesitated, and Flann asked,

"Is this because of the Cailleach?"

"The Bridgets hibernate," Raftery said to Britta, "don't you? That's what Mick told me. When the Cailleach wakes up for the winter, the Bridgets hibernate. And when the winter is over, and the Bridgets wake up, the Cailleach... the Cailleach... aestivates."

"Very good," Britta agreed. "But we have a problem. Because it's all at the wrong time, and in the wrong places, the Cailleach is not just waking up. She's trying to break out. She's getting bigger and bigger. So, Bridie and Bridget aren't just falling asleep. They are fading away."

238

Flann took several seconds to understand what Britta was saying. She still felt confused and dopey, and could not imagine Bridget, full of chat and opinions, being quiet, let alone fading.

"Why aren't you fading, then?" Raftery asked, and then added politely, "I don't mean I think you should. You're much nicer not faded."

"Thank you," said Britta gravely. "I'm not fading because I am a blacksmith. Blacksmiths belong to roads and ways and paths, not to places. I never fully sleep in winter. What the St. Maur Kers are doing to the Cailleach does not affect me so much. But Bridget and Bridie are different."

Flann sat slumped, thinking about this, and then she suddenly pulled herself together. Keer had taken Villa away, and if St. Maur Ker mischief was now leaving its sticky fingerprints on Cobwell's people, then Britta did not have time to sit about waiting for Flann to gather her wits.

"So what do we do? How do we get Villa back? Stop your sisters fading?"

"First thing is to get you back to Cobwell," Britta stood up. "Mick and Ray have gone to try and negotiate with the Storm Kelpies, or at least clear up a bit of the mess, now that the storms are hitting the coastlines. Lou and Mr. Gabriel have gone to Inishcanara, to try to get onto the island, without killing anyone."

"Who is in Cobwell, then? Peg and Jolyon?"

"Soon everyone in Tubberlue will be there," said Britta, "the winter is setting in with a vengeance. Cobwell will have to host the village and the surrounding farms. It's going to get cosy."

Even as Britta spoke, Flann shivered, and realised that for the first time in months, she was chilly. Britta went upstairs and came back with a blue woollen cardigan, and handed it to Flann.

"It'll be a bit big, but it's warm. Right, I need to find something. Jolyon asked me to…" Britta trailed off when she started looking at the shelf. Flann asked if she could help, and Britta told her she was looking for a book about harps.

"Harps?"

Britta nodded.

"Jolyon is fixing an old harp that Villa found upstairs. Bridget thinks she has a book on ancient harps, but her memory isn't the best, what with the fading."

"He's fixing a *harp*?" Flann repeated, as Mrs. Danvers clanked back in with a plate of apple-tart. "The world is cracking open and he's fixing a harp?"

"If the world were really cracking apart," said Mrs. Danvers, "you may as well go with a song as a shriek. Music is better than money any day of the week. It was Lou told him to make the harp, so there must be a reason."

"Who *is* Lou?" Flann asked.

"Lou is the reason that Cobwell is here," answered Raftery. Finding them all staring at him, he added, "Mick told me."

Flann was not quite satisfied with the answer, but the apple-tart required her attention. She went to the shelves on the other side of the room, where Bridget kept her books on music, and found some books about fixing harps. Raftery, following her, said,

"When I was beside Littlefish Water, Keer told me a story, so that I wouldn't worry about Decker chasing you and Villa chasing him. She told me the story of the hazelnut tree that grew beside the Well of Knowledge, and how nuts fell into the Well, and fish ate them."

Flann gave the books to Britta, and they all sat down again. Seeing that Raftery was eyeing the apple-tart, Mrs. Danvers fished an extra spoon out of her arm, and gave it to him.

"You already knew that story, Raffles."

"But Keer told it like she was there," Raftery said, through apple and pastry. "Details. What birds were singing. What plants grew there. And how frightening it was when Boann picked the nut. She said it was like the garden shattered into pieces and was flung hither and yon across the country. The water from the well turned into a raging river, miles wide and sweeping all before it, and everything in the garden was swept away."

"That sounds… very exciting," Flann wondered if it perhaps had been too vivid for a seven-year-old. Raftery seemed as placid as ever.

"She said the flood had—" Raftery stopped to recall the words, "—a casual brutality."

"Oh, my," said Flann hurriedly, but Britta said

"Let him tell it."

"So there's Littlefish Water and that's magical," Raftery carefully cut in two the last piece of apple-tart, "and

241

there's The Pot which is as deep as a hole that was made when a chunk of magical garden landed on it, and there's the lane between here and Littlefish, that no-one would let you walk down on your own. Ciarnat said the lane is in the otherworld as well as in this one. So it was probably made at the same time. The chunk of Garden might be Eightfoot Island."

"And what, Raftery *a mhic*," asked Britta, "did you conclude from that?"

"What did I what?"

"What did you conclude? What did you decide must be the explanation for all this?"

"Cobwell," said Raftery. "A cob is an old word for a hazelnut. Mick told me that. Hazelnut Well. Cobwell is where the Well of Knowledge was."

He ate his last spoonful.

"Or still is," he added. "Otherwise, what's all the fuss about the Salmon?"

"Raftery, how did you know Littlefish Water was enchanted?"

Raftery raised his eyebrows at Flann.

"Sure, wasn't I in it," he said, and licked the spoon. "I might be seven, but I'm not blind. Sea-Centaurs? Merpeople? Blackstar Whales *in a lake*?"

Britta laughed.

"You take after your grandmother Gale," she told him, and then added to Flann, as Raftery went out with Mrs. Danvers to get some lemonade, "Your mama's going to love that, she likes to pretend you are all completely human. No," she said, as Flann was poised to launch a flotilla of questions, "we haven't time. Tell me what you found in Decker's laboratory. I presume that's why you were there."

Flann sighed, and looked around for her bag. From it she pulled Villa's camera, squashing down a rush of dreadful anxiety about where Villa had been taken to by Ciarnat. Carefully, she unhinged the viewer, and held it out to Britta, and pushed down the lever. Britta made a face, but said nothing, as image after moving image flicked by: jars full of cloudy liquid full of thumping fists and rolling eyes; the panting creature with its chest incision, still on the operating table; a terrible pit, filled with scraps that still had fingers or a tail attached, hidden behind some leafless thorn-trees. Finally, Britta snapped the camera shut.

"A present from her grandmother, I expect," she remarked as she handed it back. "I presume Mrs. Danvers has all the jars and the cages opened by now and the place empty?"

"Yes," Flann agreed. "She wouldn't let me help, she said it was more important that I take away the proof of what Decker was doing. It was lucky for Decker that he was turned to dust," she burst out, "he'd have been ripped to shreds if he had gone back to High Tide House."

"When Decker was not able to run the conference in Prague," Britta said, "what happened?"

"What do you mean, 'what happened'?"

"I mean, when he couldn't be there, did the conference have to be abandoned?"

"Well, no, of course not," Flann said, folding up the camera, "they got my mother to do it."

Britta was looking at her, expecting something, but Flann just frowned at her, uncomprehendingly.

"Decker wasn't some sort of rogue," Britta said, "St. Maur Ker depended on him, and on people like him. Why do you think he rose so high in their ranks? Because he was what they needed."

"St. Maur Ker always deny that they use elf-parts," Flann said, and Britta raised her eyebrows.

"If you believe everything told to you by people who have power," she said, "you've learned nothing from your books. People want the things that are produced by the very things the same people claim to reject. The St. Maur Kers say the use of elf-parts is reprehensible, but they thrive on machines that have to be muted. They say they protect nature, but what they don't cut down, they dig out, or kill so they can sell it, technomance it, or eat it. And the really important thing is this: the St. Maur Kers will always find someone who will do what the St. Maur Kers need to do. There will always be a Decker; dust one Decker, another one rises."

Flann looked away. She felt cold as ice, and shaky and, dimly, somewhere, she felt angry.

"I'm sorry to say it," said Britta, sounding actually sorry, "but St. Maur Ker gets stronger each time people turn a blind eye in exchange for comfort. If that doesn't stop, they will burn down all our houses. And we don't have time anymore for your finer feelings."

She paused for a moment, and added,

"Come on. We'd better hustle our bustles. I've Bridie's jeep outside, and we've a lot of work to do on Cobwell, if winter is to be earlier and longer."

Twenty-Three

They went out to Bridie's car, and Britta told them to pile in. She fished something out of her pocket, a small angular shape made out of reeds. With a single blow of her fist, she hammered it into the door of the house. Then she climbed into the jeep, saying happily,

"I don't often get to drive one of these."

Flann closed her eyes as the jeep heeled over onto its wing-mirrors first on one side, then on the other as it flew round corners. Miraculously, there was nothing else on the road, and they sped on without interruption, or slowing or even, Flann noticed, changing gears. Britta took them through Tubberlue so fast that the single signpost spun around and forever more pointed the wrong way. Up the road out of the village they went, leaping the potholes like fences. They leaped a couple of hedges, too, to cut out a curve in the road. Over the bridge on the river, sideways through the little copse of trees that marked the boundary of the farm, and over the gate into the yard at Cobwell. As they screeched to a halt, the doors sprang open and everyone was tumbled out.

Once in the house, the fear that Britta's driving had instilled in Flann grew stronger. The kitchen was full of people, but it was very quiet, and tense. Peg was making heroic amounts of tea, and Jolyon was buttering toast as though tomorrow saw the end of all buttered toast. Flann watched, and then was startled to realise that she couldn't stand around with empty hands. She went up to Peg, and said,

"What's going on? Who is coming? What can I do? God, I sound like Villa."

Peg looked briefly surprised, but adjusted immediately.

"We don't know how long this winter will last, nor how killing a season it will be. We're bringing our neighbours in here, into Cobwell's protection, so we need to house the animals and the people, and we need to feed them."

Herds of animals were on their way up from the farms around Tubberlue, and all the farmhands were busy with these new arrivals, with preparing housing for those with young, puzzling over which fields the others could go into, and sorting out shelter and water-supplies. It being Cobwell, some of this was surprisingly easy, as shelter-belts of trees popped up like mushrooms when Britta went by, and she had a convenient capacity to multiply the bales of hay and the buckets of feed so they could be stretched to feed the multitude. Peg whisked by with extra crockery and soup tureens, and asked Flann if she'd mind putting clean linen in the spare bedrooms on the second floor; the extra linen-presses were in the junk-room at the top of the house. Raftery went with her. He was too small to manage the sheets, but he brought the blankets, and put towels and bars of soap in the bathrooms, and he had the bright idea of putting some books in each room, in case the visitors were lonely. Britta came upstairs to help. So many people were arriving that extra sleeping space had to be squeezed into each room. Britta dug out sleeping-bags and camp beds, and Flann helped move furniture to fit in as many spaces as possible.

"Britta," she said, when they finally decided they deserved a break, "why can't Lou just rescue the Cailleach? I mean—I don't exactly know who Lou is, but…"

"The humans have had help." Britta said, holding open the kitchen door for them, "we think. They are using a form of magic in which connections between things are so tiny, and so multitudinous, that it is extremely risky to touch anything. We don't know how they are doing it, they do not genuinely have half enough magic for that."

"Who is helping them?"

"We don't know," said Britta, "we don't know who it is. Or where. But if Lou just broke through the St. Maur Ker defence grid around the island, the Cailleach might be killed."

Flann made three mugs of cocoa, and Britta refreshed the toast with a snap of her fingers. Afterwards, Britta said they needed to start seeing to the food stores.

"I'll ask Mrs. Danvers to help," said Flann, scoffing down the last of her toast, "you finish your cocoa."

Before she went out into the yard to find the automaton, Flann hurried to the porch where she had left the bag she had brought with her to Littlefish, and took out the camera.

Villa was a good swimmer, but with the Blackstar in her pocket, she glided through the water of the caves like a dolphin. Her first plan was to swim out from the caves, into the River Fass, and up the river to Cobwell. Then she realised that this would lead Keer closer to The Wilderness. There was no time to stop and think, Villa kept choosing the smallest of the branching hollows and corridors, too small for Keer's boat. She swam for the nearest pinpoint of light; once there, she could get her bearings, and take the Blackstar out of her pocket.

But as fast as she swam, the Fuath were faster. As soon as she reached daylight, Villa rose out of the water for the first time to get some air, and gagged on the stench that accompanied Keer's soldiers. Two of them rose up out of the water, shoulder to shoulder, and blocked her view of the river. The water was oily and dull green around them. Villa dived backwards and started to swim away but she was too late. Keer's boat came speeding along beside her, and Keer, leaning out the starboard side, scooped Villa up by the scruff of the neck and dumped her on the floor of the boat.

The path they had taken through the caves had brought them out north of Cobwell, to the River Cora, one of the tributaries that flowed into the Great River. Now that they were away from Cobwell, they had no protection from the storms that the Kelpies were whipping up. Villa was shivering violently, hardly able to open the latch of the cabin. Once in, the brief respite from the lashing rain and the blades of wind was such a relief that she hunted about with renewed vigour to find something dry to wear. She even managed to find a towel, and she warmed up her hands and feet by scrubbing them till they glowed pink as a pigeon's. She took off what she was wearing, took the Blackstar out of her pocket, and clambered into the dry clothes she had found. They were too big, and made of very rough cloth, but they were dry, and warm, and better designed for withstanding inclement weather. She pushed open the door and went out. Keer glanced around, looked at her, and started to laugh.

"Sorry," she said, wiping tears from her face, and slapping her thigh. "Oh, a good laugh is as good as a medicine."

"They're proper clothes for sailing in," said Villa, with dignity.

"You look like you're moulting."

Before Villa could respond, a violent gust caught the sails and drove the boat forward so fast that it left the surface of the water, and crashed down with an enormous splash into the middle of the river, tipping so much to one side that the sails smacked the water. As soon as the sails had begun to bell, Villa had wrapped her arms around the mast, and Keer clung to the other one, so though they were badly shaken, they were still on board. The wild wind made the waves billow, and as the light boat turned sideways on to the next wave, Villa scrambled like a crab over the floor and grabbed the helm, and shouted at Keer,

"Pull the headsail around!"

"What??"

"The headsail! The headsail, pull the headsail!"

Villa pointed wildly, and by blind good luck, the bar which Keer grasped belonged to the headsail. She swung it around. The boat slewed around and instead of being swamped sideways-on to the wave, the prow tipped up and the boat skimmed the top of the wave, wavered vertiginously on the crest, then sped down the other side like a skier.

"Some feckin' water-divinity you are," Villa said grumpily, "can't tell a headsail from a bucket of bilge-water."

"Excuse you me!" Keer retorted, "I'm used to swimming with whales and dining with Neptune, not taking orders from some ragamuffin boat-wrangler!"

Most of their angry words were lost in the whining wind. The sails were snapping like beaks, and the usually placid river was smacking the boat left and right with waves that threatened to turn the vessel over. Villa struggled with the helm, keeping the boat's prow pointing towards the waves, and Keer struggled, barely able to hear Villa's shouted instructions, to manage the sails.

With the wild wind behind them, the boat leaped and crashed its way down the river, and skidded sideways into Lough Farderg, where the river ended.

The Kelpies were stirring up several storms, winds came from every direction, all Villa could do was try to make sure that the boat skimmed the top of the waves, and did not get caught in the trough. The rain lashed them and the storm-swollen sails battered Villa and Keer about the fragile craft. The giant waves washed them to the middle of the lake. Villa couldn't decide where they should aim for: aiming for the open lake brought them into the teeth of the storm, steering for bank risked being broken to bits on the shore. She finally hauled the helm round to the north, but in the event, it made no difference.

The wave rose, and rose, and crashed. The boat was flung about, and as they spun along the trough of a wave Villa feared that the weight of the water would swamp the little craft, and tip them out into the riotous water. She turned, and as she did she saw the flash of scales: emerald, amber, and ruby, underneath the green-grey mud.

"Oh don't tell me," she said aloud, "is there a single lake in this whole country that doesn't have its own freaking monster?"

She seized the helm and pulled to the west. The boat struggled against the rising of the water, cut through a swell of a growing wave, and crashed into a solid, scaly block. Villa yelled at Keer to take the helm, and keep the boat pointed westwards and the prow up and over the back of… whatever it was, circling under the storm.

Villa wrestled with the sails. Keer kept the boat's prow upwards, levelled it, to keep it safely cresting the waves, but a scaled tail thrashed about, a scaly back circled, searching, so the boat was knocked clear of the water, and sent skipping like a stone over the waves. Scales heaved and flashed past the port side—whatever it was, was trying to lasso the boat. Villa squinted through the rain to the starboard side and stared straight into an eye, rising above the water. The eye was as red as fire, the iris white as pearls, the pupil vertical like a goat's eye. The skin of the face that held the eye was red too, bright like a poppy, deep like a gem, and the hand that came down through the water was red, with a palm that blazed orange like lava.

Before the spasm of terror that gripped Villa had passed, the vermillion palm had lifted up the boat, and the ruby-red figure took the craft out of the water, and with two gigantic steps, took it to the edge of the lake, and pushed it out the mouth of the river, and into the sea.

While Flann was setting up Villa's camera in the kitchen, she heard a burst of static. Startled, she looked about, uncertain what she expected to see. The sound came again, and a third time. Flann, darting about the kitchen like a bird in search of egress, hunted the sound down to the radio in Jolyon's workroom. When she went to it, the camera under her arm, the radio began beeping, the faint, familiar sound that preceded Bram's Eye-Gram making contact. Rolling her eyes, she fiddled with the dial, and Bram's face flickered into sight, an incomplete face, in streaks like heavy rain on glass.

"Just letting you know," he said crisply, "St. Maur Ker decided to send a team to Inishcanara, and Dr. Breck asked me to be on it."

Send a team in, Flann thought, fumbling with the camera, *drama queen.*

"I'm on the boat now," Bram added curtly, the tone he used when he felt very important, "St. Maur Ker's private schooner."

"Don't fall overboard," Flann said equally curtly. "And while you're hobnobbing with the St. Maur Kers, have a look at these."

She flipped up the camera's viewing lever as Villa had shown her, pressed the silver button, and closed the lid shut.

"What are these?" he said, reaching up to adjust the receptor on the EyeGram,. "Where did these—"

The hologram shrivelled up so abruptly that Flann knew Bram had yanked the gadget off his face.

Thrusting from her mind the fact that Bram had, in effect, slammed a door on her, Flann left the camera safely on a chair, and went out to find Mrs. Danvers.

"What's eating you?" Mrs. Danvers said, opening the first of the storage presses in the pantry behind the kitchen, "You're radiating rage."

"Nothing."

"You shouldn't tell lies. It's not good for you."

"I sent the photographs I took to Bram," Flann blurted out, "the photographs from Decker's laboratory.

And he shut down his EyeGram. That's like pressing someone's mouth shut."

Mrs. Danvers said,

"He's probably had a shock. You know. They're not pretty photographs."

"I don't want to have to do stuff like that!" Flann growled, "I just want to be left alone. But I'm the one that has to go and take nasty photographs as evidence, and he gets to go swanning off with the St. Maur Kers while I'm stuck here changing bed linen. Villa does whatever she wants, and I'm left in a pantry counting jars of beans!"

"I didn't think you'd want to be in the middle of the action," Mrs. Danvers said mildly, and Flann retorted,

"I don't. I want to be left alone. But if I can't be left alone, I'm sick of being the one that has to tidy up after people, has to keep an eye on them, keep them out of trouble."

"You could always refuse," Mrs. Danvers said, but Flann protested,

"I don't want to have to refuse. I want not to be asked."

"Welcome to the world, darlin'," Mrs. Danvers said, impatiently. "Why do you think Villa blew up the rugby pitch?"

"How did you know about that?"

"You've never lived in a village, have you? Everyone in a two-mile radius knew half an hour after Villa told Cobwell. She didn't like the way things were, but she didn't expect to ask and to get."

Flann said nothing. It had never occurred to her that Villa might have been justified.

Blowing up rugby pitches, she thought, resentfully. *Goats.* Aloud, she said,

"Sorry for grousing. Where do we start?"

Twenty-Four

Bram flicked through the pictures that Flann had sent to him, hardly able to look at them. He was shaking, both at the photographs themselves, but also with anger, obscurely furious at Flann. He felt rather than heard Breck approach him, and she glanced down at the screen, too quickly for him to be able to shut it off.

"Oh," said Breck, looking from the screen to him. "Who sent you those? Your sister?"

Bram nodded, suddenly and mortifyingly uncertain of where he stood.

"Well," Breck said mildly, "you know we only do what is necessary. Nothing more."

Bram looked around the boat. He had no idea if it was a schooner or not. It could have been a tub or a dreadnought, he just said schooner so as to sound confident.

"Some lessons are harder to learn than others," Breck said, stepping round slowly so that she stood in front of him, and she put her hand on his arm, "and sometimes —how will I say this? Sometimes you grow up slowly and at an easy pace. And sometimes you grow up in a big lurch, when you find out something you weren't expecting, but that you must, you must absolutely, accept and understand."

Bram said nothing, and neither did Breck. The boat whipped through the water and the fog. Bram could see the ferocity of the wind, and the piling of purple clouds on black, the vicious storm that would snap him off the boat and drown him in the grey sea, if it were not for the glimmering, protective glamour with which St. Maur Ker had shrouded the boat.

"You have to have the right priorities," Breck said, sympathetically, "you know? Even if it's a bit of a shock to find out what they are. We can't tell everyone everything. We need to know that you are singing in the same choir as the rest of us."

Bram sighed.

"I know," he said, "I know."

He deleted the first image, and Breck smiled, and squeezed his hand, and with the other hand, he went on deleting them, one after another, until the screen was clear. Then he flipped the screen shut, and put the Eye-Gram in his pocket. Breck slipped her arm through his, and squeezed it.

"We'll be at the island in a few minutes," she said, "I'll show you around the yacht. You'll love it."

The storms were still raging. The wind was whipping the water to a froth, and the clouds to tatters. Villa glimpsed what might have been shadows and the rags of thick clouds, but that looked like figures of people, wheeling within streams of misty hair, stretching out powerful arms and letting their long fingers mingle with the clouds. To the south was a dark streak that was Inishcanara, so blurred by brume and cloud that it might have been made of felt. Just visible against the charcoal of the cliff was a flake of brightness, a large boat bobbing on the cinder-dark waves.

Villa seized the spar of the headsail, and began to draw it in, so that it would not take up so much of the wind. As she worked, she looked about it, blinking cascading rain out of her eyes, trying to spot somewhere that might act as sanctuary. From horizon to horizon, there was thrashing sea, and the sky heaped with rain-clouds, veiled with lashing rain, and boiling with angry, angry Storm Kelpies.

She had no idea which direction would be better or worse to sail in, but though further out to sea took her further into the storm, it also took Keer further from Cobwell.

Flann was counting up jars of pickled eggs and dried apples, and writing down the figures in a 'Cellarer's Notebook', which was the size and weight of a hearth-stone. Britta was in the cold store. The wind rose to a whining hum, the clouds hung low and dark, and rain drummed like hailstones on the window. Raftery was sitting by the fire with his *Maps of Impossible Lands*. Flann put the jars back onto the top shelf of the press, and started on the next shelf. She glanced over at her brother.

"Find anywhere interesting, Raffles?" Flann asked. "Anywhere we might go on our holidays next year?"

"No," Raftery said absentmindedly, "these are maps of countries under the water."

"Really?" Flann said, beginning to return the jars to their press, "Like where? Atlantis?"

"Atlantis is further away," Raftery said, turning the page, "these are all near Hibernia."

"We won't run out of beetroot, anyway," said Britta coming back in, "and Mrs. Danvers tells me the carrots have been harvested and we have a few tons of them sanded down in the clamp."

"Where in Hibernia?" Flann said to Raftery, and wrote down *beetroot fine, carrots 'sanded down in the clamp' whatever that might mean.*

"Off the west coast," Raftery said. "There's a map here of roads from Lough Farderg to Inishcanara, Hy-Brasil, and to another place called the Isle of the Dark."

"How are we for peas?" Britta asked. "Peg pickled a peck of peppers earlier, count those in. And the kale and the cabbages can..."

Her voice trailed away. She put down the jars she was holding, and went over to the fireplace.

"From Farderg to Inishcanara, Raftery? Can I see?"

Raftery held out his book. Britta knelt down beside his seat, and frowned over the page, pinching her lip thoughtfully. She turned over a few pages, and turned back to the page he had shown her. Then she stood up.

"You're a handy man to have around, Raftery. I'd better get away."

"Away?" Flann said in alarm, "Away where?"

"I know how we can get to Inishcanara," said Britta, "thanks to Raftery."

"What?"

"Look at his book," Britta said. "There are old ways all across this island, the Great Way west to East, the roads that Queen Meadhbh travelled, the wild horses of Tinnybearna. But I should have remembered—there are old ways in the sea, too. Look."

She drew her finger along the paths drawn on the map, some as big as main roads, with many smaller ones branching away and either leading to islands, or joining a current or a tide. She traced the line of a path out of Lough Farderg, and tapped the island where it stopped: Inishcanara.

"What good is that to us?" Flann asked, "At the bottom of the sea?"

"I can borrow the lend of a horse, from the stables of a sea-god. A horse who has the invaluable ability to travel as easily through water as it can through grass."

"Enbarr," exclaimed Raftery, bouncing to his feet, "the horse owned by Manannán Mac Lir? He let his foster-son Lúgh borrow it. I read that."

"Lou?" said Flann.

"Yes, Lúgh," said Raftery. Flann felt light-headed.

"Well, I wouldn't say Enbarr was owned by anyone," Britta said, "but what Lou can borrow, Cobwell can borrow.

From what Lou says, the St. Maur Kers have tied up every way in which the island can be reached from the sea or the air. But maybe not under the water. They might not have expected that. We may be able to get to the Cailleach yet, and still dodge the Storm Kelpies."

Neither Flann nor Britta had noticed Mrs. Danvers rolling up beside them. It had been listening attentively, and when Britta finished speaking, Mrs. Danvers said,

"St. Maur Ker will have the island infested with auto-mata. They'll be everywhere—in the sea, in the belly of the island, in the air, over every inch of the place."

"We'll have to... deal with them," Britta said, "I'm sorry, but..."

Mrs. Danvers' metal face creaked and shrieked into a smile.

"I've a much better idea. Flann, have you got that screwdriver handy? It might be time for a lesson."

Once Villa had finished taking down the headsail and tying back the mainsail, the boat caught less of the wind. Though it was still flung about on the waves, Keer was able to steer it, keeping the prow at the crests of the waves, to let the vessel skate over them. The wind was hooting, the water hissed and crashed. Villa inched down the length of the boat.

"Let me take it," she shouted. Keer shook her head.

"Stronger than you," she shouted back. "Wouldn't want you overboard—you're not a semi-immortal."

"I'll bail out then," Villa shouted, and as she started to inch her way back up towards the gunwale, Keer shouted after her,

"You're fairly handy in a boat."

Villa looked back at Keer, startled by being complimented by someone who had kidnapped her, and was threatening to incarcerate her for eternity in a portal. Keer was looking out over the wild sea, and her strange, frosted blue skin seemed peculiarly shining, white stars sparking from her fingers and being whipped from her streaming hair by the wind. Villa hunted under the gunwale, and found a small wooden bowl, and she started to bail out: the water was ankle-deep on the rocking floor of the boat. When she had finished, Keer called to her to come and take the helm. The Storm Kelpies seemed to have withdrawn a little, to the far side of Inishcanara, and though the sea was still high and wild, the crests of the waves were not so high, nor the troughs so deep.

"You'll be alright for a few minutes."

"Where are you going?"

"I'm going for a swim," Keer said, "I have been caged for I don't know how long."

"Are you coming back?"

"I am, you needn't get your hopes up."

She stepped onto the edge of the boat, so lightly that it barely tipped, and dived into the water, causing a swell that washed the craft to one side, spinning it so that it was sideways-on to a coming wave, and Villa had to wrestle the helm, and adjust the mainsail so that the boat was not swamped. Along with the dry clothes she had found in the cabin, Villa had also found a pair of binoculars, and she trained these on Inishcanara. The Storm Kelpies were circling the island, and clouds swirled around them, heaping down rain. As Villa watched, the clouds broke up and the Kelpies began to stir the wind and the sea in wider and wider circles around the island.

The boat began to bob vigorously, as the water rose, and then it tilted to starboard. Guessing that Keer was climbing back on board, Villa cursed herself for not having taken out the Blackstar immediately, so that Keer would be unable to find her way back. The boat tilted to port, so far over that it took on more water. Villa did not dare leave the helm when the water was so rough, and even as she said to herself that she would make Keer bail out the water, Keer rose up in front of the boat's prow, and shouted something at her, but the wind and the rain were too noisy, and Villa couldn't hear.

"What? What?" she kept shouting. The waves began to rise but to her alarm, however much she turned the helm, the boat did not turn, and instead it seemed to go backwards. Keer swam alongside, and hauled herself in.

"I tried to warn you!" she said. "We can try and row—"

"Warn me about what?"

"That."

Villa lost her balance when the boat jolted violently, but even as she fell she saw what Keer meant. The St. Maur Ker yacht emerged from the sea-fret, right behind them. Leaning over the railing was Sylvestra St. Maur Ker, and Dr. Breck.

"Hey there," Breck yelled at them, waving vigorously, "nice to see you! It's very good of you to agree to give us your Blackstar, Villa!"

Breck vaulted over the side of the yacht and landed feet first into the boat, driving the light craft under the surface of the water. Villa went down with it, and forced her eyes open so she could grab hold of a mast. Breck seized her around the waist, gripping her so tightly that Villa could not so much as kick, and swam them both to the surface. She dumped Villa across the side of the boat so that the oar-brace punched her in the stomach, and Breck, treading the stormy water easily, began tearing at Villa's pocket. Then, with a loud and vulgar yell, Breck disappeared under the water.

Villa scrambled the rest of the way into the boat, and, peering down, could just see that it was Keer who had wrestled Breck away. But Breck was not delayed long; she slithered out of Keer's grasp, and boarded the boat from the other side. Climbing on board, she did not hesitate to punch Villa hard enough to spin her round, and while Villa was lying, stunned, on the bottom of the boat, Breck ripped her pocket away in its entirety, grasped the Blackstar, and flipped Villa easily overboard. As soon as she saw Villa flail her arms and go under, Breck started hunting about for the emergency axe, so as to scuttle the boat, when Keer rose up out of the water, six feet, seven feet, over her. Breck dropped the axe, and lunged for the rope swinging over the side of the yacht, and was up it as fast as a rat up a drain. The yacht reversed, turned briskly, and sped towards shore.

Villa recovered her senses, and sat up. After a minute or so, the sea ruffled violently as Keer strode angrily through it.

"I can't see Breck's face," Keer said, shrinking a little and climbing on board, "without wanting to punch it."

"I thought you were planning to join in with them," Villa said abruptly. "Control the portal at Cobwell. Trade elf-parts with them."

There was no answer, and Villa looked up.

Twenty-Five

Keer was frowning at the bilge-water channel. She looked very uncomfortable, and—surprising in a semi-immortal —a bit sheepish. Villa sat back on her heels. The boat was beginning to dance a little on the rising waves, and the sails began to snap dully.

"You kidnap me," she said very loudly, "you claim you're going to try and take over the portal at Cobwell, you're going to make a slave of me, you drag me out into the middle of a storm, and now you aren't even going to turn out to be one of the VILLAINS?"

"Don't yell," said Keer.

"I'm not yelling," Villa yelled, "I could have been home by now! And that bollocks Breck has my Blackstar!"

Villa stopped abruptly, hearing a terrible quaver in her voice, and having the awful feeling that her rage might liquify and emerge as tears. She pressed her lips together and swallowed. It would have been easier if she had been a goat. She could have head-butted something.

"I'm sorry," Keer said, "I'm really sorry. I meant to turn evil, I promise. I really meant to be one of the villains.

I told you the truth. But… things have changed."

"What? What things?"

"We don't have time now," said Keer. "I don't want to alarm you, but on top of Breck and St. Maur Ker having your Blackstar, they have Fuath in their crew. If the Fuath told me about the portal at Cobwell, they will have told St. Maur Ker as well."

Villa sighed, feeling suddenly as limp as a wet sock. "We'd better get going," she said, "come on. Get the oars out."

"You steer, I'll row," said Keer. "You could do with a rest."

They clipped the oars into the braces, and Keer settled down to row, while Villa began to pick her way towards the steering paddle. Just as she sat down, the radio crackled violently, like an overturned hen. She and Keer looked at it in astonishment. The boat was small enough that Villa could keep one hand on the tiller and still step over to look more closely at the radio. Tied to one corner was a label, that read 'Call-Sign: Wave-Sweeper'. The burst of static and noise came again. Villa picked up the head-set, flipped the switch, and said,

"This is Wave-Sweeper. Come in, this is Wave-Sweeper. Who are you? *Who??*"

Inishcanara was virtually hidden in the brume rising from the storm-whipped sea. It was a small, compact island, with several beaches suitable for landing on, but the sea was so wild that there was no possibility of the boat getting anywhere near it. The mist and the spray from the thrashing sea were so thick, and rose so high, that they mingled with the low, ashy clouds. Here and there, where the clouds were higher or the whipping wind blew holes in the mist, the wispy shapes of the Storm Kelpies were visible.

"I'll see what I can do," Keer shouted. "Just try not to drown."

The light was so murky that Villa barely saw the flicker of sapphire-blue as Keer slid over the edge of the boat and disappeared into the water.

The water was still heaving, but a channel was forming between two rough billows, and Villa wrestled the boat onto it. The water glittered like fish-scales, and battered the boat as it sped along. It crashed up onto the sandy beach, and Keer crashed up after it. Villa looked around, afraid to land the boat properly, remembering what she had been told about the 'subtle devices' the St. Maur Kers used to stop anyone getting onto Inishcanara. She looked around. It had been Bram who called the Wave-Sweeper, who gave them a hurried and garbled story of why he was on Inishcanara, and who told them to join him there. Between Keer's sudden change of heart, and Bram apparently defying the St. Maur Kers, Villa did not know what was best to do, but under the circumstances, she had not had much choice. She had turned the boat towards the island, and hoped that Bram would turn up. To her inexpressible relief she saw him, shivering and drenched, emerge from the shadows of the cliff-face.

He helped them pull the boat up out of the reach of the sea, and they hurried, struggling against the wind, up the slope to a large pair of metal doors. Bram pushed one open, and urged Villa and Keer inside. Before she went in, Villa glanced back down to the shore to see if the boat was still safe. She seized Bram's arm, and tugged it, pointing.

The water was shining. Light moved fast, branching out like lightning, turning channels of water white for a moment, and then moving on, and the water dimmed but only to the colour of diamonds. Villa looked at Bram, and they both looked at Keer, but Keer shook her head and shrugged.

"Get in, then," Bram urged, "we haven't got long. And who knows what those lights are."

"How are we able to get onto the island?" Villa asked breathlessly, as Bram rushed them through dark, narrow passageways. "Lou said—"

"I know what Lou said," Bram opened a door, "but before she left for Cobwell, Dr. Breck showed me how to shut off the security system, so the alarms would not ring every time I left the laboratory. But that's only the ground system. What is keeping Lou away is enchantment. I can't do anything about that."

Bram shut the door behind them, and opened another. They walked out onto a circular mezzanine floor, above a large glass tank. Villa peered down into it.

At first, all she could see was what looked like a circuit board, with sheaves of wires coming out of it. The wires—some as big as her little finger, but most as thin as pins—curved up over the railing around the tank, where they attached to bigger and bigger tubes, that plugged finally into huge glass containers attached to the ceiling. The containers were too high overhead for Villa to be able to guess the contents, but they were strongly coloured, every shade of the rainbow, and one that reminded Villa of Lou's coat, an indefinable brightness. She looked down into the tank again, and then crouched down to see what lay beneath the circuit board. Seeing it didn't tell her anything. There was a flat disc of shining metal, with what she knew at once was an orrery, but she was puzzled by the models of the planets. They did not look familiar. Under this disc was a what she guessed was a machine, a blunted triangle of tiny plates of metal welded together, with tubes and valves sprouting from each side. The whole thing had a dense covering of tiny tubes and channels, some filled with a blue and gold liquid, some with red and silver.

"What is it?" she asked, pointing, "Why are we here?"

"I may as well tell you now," Bram said, "I don't know what is going to happen. I don't know exactly what this thing is, but I believe it is the key to the steam-god Lou told us about—as far as I can guess, it's like the heart."

"Is the Cailleach here?" Villa demanded, "Where's this machine? Have you seen it? Where's the Cailleach?"

"I don't know, Villa," Bram said tensely. "Stop asking questions. I don't know. They didn't tell me. It's a guess. I think the machine is right down in the middle of the island, and I think the Cailleach is in it. They wouldn't show it to me, so it's a guess."

"What are we going to do?" Villa said, and Bram said,

"I'm going to break the machine," Bram said, and Villa goggled at him. He was pale, and sweating.

"Then we are going to run away as fast as we can in your boat," he said, "because I think the minute it happens, we're going to have the St. Maur Ker down our throats."

Bram reached the jars, and Villa trotted up behind him.

"What do we do?"

Bram sighed, and then pointed to the wing-nuts on each of the tubes coming out of the jars.

"Turn them, all of them," he said, "they'll open the valves. They brought me here so that I could help them get the machine started up. I was only supposed to let this thing have three drops at a time."

"What do you think will happen?" Villa said, opening valves as fast as she could. Bram's hands were flying over them, and different liquids began oozing through the pipes.

"I think it'll have a massive coronary," Bram said, rather dismally, "and that I will never have a career."

Twenty-Six

When finally the Wave-Sweeper limped up the River Fass to Cobwell, her tattered crew of three was greeted by pitched battle. The St. Maur Kers' *Triumphant* was moored already, so Villa kept well behind. Keer tied the painter to the starboard cleat with a very neat bowline, and Villa scrambled out, dragging the painter, and tying it to a fence-post with a mooring hitch knot. Bram, who had been bailing for the entire trip, put down the scoop in a dazed manner. Villa scuttled down to the boat, and she and Keer and Bram stood looking up the slight slope from the river to Cobwell. It was difficult to see much through the trees, but there was smoke rising from something, there was a lot of shouting, things clashing, cracks like thunder, and flashes of sparks like fireworks.

"We can go up through the trees," Villa said, but Keer shook her head.

"I can't go beyond the water's edge," she said. "Remember Decker? I don't want to be a pile of seaweed."

"Oooh," Villa said, "I forgot that."

"I'll tell you what I can do, though," Keer said. She

picked up the axe that Breck had dropped, twisted it as though to unscrew it, and the axe sprang and snapped, and was instantly three times its size.

"I'll go in under their boat," she continued, "and sink it. They've only left one of the Fuath on board, and I'll get it to follow me. With any luck, the rest will follow it. At least that way, you'll only have St. Maur Ker to deal with."

She clambered over the edge of the boat and sank without a bubble under the water. Villa waited till she had disappeared, and then she and Bram started off through the trees towards the farm.

St. Maur Ker had not been expecting so many people to be on Cobwell, but without the Bridgets, without Lou, without Mr. Gabriel or Mick, Cobwell's defences were considerably reduced. St. Maur Ker's automata were breaking everything apart. When Villa and Bram emerged from among the trees and into the open grass of Home Farm Field, an armoured Fuath was pulling a beech tree out of the ground and using it to fend off Oscar the boar. That Oscar was now the size of a small horse, that his tusks were huge and numbered six, was, by this stage, no surprise to Villa. The Fuath knocked Oscar right off his trotters, but in moments, the boar had twisted the tree out of the Fuath's iron pincers, and flung it away. Villa ran between Oscar and the Fuath and, holding her nose, she gesticulated violently towards where the St. Maur Ker boat was sinking, and where Keer and the last Fuath were swimming away. The Fuath saw them, and surged, then sped away. Oscar shook some bits of tree out of his tusks, and thundered away through the broken fence into the yard. Villa and Bram followed.

The automata were breaking open the walls of the sheds, ripping rooves away and throwing the girders and the corrugated iron around the yard. Others seemed to be trying to set fire to Cobwell House, but every time a window smashed to let in a bottle stuffed with a burning rag, the rag was doused and a shower of glass returned. The wooden sheds where Mick had kept the seeds had been torn to bits and the containers smashed, their contents scattered across the yard. The vegetable patch had been torn up, a hedge ignited, and small birds came shrieking from its burning branches with their feathers alight. One of the dogs lay dead near the carriage, and there were other bodies, too, huddled and slumped and bleeding. One of the horses was on the ground, alive, but thrashing and frothing, with a broken leg.

Villa bolted for the house, and Bram raced behind her. The kitchen door was bolted and they had to hammer on it before Jolyon heard her and let them in. The kitchen was crammed with people, as soon as one rushed out with some new bandage or a replaced weapon, another one rushed in. Villa hopped from tiptoe to tiptoe, trying to find Flann, but it was Peg who finally spotted them, and dragged them both out into the quieter scullery.

"Hallelujah," she said. "Raftery keeps asking."

"What are St. Maur Ker up to?" Villa demanded. "Are

they just breaking everything?"

Peg scrubbed her face, and said, "St. Maur Ker know about The Wilderness. They know about the Well."

"They know that the Well is a portal," said Villa, and when Peg nodded, Villa said, "So that is why Breck took the Blackstar."

"They need more than a Blackstar to keep the portal open," said Peg, "they need one of the aos sídhe."

Peg said nothing for a moment, and then, very uncomfortably,

"Or someone who is even part-sídhe."

Villa waited, and then said,

"What? Who? Murph? Who else is aos sídhe? Or part aos sídhe?"

"Raftery. All of ye, actually, but they're looking for him."

"But we're not part… oooooh."

Bridie saying *you're just like your grandmother*. Mama saying *my mother's… different…* Villa thought *that's how I got into the Wilderness.*

"No," Bram protested. "no, no, no, no, we're not. We can't be. Please. I don't want to be part-sídhe. Not even a tiny part. I'll never work for St. Maur Ker if I'm part-sídhe."

"You don't choose your granny," Peg said bluntly. "Your grandmother Gale is who—or what—she is."

"You've just destroyed St. Maur Ker's shiniest new machine," Villa reminded him cheerfully, "so your chances of working with them are not good anyway."

"Why Raftery?" Bram said, suddenly. "Why not Flann? Or even me?"

"Raftery rather than ye because St. Maur Ker feel safer with someone unable to defend himself."

Villa said nothing. Having reached Cobwell, they had, she thought, reached sanctuary, safe from the Storm Kelpies and the wild sea, safe from St. Maur Ker. They had come with the good news, that the Cailleach was free and the Storm Kelpies cooling down, but now that wasn't enough. The St. Maur Kers were at their door, and Cobwell was not properly defended. Villa thought she knew where Lou was, the Bridgets, maybe even Mr. Gabriel and Mick by now. But she was not sure, and now she would have to take a chance on her guess.

"There's only so long we can keep them back," said Peg, and Villa said,

"They're not getting Raftery."

She reached for the door, and Peg pulled her back.

"Don't," Peg said angrily. "we can't deal with the St. Maur Kers and take care of any heroics."

"It's not heroics," said Villa, wriggling away, "it isn't. Trust me. Bram, can you see if Murph is back yet in her bathysphere? If she is, get Raftery to The Pot, and Murph can hide him in the caves."

"Murph is on her way back?" Peg repeated. "Murph?"

She sounded unbearably relieved. In the hectic bustling of the kitchen, she stood absolutely still, not speaking.

"It's a long story," Villa said. "Britta arrived on Inish-canara, and Murph had followed her, in the bathysphere, as a wing-man—well, a wing-púca, just in case."

Bram picked up the tale. "But St. Maur Ker security was everywhere the minute they landed. Britta said the action was just starting, and that we were to make our-selves scarce. Can't pretend I needed much persuasion. Murph said she'd come back to Cobwell as soon as she could."

"What exactly were you doing on Inishcanara?" Peg sounded suddenly suspicious.

"It's a very long story," Villa said, "and it's probably not a time for story-telling."

"I'll go and see if I can talk to Murph," Bram said, weary but decisive. "Peg, where are Flann and Raftery?"

Peg sighed. Then she took another deep breath, and said,

"So, there's a bit of hope, but it's not all over here. You'd better stay here. Bram, we'll go together, and see about getting Raftery to The Pot."

Peg hurried away, and Villa pulled open the kitchen door before anyone spotted her, and started to trudge across the freezing, muddy yard.

Sylvestra St. Maur Ker was standing well back from any of the fighting, contenting herself with throwing in the odd glamour or curse. Villa walked up behind her, and, just to be annoying, drew Sylvestra's attention by booting her hard in the ankle.

"You can't have Raftery," she said, as soon as St. Maur Ker stopped hopping about clutching her bruised ankle.

"But you can have me," Villa said, loudly so that her voice did not quaver. "I'm not that much older than him. And the Blackstar works with me. That's why Keer kidnapped me. She had the same idea about the portal as you."

"Oh that's why she wouldn't let Breck take you away!" St. Maur Ker said. "I wondered about that. I see. Well, you'll do for the time being, once we... persuade... one of these Cobwell thugs to bring us to The Wilderness and the Glasshouse."

"I can bring you to The Wilderness," said Villa, "but I have to have the Blackstar. Otherwise, we can't cross the boundary."

St. Maur Ker looked at her for quite a long time, not seeming to hear the crashing and yelling going on around them. Then she caught a passing automaton, and flicked open its back-panel. Villa turned away, unable to look at the desperate eyes of the sídhe struggling inside it. Whatever St. Maur Ker did to it, the automaton rushed to the nearest automaton, and cleaved to it like a magnet, and an electrical current leaped from machine to machine, immobilizing the automata and making an electric fence that penned in the Cobwellians. Breck ducked out from under a slumping shed, and joined St. Maur Ker.

"Villa is going to show us how to find The Wilderness," Sylvestra said, "but since that means we have to let her hold our precious Blackstar, I would feel much safer if I knew she could not escape."

Breck snapped her fingers, and immediately held a long, slender piece of rope.

Villa stepped out of the frosty long grass, and rattled over the frozen and churned soil to where this way through the forest began. The silence was absolute, as petrified as the darkness down a well. She breathed through her mouth, afraid that even the silky rustle of air through her tubing would cause a disturbance. St. Maur Ker and Breck crashed out of the grass, and their boots rang against the icy clumps of soil. Villa stopped, jerked to a halt by the length of rope between her wrist and Breck's. She waited. She faced them so that it seemed like she was waiting for them. She was waiting to see what The Wilderness would do.

"Perfect," St. Maur Ker said, striding past Villa and fishing out a little knife, "absolutely marvellous. Oh, I can see this working very well indeed for us."

Villa heard a very faint sound like the swift scrape of a blade over ice. St. Maur Ker was smiling, she looked very happy. Breck's eyes were very bright, and she was on the cusp of smiling, but hesitant, as though she could not quite trust St. Maur Ker's happiness. They had heard nothing.

The sound came again, this time from the trees behind them. Spiralling down like an autumn leaf and scratching out a sound on the frozen air. Deaf to the faint sound, St. Maur Ker beckoned Breck brusquely, not for her to approach, but for her to snick open the specimen bag. Little glass jars clinked softly as they were handed over.

Overhead was another sound, not quite so swift now but a flurry of fractured, noisy notes, indistinct but shrill: ghosts of notes. Villa inched backwards to the edge of the path, away from the open sky. She began picking at the rope that tied her. It was a lousy little half-hitch knot that she could have undone in a minute, but she did not want to alert Breck. Everything depended on Villa being right about The Wilderness. St. Maur Ker, beaming ecstatically, looked around at the forest.

The forest looked back.

Twenty-Seven

The sky was being muffled in evening but there was plenty of light to see by, plenty of air to carry scent and sound, plenty of earth and wood to carry tremors. Grit and small stones ground together, and resounded like cymbals; under every step of St. Maur Ker's kid-skin boot, the ground reverberated to the strike of her heel, and the frozen leaves cracked like gunshot, springing apart when the foot moved on.

Branches, dwindling down to twigs and leaves, were alert to the currents of air that eddied with each movement of something down around the roots, something walking around in increasing circles, then stepping back and forth, one approaching to hand over another glass jar, another retreating a little further to the edge of the path, to where the shadows were. The figures themselves were so tiny beneath the trunks of oaks or the branches of yew as to be barely visible, blurred shadows appearing and disappearing.

There was the smell, too, metallic, but not like petrichor that announces the approach of rain. This was metallic with a tang, not just of human sweat, but of an unpleasantness, like corruption, but not the necessary corruption of death, but of something baser and more alarming, of fear, and despair. Wolves and bears, deer and hares, predator and prey alike stopped to investigate the smell, still as statues, reading the air intently. Predators circling down from their green sky towards the pink and purple of the trees' crowns, saw infinite detail: the knots of shoelaces and the gleam of eyelets, a finger-plaster, buttons, a zip with its twinkle of fading light, a flash of teeth in a satisfied smile, all in shades of grey, or piebald black and white.

Villa took one last step back, and was off the path. St. Maur Ker snicked open her knife, and dug it into the ground—

> *and Villa heard it if they did not, it was a boom, the indignant shout of one who has cracked their knee on a sharp corner, but indignation magnified many thousands of times*

—and as she cut a square, she said to Breck,

"There are more living things in a square inch of good soil than there are living on the surface. Did you know that? There are. Billions of the little beggars. Now just think of this."

St. Maur Ker gouged out the square with an expert flick of the knife, and held it up between her fingers, crumbs trickling down her arm like water.

"Just think of this in our laboratory—we have to replace poor dear departed Decker of course—"

It was astonishing to Villa that they could hear nothing, St. Maur Ker and Breck in the middle of the path and not hearing the boom repeat in a halo of blurred and shrill sounds, icy and distant, quavering like sirens, or the sudden brief storm of short noises, like a bow dashing too fast over a string to make anything but the briefest contact, or those truncated, random, notes exploding into the air like birds startled out of a tree

"—choice of replacements, really, Dr. Hanson, or Grace, or Braithwaith, anyway, whoever it is, give them that magnificent laboratory, and give them even just this sample, and see what new creature they can create out of the billions of microscopic opportunities we have here."

St. Maur Ker deftly tossed the soil into the jar and closed the lid.

"And as for the rest of it," she said, "as for when we take it all, and we have the Glasshouse portal permanently open—"

She handed the jar to Breck to put into the bag. Breck reached out to take it.

The ground split open, and the air twisted like a spinning top, sucking the soil out of the closed jar, and spinning St. Maur Ker off her feet. Breck had only the three seconds during which St. Maur Ker was in midflight towards the fissure, and she leaped like a pouncing fox, landed on St. Maur Ker's feet and clung on, dragging her back, clawing her out of the grasp of the vacuum.

The path through The Wilderness heaved, up-pausedown, up-pause-down.

"Come away, human child," said a voice behind Villa and so heightened was every sense that she was not as petrified as she might have been. Even at that she let a terrible shriek out of her and bolted, but her path was blocked by what had been behind her. It was the horned figure she had seen on her first visit to the forest.

"This is no place for you," it said. "Come away with me now, to where you will be safe."

It held out its hand. Villa's eye flittered over the figure—lots of ivy, great thick ropes of it, twisted and cracked. The horns were great branching things like sharp-tipped antlers. Its eyes were as dark as the earth, with a splash of gold, and they glittered in the depths of the leaves and twining wood. Was it even a person? Flesh and blood and all the rest of it? Or was it made of ivy? The leaves, though—ivy, yes, but oak and beech, elm leaves like moorhen's feet, ash leaves and their seedkeys drooping like empty gloves. Its hand was definitely hand-shaped, the reaching fingers, though veined with narrow ivy, looked flesh-and-blood. And bones, too, of course. Villa dragged her mind away from the construction of hands, and took the one offered.

"Where are we going?"

"To somewhere that you can be safe," the figure repeated.

"But I want to see what happens to St. Maur Ker! And Breck!"

"No, you don't," said the figure, taking Villa's hand. "You really, really, don't."

The booming had stopped but the ground was, very slightly, pulsing. The trees behind them as they hurried away from the path were vibrating their branches, swaying their trunks. The leaves, already doused in their autumn finery, whispered, hummed. Random gusts of wind blew up flurries of dead leaves. The booming started again, very low, very fast, like extremely distant and extremely large wooden drums. The humming became a little louder, a little higher. Villa was hurried a little faster, a little deeper amongst the trees. The trees began to strike their higher branches against each other, slowly, steadily, one–pause–two–pause–three–pause. Villa could no longer see the path, and the horned figure was setting such a pace that she had to keep her eyes on the ground so that she didn't take a tumble over a fallen log.

The blurring, scraping sounds that she had heard first were more frequent now, figure-skaters on the frozen air, notes of music struggling to take form. The booming, and the humming, and the rhythmic beating of the branches continued without interruption, and the blurred, icy sounds were more frequent but very irregular, and now there was a new sound, a soft but persistent hissing. Now and then, a high, clear sound rang out, like a single note struck on a piano, and, happening to glance up at the right time, Villa saw the cause: a drop of water fall from a leaf and hit the ground. She was breathless and too hot when finally the horned figure stopped, and said,

"You'll be grand here. Climb up."

They were standing in front of a yew tree, as wide as a bus and as tall as a turret, but long-dead, split in two to within a few feet of the ground. A chunk of trunk as big as a boat had broken away, and the rest of the tree was dead too, bleached to the colour of cream, its stripped trunk shining in the dull light, and its few, leafless branches breaking off abruptly.

"It's both dead and alive," said the horned figure, above the clattering of branches, and the distant screeching. "Above the ground, it is dead from a lightning strike, below the ground, it is still connected to everything else in the forest. You'll be safe here. Well, as safe as I can make you."

Villa looked up into the tree, the torn wood bright as a primrose, and the bark as dark as storm-clouds, but with splashes of bright red and yellow lichens. She shifted her gaze and looked up at the horned figure. Its face was thick with leaves and vines, and a chaplet of holly drooped to one side, dangling berries over the eye with a blade of gold through the brown iris.

"Are we in danger?" Villa asked.

"Of course. Up with you into the tree."

"Should we leave? Go back—"

"There's no leaving now," said the horned figure, "there's no getting out. St. Maur Ker threatened The Wilderness. What has been started must be finished. Then, presuming we are still... you know..."

"Alive?"

"Then we can leave. Get up into the tree."

Villa clambered clumsily over the vast hillocks of the yew's roots. The ground trembled gently in time to distant booming, behind them, from where the path was. The ripped insides of the tree had been so churned by the lightning that they would be easy to climb. She found a foothold, but stopped.

"But why are we in danger? That's not fair. We haven't done anything wrong."

"Get into the tree," urged the figure, glancing round as the trees closer to them took up the forest's noise, beginning to strike their branches together, shivering their leaves and making them hum. "We're in danger because we're here. The Wilderness is not concerned with fairness, or even justice. Things have been done, and they have consequences. You hear The Wilderness as music, and not as the St. Maur Kers do, as something to be returned to silence. So, you get to take refuge in the split yew tree. But that's all you get, without Lou or one of the Bridgets here. Now, stop talking and start climbing. I have work to do. I have to get back to a path."

Villa climbed quickly, and very carefully. She was a good climber, but she knew that the horned figure was gone, and that if she fell now, there would be no-one to help her. A few feet from the truncated top of the tree, there was a narrow ledge where a branch had broken away, and where the shattered surface had been transformed by weather, and by moss, into a reasonably comfortable seat. She tucked her coat under her, pulled up the collar, and wished she had brought a hat. Then she sat down, to wait.

The yew was shorter than the other trees, and sheltered from the rising wind that was shaking the crowns of the beeches, oaks, and elms—that, Villa realised, was the hissing sound, the trees sweeping like besoms against the sky. The twilight was increasing very slowly, endlessly splitting the seconds between day and night. The darkening of the sky smudged the finer details of the forest, but the intense, tremulous blue illuminated it. Colours stood out as though lit from inside. Where stems were hidden, turning leaves shone out like falling stars, shining white or gleaming red tree-bark slashed the gloom as far as the eye could see, and ferns and shrubs and long grass glowed under a slick of moisture. As things usually silent were now being heard, so things usually hidden could, in this peculiar, hovering, light, be seen.

For the duration of this extraordinary day, Villa had felt little fear. She had been rushed from one place to another, bundled into boats, hauled out of the water, threatened, attacked, washed out of a lake by its occupant, befriended and kidnapped, and each time she had coped as best she could as fast as possible. Leading St. Maur Ker and Breck into The Wilderness, even running through the sparse growth at the edge of the path, climbing up into the dead yew tree, she had not been afraid. She had been badly startled by the horned figure. She had been uneasy amid the strange noises of the forest, the agitated, tense feeling that all these noises were trying to get somewhere, trying to break out, or climb up. Clinging to the relative safety of the dead tree now, she was terrified. St. Maur Ker and Breck had disrupted The Wilderness, and that had been bad enough. The Wilderness had worked out its answer now, and that was even worse. *Things have been done. There will be consequences.*

Villa drew a deep breath, and clung to the yew tree, as much for comfort as for safety. The mouldering, rotting smell had gone now, and there were surely as many scents as there were sounds. The yew tree smelled very strong for a dead thing, sweet and dusty. As the forest below moved—clacking, cracking branches, running animals, swooping birds, vibrating earth—pockets and waves of air washed up around her, opening and breaking and each smelling strongly, but changing so quickly and so absolutely that she hardly had time to name them: spice, honey, resin, pepper, lemons, nectar. Even these fleeting scents were overwhelming. This is what it is like, she thought, The Wilderness, this is the nature of it, its particular fairness, its particular justice rising up like a wave, and the wildness running on like an everlasting sea. There was nothing more she could do, except to cling on. The Wilderness would do what it would do, and that would be that.

The noises continued to rise, in number and in volume, and Villa remained hunched up into the split yew.

She had no idea how long she had been there, but the sky was black and freckled all over with stars. Villa, stiff and sleepy, wondered why a woodpecker had chosen this moment to start rapping on the dead trunk. She turned over to see where it was, but instead of the short, thick beak of a hard-skulled bird, she was face to face with Britta. Fifteen feet high Britta, looking at her with a mild blue eye that was the size of Villa's head.

"Didn't mean to startle you," Britta boomed in a whisper. "Let's get you back to Cobwell."

She scooped Villa up into her armchair of a hand, and set off through the trees, Villa wondering at the way the trees and Britta both swayed and bent out of each other's way, the air seemed to part into rivulets. When they got to the path, Britta strode off towards the exit to Cobwell, walking as serenely and briskly as if the ground was not vibrating and heaving into little hillocks, and the trees were not banging their branches together, drumming their roots.

"Can I get down now?" Villa whispered. "I don't really like being carried."

Britta hesitated.

"Alright," she said, and shrank about seven feet. "You have the Blackstar, you should be safe enough, even here."

Villa struggled to keep her balance on the roiling ground. The air was weirdly dense, Villa felt like she was pushing through columns as weighty as tree trunks. She managed not to fall, but though Britta looked quite unconcerned, Villa had to steel herself to even glance sideways into the darkness behind the trees, and see the flash of fur, and the harsh glint of eye. Once she stopped to look around, but Britta caught her arm instantly and pushed her in front.

"Don't look back," she said. "You'll never unsee it."

Villa set a brisk pace back to the stile.

Twenty-Eight

On the other side, Villa perched on the wooden step, and Britta sat on the ground of the path back to Cobwell. Everything was very still, and evening was just gathering in, the sky and the fields growing dark at the usual rate. There was not a breath of wind, and the air was frosty.

"How did you know where I was?" she asked.

Britta took a sprig of some plant out of her mouth.

"As soon as Bram destroyed the central part of the machine," she said, "we were able to get the Cailleach out, and the Kelpies surrounded her. Once she was safe, it didn't matter who saw us, so we had Lou, Mick, the whole gang. Bridie, and Bridget came back to themselves, as you might say."

"When we were leaving the island, we saw that the St. Maur Kers were sending security back already."

"Oh, they did. When the alarms started to ring, the St. Maur Kers were everywhere—military ships out at sea, their automata all over the island. Have you met Mrs. Danvers?" Britta added, and laughed, "An automaton that used to be in High Tide House? Your sister Flann reconnected it, so it could speak."

"She's always doing that class of stuff—Mama gets wild about it."

"Well, your Mama better sit down for this one," said Britta. "Flann didn't just reconnect Mrs. Danvers' voice. She reconnected the entire nervous system. Mrs. Danvers is not an automaton now. She's a luchrupán with an exoskeleton."

Villa was gobsmacked.

"I'm gobsmacked," she said. "Who'd'a guessed it? Flann! Leave-Me-Alone Flann! Books-Or-Bust Flann!"

"She taught Mrs. Danvers," Britta went on, "and Mrs. Danvers has her own magic. So between the two, when we got to Inishcanara on the back of Enbarr, Mrs. Danvers reconnected all the automata! Hundreds of them."

"And?" Villa was agog.

"And they turned on St. Maur Ker. Drove them off the island. Sank their warship, too."

"Oh, I'd have paid good cash money to see that!" Villa hugged her knees, picturing the sídhe in their armour, hunting the St. Maur Kers out into the wilds of the ocean.

"Lou and me helped the Storm Kelpies to get the Cailleach back to the Whirlpool," Britta went on, "Mr. Gabriel and Mick fixed up everything that the Kelpies had vandalised. Bridget and Bridie came straight back here, and the rest of us followed."

Villa was silent, thinking of The Wilderness. *Don't look back. You can never unsee it.*

"We could tell, of course, that The Wilderness was up in arms. Keer told us you'd gone in too, she was in a right panic about you. So, while the others were— busy with The Wilderness, I came looking for you."

They started the walk back to Cobwell. Villa was so cold she was sore, and she could feel neither her fingers nor her toes. She was queasy, and ravenous, and parched with thirst, and more than anything, she wanted to get to a toilet—or even behind an unenchanted tree—and then go to bed and sleep for a week. But she had asked Britta not to carry her. She had to make it back to Cobwell on her own two feet, blocks of ice that they were.

"Britta," she said, as they passed the little haggard where Mick had shown Raftery how to plant autumn bulbs, "whatever happened to Sylvestra St. Maur Ker— it's really my fault."

"How do you reckon that?"

"I brought them to The Wilderness," Villa mumbled, "her and Breck."

"You didn't know what would happen."

"I kind of did," Villa said. "I guessed that The Wilderness would take care of itself."

"They were a danger to Cobwell," said Britta. "That was not your doing. Sylvestra wanted to find what was in there. Her arrogance was not your doing."

Villa sighed. She wanted Britta to be right, but she could not quite shake the feeling that she should have said something.

"They wanted to find out the true nature of The Wilderness," Britta reminded her, "that's what they wanted. It is not your fault that they did not know what that meant. Because it was exactly what they got."

"Is she dead?"

"Very."

They crossed the yard in a dense gloom, Villa yawning so hard that her jaw cracked.

"What will happen," she asked, "when St. Maur Ker find out what happened to Sylvestra?"

"When will they find out?" asked Britta, shrinking so that she could fit in the door of Cobwell.

"Well, she'll have to be buried," Villa said, feeling thick-headed with sleep, "you know."

"I don't think so," said Britta. "No ground would receive her. Even assuming there is anything left."

Villa opened her eyes, that seemed to be gummed together. She leaned up on her elbows, and saw that her three siblings were sitting at the foot of her bed, playing cards. Raftery was winning. The room was dim, but the curtains behind them were bright, so it was late in the morning. Raftery heard her moving, and knocked over the card-game scrambling to hug her. Flann and Bram stood back a little, letting her struggle into the upright, and wake up properly.

"How's it going?" Flann asked, and Bram added, "You alright?" plumping up the pillow behind her.

"Could be worse," said Villa, feeling very stiff and sore, "but I couldn't be hungrier. Any grub going?"

"Leave it to me," said Bram, and scuttled out. "Breakfast in bed for the homecoming hero!"

Villa muttered something, and looked around for something to put on, as the room was chilly. Flann handed her a jumper.

"Is it all over?" Villa asked, as soon as her head cleared the neck of the jumper. "Are we back to normal?"

"Normal for Cobwell, I suppose," Flann said. "The Fuath are gone. The storms have stopped, and so has the freezing. The Bridgets are back. Lou, too. Mr. Gabriel. Mick."

"Where's Keer?"

"In Littlefish Water!" Flann said, and laughed. "She went off there with Murph in the bathysphere, like the best of mates. Murph stayed in High Tide House to help Mrs. Danvers clear up, but I think Keer stayed in the water."

Villa stumbled out of bed and went next door into the bathroom. Flann idly started picking some clothes up off the floor, and then, with sudden recollection, she dropped them again and left them there.

Villa clambered back into bed.

"What were you up to while I was gone?" she asked. She felt a bit awkward. It seemed a very long time since Flann had not found her irritating, even before Villa capsized Flann's cherished plans for the Klementinum in Prague.

"I was thinking," Flann said. "Well, other things, too, getting Cobwell set up in case we did end up in the winter of a millennium. But thinking."

"What were you thinking about?"

Flann sighed. This was not going to be easy.

"I was thinking about you blowing up rugby pitches," she said, "and getting expelled. And I realised that I was being unfair on you, being sniffy about you looking like a tatterdemalion."

"You think it's a good look?"

"No, but I think it doesn't matter. If we lived hundreds of years ago, you would be out getting arrested for punching politicians and smashing windows because you weren't allowed to vote, or because it was illegal for you not to wear sixteen wool petticoats and a dress. I wouldn't. I'd think it was unfair, but I wouldn't go punching anyone about it. But when changes were made and rights were won, I'd still get to vote, and study for degrees, and wear what I want, and get equal pay. I'd get given all these things, but I wouldn't ever have had to put up with anyone telling me I was a disgrace and a reprobate."

"So you don't think I'm a reprobate?" Villa said, uncertain (as she often was) of what Flann was getting at.

"I do. You are," said Flann. "An unrepentant, dyed-in-the-wool, trouble-seeking rascal."

"Ah, Flann," Villa said, "you're making me blush."

"What I'm getting at is…"

Flann trailed off, uncertain of how to sum up everything she had thought.

"What I'm getting at," she started again, "is that some trouble is good trouble. Some trouble is necessary trouble. And I'm grateful that you're willing to kick arse, because I can't."

To the immense relief of both sisters, Bram pushed open the door with his foot, and carried in a majestically laden tray of breakfast. Being a considerate sort of brother, he had ensured that there was plenty for Villa to eat despite the fact that he had every intention of stealing food from her plate. As she ate, she and Bram told Flann and Raftery how, with the steam-god fatally damaged, the captive Cailleach broke free, and rose up from the sea, how the Storm Kelpies had instantly surrounded her, like a spinning-top on the water, how a twisted column of smoke and lightning, brightly coloured, had surrounded the Kelpies.

"Bet that was Lou," said Raftery, sneaking some fried potato. His siblings looked at him, reluctant to contradict him.

Villa told them what Britta had told her—arriving on Enbarr, and Mrs. Danvers turning the St. Maur Kers' automated army against them. The sea they set out on for home had been calm as a millpond, Bram said, but the boat was so battered and leaky they had feared they wouldn't make it. Meanwhile, Flann said, Cobwell had been so well stocked that they could survive a winter of a thousand years, and she never wanted to change bed-linen again.

"Then you disappear off," Flann said indignantly, to Villa, "and when you get back from The Wilderness, you fall asleep halfway through a sandwich so we can't ask you a thing!"

"Before anything else," said Raftery, "I want to know what you did to the steam-god, Bram."

Bram slumped, and put his head in his hands. Flann patted his shoulder.

"He's distraught," she said to Raftery. "He's terrified that someone from St. Maur Ker will find out what he did."

"What did you do?!"

"Look," Bram said, sitting upright, "St. Maur Ker's Rain-Maker was bad enough. They took the machine that the O'Connell Beare had made, and they added their own attachments, so make it more effective. But of course, the added attachment—the glass harmonica and the amplifiers—they were built so that one of the sídhe could be trapped in it."

He rubbed his face again, and did not seem too keen to continue, but Villa said,

"The steam-god? On the island?"

"The steam-god. That is what they did with the island, they turned the whole thing into this mechanical Zeus. They had hollowed it out, from underneath the original astrolabe, right down to under the sea-level. The Cailleach was in the middle. Sylvestra and Breck brought me to the laboratory where they had put the machine that acted like the heart, the central pump that made the whole steam-god work."

Flann said,

"What did they mean by *work*?"

Bram hummed and dithered, and didn't answer at once.

"They didn't explain it to me," he said eventually. "I've never seen anything like it. I don't know."

"I know you don't know," said Flann. "What do you think?"

"I think," Bram said very reluctantly, "that their plan

was to make a steam-god that controlled other machines. At a distance. Like a brain, making things happen everywhere in a body. I think they were going to keep the Cailleach, the winter immortal, in Inishcanara, but then have the Bridgets, and anyone else they needed, somewhere else. Balance one against the other, pit countries suffering drought against countries suffering eternal winter. A fine circus of wars."

"Well," Flann said, astonished, "no-one can accuse the St. Maur Kers of thinking too small."

"What about the Rain-Maker?" Villa asked, "How did that fit in?"

"It didn't," said Bram. "At least, if it does, I can't see how. I think it was probably a blind. The High King—all the local rulers—are very suspicious of people who are so close to the Pharaoh's Court. I think they used their idea about the Rain-Maker as an excuse to allow them into Hibernia, and close enough to Inishcanara."

"What did you do," Raftery demanded, "about the mechanical heart?"

Bram sighed, and said very sorrowfully, "The machine —the heart—was started up by electricity, but it was kept going by a sort of soup of chemicals being dripped down into it. Breck brought me into the laboratory where they had this set up, the heart in the middle and above it, the demi-johns of chemicals, each one with a tube coming from it, and each tube with a valve to shut it off or open it. There was a timetable, the valves had to be closed or opened regularly to control what was being fed to the machine."

301

"Or control whatever they had trapped there," Flann said. Bram looked miserably at her.

"I didn't look. I *couldn't*."

"Whatever was in there, isn't in there anymore," Villa said. "When we turned on all the valves, the heart had a sort of seizure and it split open, all this, sort of, oil and thick green and black stuff came out, but in amongst it was… I don't know. We got only a faint glimpse of it."

"What did it look like?" Raftery said, entranced, but Villa shook her head.

"I only got the briefest glimpse, Raffles," she said, "it was out and back in the sea before you could say 'jumping jack flash'. It had fins, is all I can say, but it was so fast. It was about eight foot long."

A knock came on the door, and all four of them looked over at Jolyon, standing half in and half out of the door, jangling his keys.

"If anyone wanted to go down to Littlefish Water…" he said, and Flann grabbed the tray just in time to stop the crockery being smashed in Villa's heedless hurtle to get ready. They left her to it, and she joined them in a very few minutes in the yard.

Twenty-Nine

The four Graces were briefly subdued by the sight of the damaged farmyard. The display of bright wood inside smashed fences looked as wrong as protruding bones. Grey mud was smeared over the ground and heaped up in corners and gutters, and branches sheared off their trees were tossed about, hooked over the rooves of sheds, or half-way through broken windows. But once in the carriage and on their way, they cheered up again. The cleaning-up had already begun, Bridie was busy with the injured animals and the wounded trees, and Britta and Mick were shovelling the filth and sludge away into bins. Settling herself into the carriage, Flann struck her foot against something under the seat in front of her.

"You got your harp finished!" she exclaimed. "Despite everything!"

Jolyon laughed.

"I did," he said. "There were times when there was nothing I could do to help, so better do some work. Anyway, Lou seemed keen for it to be done."

It was a dim day, and very still. When they reached the

sandy sweep that led from the village to Littlefish, the horse hesitated.

"Stay where you are," Jolyon said to the Graces. "Let's see what happens."

The horse snorted, bowing and raising its head, taking a few steps forward, and then a few sideways. It stood quite still for over a minute, before looking over its shoulder at Jolyon, and saying,

"Does that young one still have the Blackstar about her person?"

"She does," said Jolyon, adding over his shoulder, "You do, don't you, Villa?"

"Well, we can go for it so," said the horse. "The Blackstar will keep our boundaries steady."

Bram put his hand over his eyes.

"Cobwell," he said, with a smack of despair in his voice.

The land remained quite peaceably in one world only, and the horse cantered briskly along without upset. As Littlefish Water came into view, Villa stood up and Bram and Flann held on to her as the carriage bounced over uneven ground and Villa waved with both arms to Murph and Keer.

They had been fixing the bathysphere, and Murph let them in two at a time to see how the work was progressing. She pointed over at Eightfoot Island, where they could see the shining blue figure of Keer making her way back through the water.

"Keer's been brilliant," she said. "Doesn't know beans about bathyspheres but she's been able to find all sorts of gems and metals for me, it's like she can smell where they are in the water, and just sort of sieves them out for me."

Lou was on the beach, shabby and shadowy as ever, coat as weirdly coloured, hat as concealing.

"I hear you did well," Lou said to Villa, and cuffed her shoulder gently. "Thanks."

Villa muttered something, and kicked a couple of pebbles.

"News for the Graces," Lou said then. "St. Maur Ker's in uproar now, with first Decker and then Sylvestra St. Maur Ker all gone to their reward, we hope, and then Breck—"

"What happened to Dr. Breck?" Bram asked quickly.

"Breck got out of The Wilderness through the cattle's watering-place," Lou said thoughtfully. "Abandoned St. Maur Ker at the first opportunity. We don't quite know how she got away. Though... she probably met up with the Kelpies, if she went out to sea."

There was a long silence.

"So—"

"Roused, the Kelpies were," Lou interrupted Bram, "strong feelings, you know. Angry about the Cailleach, and abducting the Cailleach had been Breck's idea, first to last. The Kelpies are very persistent."

Bram went a little pale. But he remembered that Breck had tried to drown Villa, and had threatened to imprison Raftery in a portal, and that she knew what she was doing if she outraged Storm Kelpies and winter immortals.

"So, as I was saying," Lou went on, "Decker gone, St. Maur Ker gone, Breck gone. Place is in uproar, they've

305

had to find replacements for everyone. Sylvestra's cousin on their way to the High King to ask permission to move the laboratory off Eightfoot Island. They don't have a new Breck yet, that's a whole new hunt."

"Who is the new Decker?" Bram asked.

"The new Decker is on her way here," Lou said, "to collect her four children before, as she said, they're eaten by the sídhe."

Raftery dropped his bag, and looked at Lou.

"Mama? Poppa?"

Lou nodded, and Raftery burst into tears. His siblings stood looking at him in astonishment, because Raftery was not a crying sort of person. Villa, who was nearest to him, put her arm around him, and patted his shoulder, keeping time with his sobs. When these eventually died away, Bram fished a handkerchief out of his pocket, and he helped Raftery mop his eyes. Flann hovered, and gave Raftery a hug when he was dry again. Raftery said,

"There was no point saying I missed them all the time. But I did. And you were fighting. And then everything turned to winter, and you nearly lost Villa on me."

He sniffed a few last times, and looked in distaste at Bram's sodden handkerchief. Lou came over, and with a faint crackle of sparks, the handkerchief was dry.

"The real reason I came stumping it down here," said Lou briskly turning to Keer, "was to see you. I know you know who I am."

"The last time I saw you, you old pagan," Keer said curtly, "you were too busy giving orders to the Salmon to save me from drowning."

"I was," said Lou, scratching beneath the slouching hat. "If I had not dispatched the Salmon to get back the fruits of the Tree, we would all be in an awful lot more trouble than we are. But I always felt bad for you."

"Hmph." Keer sounded very unimpressed.

"Well, I'm not going to apologise. Getting the Salmon on the track of the hazels was literally the most important thing in the world, in any world, at that moment, and I only had a moment."

"Well, thanks for that not-apology."

"You're welcome," said Lou.

"I was being ironic!" Keer retorted.

"I wanted to offer you something to make up for what happened."

Keer said nothing, but blinked rapidly.

"What could make up for what happened?"

"Alright, well, maybe nothing could. But I can bring you back to the Blackstar Whales."

Keer's face lost all expression. She said nothing, but she stared at Lou, beginning to look faintly puzzled, as though trying to translate what she had heard.

"There's a grand big pod of them," Lou went on, "you could go and live with them again. You were happy there."

Raftery nudged Villa, and whispered piercingly,

"She's sparkling!"

Keer still said nothing, but very gradually, the sparkling stopped.

"I can't," she said, "though thank you for the thought."

"Are you being ironic again?"

"No! No, I'm not. But I can't."

"Because?"

"I can't—I can't understand them properly, and they can't really understand me. Not enough for me to be part of the pod. Not really. Not forever."

Waves lapped gently, and murmured over the pebbles on the beach. A long way away, a woodpecker was hammering, and in the blackthorns behind them, a robin whistled. Lou was looking at Jolyon, who suddenly mouthed *oh!* and went back to the carriage.

"And?" Lou said.

"And," Keer said hurriedly, "because I can't hide like they can. The reason they were—the reason Decker could find them—it was because of me. I met him. I didn't know who he was, I thought he just liked whales. I told him I could show him where the pod was. And then... then he..."

After a pause, Keer went on,

"I can't hide like they can. I couldn't know where they were going. I can't understand them, not really. I have no Blackstar, I'd be a danger to them."

A slight breeze rattled in the bare hedges. Jolyon's feet crunched over the sand. Villa was horribly startled by a sudden realisation. She had wondered, in passing, how it had been that she could understand the Fuath, when they spoke to Keer in the caves. It could only have been the Blackstar. She fumbled in her pocket. As soon as her fingers closed around the familiar shape, she stopped, and then she moved very quickly so that she would not chicken out.

"Take this with you, then," she said, hurrying over to

Keer and thrusting her Blackstar at her. "Wear it, or eat it or something. If it worked on me, it'll work on you."

She shoved the Blackstar into Keer's hand, and hurried back out of reach of being able to snatch it back.

Jolyon, crunching up with the harp in his hand, said to Lou,

"You know, you could have just told me what you wanted it for."

Lou said, "I couldn't be sure. There's always more than one possible outcome, as you know. Sometimes things just flip inside out."

Jolyon held out the harp to Keer.

"There you go," he said, "sling that behind you, and you can get it to make the sounds that you can't make. You mightn't speak quite like a whale, but they'll understand you."

Keer took the harp. She tilted it this way and that, and such dim sun as there was glittered over the metallic sheen of the green and the red wood, the copper screws and keys, and the thin, bright, strings. She laid her hand flat on the strings, and then drew it back, gently plucking them so that the harp chimed and trilled.

"Careful now," said Lou, as Littlefish Water suddenly churned and boiled behind them, with fish and merpeople and the eye of a Kraken rising to the surface to listen. Something silvery, and finned, and about eight foot long slithered through the water from the island.

Keer put the strap of the harp over her head, and pushed the body of it behind her. She seemed at a loss to know what to do next.

"Villa," she said, and Villa hurried forward, splashing into the lake.

"I'm sorry I threatened to incarcerate you in a portal for an agonising eternity," Keer said, and Villa muttered that it was alright, she'd have found a way to escape.

"I can't thank you for the Blackstar," Keer said, "I don't know how. But I will be grateful to you for this for as long as I planned to keep you a prisoner."

"Well, I won't try and escape that," said Villa, still keeping her hands firmly in her pockets in case, even now, she grabbed back the Blackstar.

"I know you found the Blackstar, and that you still want it," Keer said, "but if I don't have this, I can never go home."

The water behind them calmed down as the last of the harp notes died away. Only a few waves rustled gently against the stones.

"You're welcome to it," Villa said finally, and finally meant it.

Thirty

Dear Mr. Wittgenstein,

I did not know how much I missed home until Poppa drove the car through the gates of Oaklake, and I felt a terrible rush of affection for it. I even felt guilty that I had not thought about it while I was away, as though I might have hurt its feelings. That is foolish, it's just a house, bricks and mortar, but that is what it felt like. I wonder if affection makes you think of everything in human terms.

They were waiting for us at Cobwell, Poppa and Mama, which we knew from Lou, but Granda, and Grandmother Gale, too! Mama and Poppa had travelled non-stop from Prague, and they looked like it, too, all red-eyed and shaky with tiredness, rumpled. They had to go by sleeper-train to the North Sea, and it seemed like they would be stuck there, till Mama thought of chartering a fishing-boat to Northumberland. Poppa, by their account, was phoning ahead, sending messages, so they could straightaway get on more trains, and finally he finagled someone with a biplane to help them out.

Granda met them at Carrickfergus, and brought them to Cobwell. They had been trying to get out of Prague ever since they started hearing about the weather turning, and the storms, and the winter being suddenly upon us. Mama kept saying, "What were they thinking? The Cailleach!"

Bram showed them how to get breakfast out of the cooker, and while they ate, we told them what had happened, each of us telling our part of the story. When Villa said she had gone into The Wilderness with Sylvestra St. Maur Ker and Breck, Mama put down her cutlery and put her hands over her face, and Poppa kept rubbing her shoulder with one hand and saying *sure, she's grand Gráinne. Look at her, she's grand. You are grand, aren't you, Villa?* and rubbing his nose and his hair with his other hand. I didn't like to say that in fact, Villa hasn't told us very much at all about what happened in The Wilderness.

The big family news is that Mama is to replace Decker. St. Maur Ker have decided to move the entire laboratory up to Oaklake. That's all I know about it at the minute. Everyone is very happy, but I am not sure. When Mama told us, at Cobwell, everyone congratulated her, but later on, Peg said to her—a bit bluntly—"I can't see your father being so happy about this," and Mama sighed and said "Yes, but we're only human, we have to eat," and Lou said, "But do you all have to eat so well? Do you have to eat the whole world?"

I'm very proud of Mama and her being what Villa calls 'frantic with brains', but I'll buy tickets for a ring-side seat for when Mama and Granda discuss her new job. It feels very strange to say this, because I don't want to be a contrarian and I hate arguments when people get over-heated. But nothing of what happened on Cobwell is known outside Cobwell. There are a few scattered reports of Sylvestra St. Maur Ker meeting 'a tragic accident', Breck isn't mentioned, Decker succumbed 'after a long illness'. Granda always said St. Maur Ker lied but I never quite believed it. Not lie, not really—see things differently, maybe, have different priorities, but not lie. But, yes, lie. Just straight-up, flat-out lie. Lie like a bastard, as Granda says, and then says, 'Don't tell your mother I said that.' But Mama isn't a liar. Even if you wanted her to lie, and tell you some comforting untruth, she won't. So, I really want to know how this is going to work out. Not the job, I don't mean, but how the job fits into the way they see the world. I'll get to hear how she sees it *and* how Granda sees it.

Besides, people were dropping hints all over the gaff at Cobwell about how there's some connection between Grandmother Gale and the aos sídhe. Not that she is of the aos sídhe, but something. On the way home from Cobwell, Raftery asked her about the Salmon of Knowledge and the hazelnuts, and why Lou had to get the Salmon on the hunt for them, and what she told us was no fairy-tale.

Yours, in some trepidation, but not as much as I would have thought,

Flann.

P.S. To my surprise, Bram said he felt very bad about Raftery, how much he missed Mama and Poppa and we never noticed. He said exactly what I thought: we think Raftery is too young for anything but happiness.

P.P.S. I have just remembered something. I forgot to ask Lúgh about the Cobwell Hound.

BRAM: ...bringing the whole laboratory up to us! And Mama is the Senior Phyto-tekt—
RILEY: Which is what, when it's at home?
BRAM: It means making plants. Decker used to make plants and animals, but Mama is a botanist, so its only plants. I don't know if she is actually going to make plants, she says it will be improving, investigating.
RILEY: Well, she'll have to do whatever the St. Maur Kers want, won't she? They're paying her.
BRAM: Uhh... maybe. No. I mean, there are things they will need, of course, but it's not like with Decker, who went off doing his own thing ...
[Pause]
RILEY: Still there?
BRAM: Still here. I was just thinking. Oh, something else! I'm very excited about this. It'll be next summer, though.
RILEY: What?

BRAM: Well, before we left Cobwell, the O'Connell Beare came to visit. I can't believe I didn't recognise her, I met her months ago when St. Maur Ker met with the High King. But it was Villa had to remind me. Lou said that the O'Connell Beare was visiting and Villa said she owned the castle in Dunmathew, she was the very tall one with the leaf of gold... that's funny.

RILEY: *I'm not laughing.*

BRAM: No—it was Villa. So, she said that the O'Connell Beare had this streak of gold in her eye, you know, a hetero-chromia, but then she went really quiet, she looked like a stunned goat. I don't know why.

RILEY: *Still not laughing.*

BRAM: Anyway, so the O'Connell Beare said that she wants to fix up the castle's original work-room, where her ancestor made the Rain-Maker and all the rest of the stuff they invented. She's going to start it in the summer, and she asked if I'd like to have a summer job with them!

RILEY: *Oh, that's marvellous! Congrat-ulations—you'll have your head in the door of St. Maur Ker alright, between helping them with the Rain-Maker, and*

now this! That's really exciting—following
your da's footsteps. They know all about
what you did at Dunmathew, and on
Inishcanara, don't they?
BRAM ... Yeeeessss... Oh, yes. I told
them... everything.

Dear Mick,
Thank you for a lovely holiday.
  Did you know that the horned figure
in The Wilderness was the O'Connell
Beare? Villa didn't. She was so shocked
that she didn't say a word for like
half an hour. Bram does not believe
it. He kept saying "I don't believe —
no, no, it can't — The O'Connell Beare?
The O'Connell Beare? No." I did not
like to say that I don't think Beare
is a nickname.
  You were very kind. I thought that the
holiday would be awful, because no-
one was speaking to each other when we
left home. But you were really nice to
me, and so was Bridie even though
she's a bit scary. But then she's three
people so it's probably very tiring.
I thought you were very interesting
about seeds, and how things grow.

I hope that Cobwell stays safe. I am a bit sad to think that Cobwell won't be Cobwell anymore, when Lou puts the Garden of Knowledge back together again. But Grandmother Gale said that Cobwell was 'a means to an end', to keep the Well safe until the Salmon brings the hazels back. She tried to explain to us what the hazels really were. Flann seemed to understand, but she always does. Bram looked a bit unhappy. Villa looked dazed, and said she didn't understand a word of it. I might have fallen asleep.

I hope the pigs and the horses are alright, after St. Maur Ker. I know they have Bridie to look after them, but Oscar and Lucinda were right in the middle of everything, and there was that massive hound, the one that picked me up by the gansey and brought me to Murph at The Pot.

Say hello to everyone on Cobwell for me, and to Murph as well. I don't know if Murph knows the lake near where we live. She'd have a great time, exploring. It might be full of loads of cryptozoology. I'm just saying.

Love,
Raftery

CALL SIGN: Good Ship *Good Hope*

HOUR: 22:00. Am supposed to be in bed asleep.

WIND SPEED/DIRECTION: 4 knots. Autumn is coming, as it should.

TEMPERATURE: 15°C/34°F. Very cosy inside the house though; Mama let me have a fire in my bedroom. Well, in the fireplace in my bedroom. Usually, she won't. She thinks I'll burn the place down, accidentally.

CURRENT POSITION: Oaklake

MENTAL COMPASS COURSE: School

SPEED OF TRAVEL: Doubtfully, but with hope.

FATHOMS:

COMMENTS: Back again, in one piece.

When I started this entry, I meant to record everything that happened but I can't. I mean, most of it I can, about how we found St. Maur Ker's steam-god, and how Keer hauled me off in a boat, and all the rest of it. But I can't describe what was in The Wilderness. I haven't been able to tell anyone, not even Grandmother Gale, and she seemed to have some idea what it was like. When she heard I'd been in there, she rounded on Lou and said, "You let my granddaughter into The Wilderness," really fiercely, and Lou said, "I was a bit preoccupied, Gale!" and the O'Connell Beare, who had her mouth full of scone, said "I put her away safely," and at the same time Britta said, "We got her out quick as we could!" I can remember it, as clearly as it was still happening, but that's it.

Later, before we left Cobwell, I went outside for some fresh air, and to get away from the noise of people. I was just sitting on the branch of the oak tree, where it rests on the ground. The O'Connell Beare came out, and sat down on the ground beside me. She had something with her, wrapped in a bit of hessian cloth. She said nothing for a while. Then she sighed very deeply, and held out the wrapped thing. "Here," she says, "I believe you had to give away your Blackstar." So, I took it, and unwrapped it. I thought it was a lump of glass at first, and when I was turning it over, she said, "It's sunstone." "Oh," says I, "the Vikings used sunstones to find the sun on cloudy days."

I felt a bit silly then, of course she knew what a sunstone was. So, I said, just so she'd know I knew stuff, "It's a kind of quartz, isn't it, that polarises light." "It is," says she, "but this stone will show you more than just where the sun is. This stone belonged to a rascally ancestor of mine who was said to have sailed with Mael Dúin, and made it to Hy-Brasil." That's a great thing to have said about you. I love the idea of having a great-great-great-grandniece who says—preferably in that sniffy way Mama has—"This belonged to Villa, a rascally ancestor of mine." Bram isn't the only one with ambitions.

Anyway, something else: when we were getting into the carriage to go home, the O'Connell Beare was helping them pack the few suitcases we had. And she said to Poppa, "I believe your Villa was expelled from that grim Gladdish Academy. They threw me out, too." Poppa had his mouth hanging open, and then he recovered himself, and called to Mama. Apparently, they sent her—the O'Connell Beare, not Mama—to a "forest school." Then she looked at me, and said, "Don't get your hopes up, you still have to do literature and physics and all the rest of it. But they'll teach you to fix boats and track bears and build huts. Keep you out of trouble."

Even at that Mama went pffffff and said, *well, I'll believe that when I see it*. I didn't think they'd consider it, my parents being cheerleaders for book-learning, but we're going to visit the place, it's not far from here, on Friday. It might even be bearable.

Raftery asked Grandmother Gale why Lou had to send the Salmon after the hazelnuts, even when it meant Boann and Keer drowned. I don't think I understand her answer. But last night I dreamt that I was swimming with the Salmon, a big whale of a fish the size of a catamaran, and we were hunting the hazels. I was able to swim and breathe underwater, like the fish. When I woke up, I thought of Keer, swimming with the Blackstars, and I thought that when I grow up, I could take a ship to look for the Salmon. I have a bad feeling we might never go back to Cobwell. It's not the sort of place. But anything can happen in the oceans.

From Mr. Gabriel's position in the star-flecked sky above Cobwell, the farmhouse seemed distant and tiny, speckled with lights until the inhabitants started tottering to bed in the early hours of the morning. Of all the animals on the farm, only Lucinda the sow was awake. The cattle and the alpacas were settled on the ground, a scattering of blocky shapes in the dark like a fallen wall, sleeping. The horses slept standing up, except the stallion whose leg Bridie was fixing, and who lay in an enchanted sleep in the sweet-smelling straw. The goats were indoors, the poultry safely locked away and the piglets were pressed tightly to the warm flank of the sleeping boar. A mile away, a slight wind ruffled the waters of Littlefish Water, and whatever was sleeping again under Eightfoot Island, slept.

Dramatis personae

ARTEMIS (TIMA), THE O'CONNELL BEARE: Forest entity, spy, aristocrat, owner of Dunmathew Castle, where the St. Maur Kers are building their Rain-Maker.

BRIDIE THE VET, BRITTA THE BLACKSMITH, BRIDGET THE POET: The three aspects of the goddess Brigit, daughter of the Dagda.

MURPH: A púca; a cryptozoologist, captain of a bathysphere.

CAILLEACH: Winter deity, said to live in Corryvrecken Whirlpool off Scotland, rules between September and February, when Bridget takes over as Summer divinity (does not appear).

SYLVESTRA ST. MAUR KER: In charge of the St. Maur Ker Research Academy.

COSIMO ST. MAUR KER: Sylvestra's brother (does not appear).

PEG: Farmer at Cobwell.

JOLYON: Peg's husband, farmer, instrument maker.

DORIAN DECKER: A tekton, a maker of plants and animals, supposedly an adept with great magical powers.

GALE MCCABE: Mother of Gráinne Grace, grandmother of the children.

GRANDA (THELONIUS) O'MALLEY: Father of Gráinne Grace, grandfather of the children.

GRÁINNE GRACE: Botanist, parent, works for the St. Maur Kers.

TERENCE GRACE: A St. Maur Ker lawyer, parent.

FLANN, BRAM, VILLA AND RAFTERY: Children of Gráinne and Terence.

MR. GABRIEL, MICK, RAY: Helping to care-take Cobwell; archangels.

LOU: Lúgh, in charge of Cobwell, but especially of the Glasshouse; a god.

DR. BRECK: Technomancer and engineer for the St. Maur Kers.

MAGUS BOITUMELO: Working on the Rain-Maker project for the St. Maur Kers; engineer, technomancer.

SUNNY, RILEY: Friends of Bram's (appear in conversation only).

LUDWIG WITTGENSTEIN: A dead philosopher, to whom Flann writes letters.

STORM KELPIES: Water beings, including the Blue Men of the Minch, who sink ships, but some said to inhabit Corryvrecken Whirlpool where the Cailleach washes her plaid.

MRS. DANVERS: A housekeeping automaton.

KEER/CIARNAT: A marine semi-immortal.

More Books by Susan Maxwell

Good Red Herring
(Muinbeo Chronicles #1)

"Some of these stories really started decades, generations, ago, and now come to their close. New things begin to arise from the past, like phoenix feathers separating from the flame. The winding down of the old stories and the starting of the new arose from a death; a murder, if you will believe such wickedness. We warn you. We are the last—eh—people to pretend that Muinbeo is some kind of Island of the Blessed."

Those enigmatic entities, the Storytellers of Muinbeo, know that History has something waiting in the wings. To set the scene for their audience, they relate a gripping tale about a death and its consequences.

When her mentor is bitten by a rogue werewolf and "joins our hairy brethren howling at the moon," apprentice detective Salmon Farsade is assigned to Hal McCabe, Detective Chief-Inspector and vampire, just in time for a murder.

Fen Maguire has been stabbed, throwing the normally peaceful community of Ballinpooka into shock. The investigation into her death lifts the lid on more than just the name of her killer: political corruption, Outland conspiracy, academic deceit, and plain old-fashioned greed. A second murder follows: the clock is ticking, and as they seek a key to unlock the truth, the detectives are both helped and hindered by the various human and not-so-human beings that populate Muinbeo.

For readers of all ages.

Irish Times Best books of 2014 for children and young adults

A Wild Goose Hunt
(Muinbeo Chronicles #2)

*"You did not tell the Abbess a single lie," Diamond said,
"But you didn't tell her the truth."*

As a good Sombrist, Hunter Sessaire is aware that not only
lying, but curiosity, is very much frowned upon by his
community. As an apprentice archivist, he cannot resist the
temptation to puzzle out how a manuscript could have
been stolen from a room within the Sombrists' Labyrinth.
A room that opens only during a planetary alignment. An
alignment that has not yet taken place.

But this is not the only enigma abroad in Muinbeo.
Seemingly disparate occurrences remain opaque even to
those normally in the know. Detective Chief Inspector Hal
McCabe is scratching his head over the inexplicable vanishing
of his apprentice, Salmon Farsade, and the dramatic and
destructive theft of an ancient silver hand from the local
school museum.

The boundaries of Muinbeo, carefully managed to keep the
Outland and its machinations outside, where they belong,
have become a bit more porous than McCabe would like.
Not least when he begins to suspect that some of the
uncanny events may have their roots in a controversial
Outland archaeological dig in Aegypt... Once again we are
led into a maze of mystery by those not entirely reliable
narrators, the Storytellers, in this enthralling sequel to *Good
Red Herring*.

For readers of all ages.

Hollowmen

"It seems to me—and I no longer claim objective recall—that the morning on which I first arrived in Quettopolis looked much like this morning just breaking. One year ago. I was right at least that it was my last job."

The Moufet Institute's mission is to protect endangered lepidoptera, but its experts are becoming bystanders, sidelined by the 'Players' and their pursuit of corporate self-perpetuation. Cuffe, recruited to create the rhetoric to underpin a new corporate vision, finds her initial confidence eroded by the peculiarities of the Institute and its environment—the punitive *process* with its absent defendant, the disregarded but omnipotent Registry, the quarterly Hunt, the Forest as it re-asserts itself.

Then the Institute is galvanised by the discovery of a breeding pair of a rare moth species in a country in the throes of a military coup. The Institute in turn is riven by competing ambitions—the scientific specialists trying to save the moths, the Players trying to save the goose that lays the golden eggs. Meanwhile, no-one has been paying enough attention to what is happening in the basement...

Hollowmen is an intricate and unsettling work, its shifting, interleaved narratives by turns ironic, lyrical, witty, and savage.

Fluctuation in Disorder

An encounter with an alien enemy. A strange epiphany in a fog-bound park. A collector of the names of the dead faces their own death. Rebel divinities respond to the prayers of despairing creation for deliverance. Bureaucrats find their grip on reality dissolving in odd ways.

In these ten finely crafted and unsettling stories, Maxwell's slipstream style interweaves strands of naturalism, science fantasy, and the experimental irreal, illuminated by sharp flashes of wit and language of lyrical precision. Many of the characters exist in a state of slippage, alienated from a world they thought they knew by an encounter with something that is indifferent to them, but to which they cannot remain indifferent.

More than twenty years separate the earliest and the most recent of the stories in this collection, but certain persistent preoccupations provide loose thematic links—environmental crime and retribution; the ways, both overt and insidious, in which institutions can corrupt or sacrifice those within them; the interpretations and recording of past events by unreliable narrators; and the pervasive, irreducible weirdness of existence.

Death at Hallowtide
(Quill and Thornapple #1)

"What's at the back of the field?" I asked. "Beyond the stream? Where the railing is?" Dermot turned to follow my pointing finger, and smiled. "That," he said, "is your poison garden."

Corbofinn. A place where things are... different. Where Jessica Quill has inherited a house and land. And where she has just become the number one suspect in the murder of local wide boy Tony Millar.

Jessica's life has entered uncharted waters. A job she hates, a cheating partner, her unexpected inheritance, and the final straw: tripping over a corpse in the rain when she comes to rural Ireland to arrange the sale of her property.

But Herne's Acre is no ordinary place. It's a key crossing-point on the borderlands between the mortal world and the otherworlds of the sidhe. And now it is to be sold by a stranger unfamiliar with the true nature of Corbofinn, a source of considerable anxiety for Thornapple, that very civil servant of the Borderlands Commission.

Bewildered, grumpy, and armed only with knowledge of toxic plants and classic detective stories, Jessica pursues her own inquiries to clear her name. Corbofinn yields some of its mysteries along with new friends—human, canine, and... Well. You know.

Increasingly conflicted, Jessica's sensible self squares off against her dreams of a different life. But she makes enemies, too, leading to a deadly showdown on Hallowe'en, when the borders between worlds are at their most fluid and uncanny.

If you enjoyed this book…
…please consider reviewing it online.

If you want to follow me online…

Website: www.biblioref.com
Blog: bibref.blogspot.com

LibraryThing: librarything.com/author/maxwellsusan-1
Goodreads: goodreads.com/dr_susan_maxwell

Mastodon: @BiblioRefuses@mastodon.ie
Bluesky: @bibliorefuses.bsky.social
YouTube: youtube.com/@biblioref

Linktree: linktr.ee/dr.susan.maxwell

IMAGES USED IN THIS BOOK

No text or image in this work is the product
of generative AI.

Illustrations
Maps © Susan Maxwell

Cover Design
Horned Figure © Susan Maxwell

Stock images and graphics provided by canva.com